The Ladybird Flies

Edel Cush

To Sara
Can't wait for
the book club.
Thank you
Edel Cush
25-11-23

ISBN – 13: 978 – 1517445850
ISBN – 10: 151744585 X

For my Cushes, for everything

Thank You My Dear Reader

O L I V E

The Vampire Hours - Heaving and rollicking, he ejects, dislodging mucus slimed objects. Then, proceeding, he licks the tile clean, the mastery of no messy evidence, his domain. Why do dogs eat their own vomit? I nod respect to my dog but my neck doesn't tilt. Why can't I lift my head? My brain spikes with insomniac superiority. The stench burns my nostrils.

Is this how it is pulled off, Doctor?

Inspirational thoughts u-turn, I think of her and my insides expels. We favor odd numbers, mother and daughter, alike in many ways. Her number is 7. Mine is 3. I've reached all the 3s, side by side, curvaceous 33. We never discussed the probability of 7 aligning with a 7 in her vintage years.

LIAR.

Life is a lottery, random wishes join random numbers. This October day, like any other, lasts a few short hours.

Mom? I feel your warm caresses on my cheek and soft voice in my ear.

It is you. Snapshots keep flashing in my head. Overpowering lavender odours suffuse me.

Induced coma Mom? Why are you talking of final wishes?

I black out. The silence distracts me. Vampire hours trickle my reserves to a constant drop-like consistency, beating in my eardrums. There was so much blood. My eyes turned red. The taste clumps in the cracks on my lips. Her diagnosis seeps into my mind as sure as the dark seduces, Mother's disease infiltrates my blood. I wish I could pour a gin & tonic, the chilled ice with a kick. The simple joys of last night. Out of the corner of my eye I spotted the flash of red, a ladybird throttled on the back of my hand. I let her journey be. I can't feel the sensation on my skin, I almost distrust my senses, she is there; I can see her. Where did she come out of? Maybe when I opened the patio door? The outside came inside. The rules are broken. Does she know where she's going? Do any of us know where we are going? How can I tell if a ladybird is male?

Why is my brain jumbling?

Did my eyes deceive me? One instant she is there and then, she is gone forever. The ladybird flies.

Lucky girl, she has more freedom than I have.

Her hot red tinge imprinted in me. Was she my premonition of danger? Blood did spill, then disappeared out of sight.

The blip, where is that noise coming from? Blip. Blip. Blip.

What's that sound, Mom?

No one is answering me.

Discontent breeds in my mouth - The car. I remember the motion, rocketing forward. Tremors afflict my trembling limbs. I re-route the drive. My intelligence forges ahead but I drift off, cursing the natural law of coincidence. Precise commands suit my temperament. My fingers want to touch the iPad's coolness of glass, like rubbing my thumb and forefinger along a ribboned gift, sublime pleasure. Work and porn block my reality, I switch worlds, the office notes the early morning hour

4

of emails. A good day's graft at any bewitching hour compensates for my waywardness. Another satisfied client on my books, I saved her a fortune. The required client signature, a mere formality, I can arrange. That was the plan, after I checked my mother into the fancy clinic she privately selected for her treatment. Fuck, I'm thinking of that crap again.

LIAR.

Searing pain racks through me.

The triumph of my success is short lived. My tongue is on fire, dagger jabs deep on my face, slit, the draw of blood, reflecting the ladybird's vibrancy, almost chokes me. Escaping my embedded anguish is impossible; I can't fly off. My mother, Dr Lily Tully, esteemed consultant to health professionals, asked me to assist her medically today, as next of kin; confirmation of insurance more like. She has never crossed this boundary line. Blip. Crazily, the pain assimilates into me. Relieved, I pass my threshold of horror. I hear whispering in my ear. 'Olive.' She is here.

Mom?

I try to roar. My throat splits. Why can I not be heard?

'I love you, dear,' she says.

Mother has become courageous and uncontained.

I scratch anew my angst of fear. I can't feel my nails claw. I'm maxing my limits of pain, pulsing pain. The throbs rethrob and stun my ruminating, its dark, black spots on my eyeballs, drown in red. How long? Stillness surrounds, enticing me to linger, going deep into the night, where private time is not accountable, silencing the tick-tock. The whispering voices annoy me.

Frank you fucker, I can hear you.

Dawn will break, capture me and catapult me into this day, kicking and screaming, tearing and bleeding. Again.

Shrills echo, my cell phone is ringing. Nobody is answering my phone. Raised bumps on my head jab like splinters of glass. With a natural propensity to align logistics, I agreed to drive her to the clinic. She can be quite persuasive. I don't want to be near sick people. I'm confounded, and unskilled, for the ailing world my mother inhabits. Mom is the doctor, but nobody speaks of the truth. We all falter.

I scan, my ears overpower my senses, my pupils flicker and enlarge, I can't see. Disoriented, the fuzziness is frustrating, my mind jumbles, I pass out. My boy of favor is online, I moisten as he awaits, for me to complete the credit card transaction. I self-soothe. The work load is through the roof, it is the end of the year accounts. I'm a highly sought after tax specialist. My mother knows of this too and yet she asked me to be here at the clinic today. She's insistent. I tried to cancel our arrangement just hours ago. But Mom would not let me off the hook. I'm a captured, flapping fish, out of my depth. The struggle is cruel and futile, the stupid fish continues the futile smash of its head. The accumulation of time is increasing, I'm running out of hours, the night is being overtaken. Trying to orgasm now of all times, I laugh in optimism. Imaginatively, I stimulate the blood to my vulva but my problems revolt in my mind. I don't want the impending morning to arrive, but there is nothing I can do to control the rhythm of life. I can't control time. Masking my emotional upheaval, I concentrate. My vagina is squirming. Writhing, I try and outsmart my brain. It's pointless. The fact of the matter is I am ignoring the emotional facts, even now. My scalp feels no tracks when I run my fingers through my hair. Am I moving?

LIAR.

Down to the last drug trial. Ignoring the misery of her existence enables me to get lost in my own selfish world. Survival is the strongest instinct. When I get my hands on them. I shiver, I can't feel my hands. I hear humming.

Who is humming, Mom?

It's that fucker Frank. I'm drifting away, a sensation of rising, higher and higher, a unique feeling of weightlessness. My mind goes off to infinite erotica. Who would think even now, at this stage, I titillate. I can hear the hushed undertone of the day, served up on a sterile tray. Lavender fumes fumigate the room. Mom? I let the reels play unabated. The fuzziness returns. My red eye complete with the black dots indented in my eyeballs, congealed seeping I can't lick up. I try to make sense of it all. The trivia of the last few hours I would have respected if I had known to.

Mom, my body feels very light. I'm rising higher and higher.

I mumble incoherently.

LIAR.

I will begin at the start of this day, a mere twenty-four hours, as I recall it, as I understand it. I was taking my mother to her appointment. In the ordinary is the extraordinary.

*****

Change is in the air. Autumnal early mornings in Florida chill one's blood. Illusionary colors fade, I see invigorating orange and dull brown, a scene of decay or regeneration. Fallen dead leaves smother the earth. Clogging leaves block out the light; I swish the wipers but they matt the windscreen. A bit worse for wear this morning, I see the hassle in everything. I'm struggling to maintain composure amidst the deadness in nature surrounding my decomposing personal life … My beloved mother, a medical fore-runner in her field of palliative care, is disintegrating right before my eyes, ganging up with the natural surrounds. Sneaking a side view glance, Mom gingerly walks to the car, pulling a wrapped up rug behind her. She can barely manage, her wasting muscles unable to be loyal, because the motor neurons will not recharge. The mother I know is a true lady of graceful beauty, but she hobbles along these days.

Her legs are the first limbs to weaken, they folded beneath her, I could not catch her. Physical forms slip through fingers, just as I drop my cell phone. If only we were creatures of the sea, my mother could move with ease. We loved our adventure on the jet ski. I clipped her life jacket, said a silent prayer and clung to her for dear life as the machine spitted and hopped. We screamed with terror but it was too late, we were on the move. Wisps of water played on our faces. Her bravery was instant, the speed increased in nanoseconds. Scrunching my eyes shut, I screamed. I had to open them and look.

Her cap flew into the air before landing on the water. We slowed and went to turn around to retrieve it but her turn of the machine was too sharp. Both of us were chucked into the ocean. The buoyancy jackets bobbed us in the sparkling water, our laughter echoed to eternity. Mom was light as a feather, carefree and most important, pain free. How can I regain that freedom for her again? The assistance boat came to our aide and we wanted to get back on that bucking machine. There is no one to help us now. A sharp heat stings my breastbone and spreads uncomfortably over every inch of my skin. I must stop staring at her efforts and scrutinizing her ability. I hop out of the car, rush up the driveway to go to her rescue.

'Are you hauling a dead body to the clinic?'

I stun her with my fleeting remark. Mom barely smiles, I can tell she is in more pain than ever. The doctor in her will surely have a plan with the medical team today. Hobbling, she makes a few more tentative steps to my awaiting car.

'I dug up my rose bush for you, Olive,' she pants. What the? I don't want a plant, but I say nothing as I take the heavy gift from her and lug it to the trunk.

'Thanks,' I say but my head nods with mystification. 'Don't get your case,' I intervene to prevent her journeying backwards to the house. 'Let me.' I kiss the top of her head, passing her on my way back up the driveway. Then it strikes me as odd, missing. The car! Where is Mom's car? Maybe it's in for a service, that's why she has me drive today. I'm back to my car before her.

Determinedly, Mom gets in.

'Oh, the pain.' She breathes deeply, the exhales draw puffs of cloud on the windscreen.

I look away from her painful effort. Lifting her body up off the upholstery, we pretend she is content as she angles for the hundredth time to rest in the seat, trying in vain to make herself comfortable. Clutching her bag on her knee with one arm, guarding her belongings, her hunched back avoids the frame. I cannot comprehend my mother being old, it astounds me, the duality of how she is in my mind and how she is in reality. The email notice flashes on the car monitor, distracting me. I tap the screen and read.

'It's the office. Hold on.'

'Can you not give me five uninterrupted minutes, Olive?'

'None of us have that luxury, Mom,' I wink and check Twitter while she reaches for the seatbelt. 'Kim Kardashian has a new hairstyle,' I gaze. 'Nice. See, Mom.'

An idea nudges me, my inner eye treasures my mother's beauty that I grew up with, held in time, in a picture I love, that Dad took when they were dating.

9

'Mom, I must upload a photo you have in your bedroom, on the dressing table.'

Morphing reality with wishes, it is hard to believe she is the same person. As if aware of my intense gazing, Mom glances at me in return. There, I caught it. A worried frown flicks across her eyebrow before edging into her wrinkles, cementing the cracks of strain. Are my private concerns as obvious to my mom? I have worn a long-sleeved top to camouflage my flare of anxiety.

'Better still, dear, you take the original copy, and the encased silver frame.'

'I couldn't, you treasure it.' I'm about to pull off the curb when, forcibly, the back passenger door is jerked open.

'What the fuck?' I yell, as a crumpled young man lands heavily in the back seat of the car. Damn it, my BMW is going to get nicked. Unblinking eyes bulge in his head. He pulls on the headrest behind my mother. I react. 'Help!' I scream at him. Ridiculous, why am I addressing him? The back window is blank; no one is about in the early dawning hour.

'Dr Lily!' He spits a splurge of saliva onto my face. His ragged voice burns my ears. Frantically, he grabs her shoulders, forcing his agenda. She cries out in pain.

I punch his arm. 'Leave my mother alone, you fuck.' The guilt of my inadequacy cripples me. 'Get the hell out!' My rage surfaces vocally.

'Olive dear, please?' The steadiness of her tone stumps us all. Lily implores that gap to regain command. 'Let's all remain calm.'

The deranged man, confused by the tenderness, eases his grip. He notices my look of concern, and lifts his hands inches off my mother's frame, recognition of horror.

I roar at him again. 'Leave us alone, man!'

He has a lost look in his eyes.

'Drew? What are you doing at my house?' He doesn't answer mom; his attention is on my face. 'How do you know where I live?'

Glazed expressions flit across his face as he voices, 'Who are you?' I don't answer but look at Mom because she is addressing him.

'You have not met this daughter before, Drew. You and I were to meet in the office this afternoon.'

'Were you at the house?' His mind trails. 'Are you one of the team?'

'The house?' I say. Is he talking about my parents' house because we are parked outside it? He takes a cell phone out of his pocket and scans my face again and then looks at a picture on his phone. Mom's view is restricted, she is angled around, but I can see clearly.

'Is that you at Round Wood?' He points a very dirty nail at a person in the shot. I lean in. He holds up the photo and pushes it into my face. My family is on a lavish lawn, my parents and my sister Missy sit with a group of mixed ages. Drew is there and children play in the background of a luxurious New England-style house, dating back to the 1920s, by the intricate woodwork.

'No, that's my sister. I'm not in that picture.'

He doubts me and brings the image up to his nose tip. Dribbles from his mouth moisten the glass.

Repeating in a calm manner, slicing through the fear, emanating from us, in the cocoon of the vehicle, 'Drew,' she calls.

He responds to Mom's voice but I override her. 'Whose place is that?' I ask him.

'The fellowship's pad,' he recalls and becomes agitated. 'I thought you could be a witness.'

'The team will meet you.' Mom maps his way and intervenes. Short, definite answers bounce off him, his

11

overly panicked body a vessel of non-absorbent material.

'I've opened her grave,' his voice grovels. Mom's back arches stiffly. I'm grinding my teeth as I lift up my cell phone from the hold.

Mom tries another platitude. 'I will ask them for details you want to know, Drew.'

'Right now. I want to go right now, with you,' he adds rapidly, his mind racing.

'You will not,' I spit this time. 'Get out of my car, you crazed fool.'

'Olive,' Mom hounds. 'Have mercy.'

The odd turn of phrase jars in me but the term of endearment registers with him. He starts weeping uncontrollably. Dr Lily hands him a fresh-laundered hankie. Her care puzzles me.

'The team,' he croaks like a frog, in between the gaps of his distress. 'You should meet the team,' he instructs me, irony lacing off him as his head bounces off the ceiling. Then he stares through me.

'We won't meet the team if we don't get going,' I say. His eyes alight with lunacy.

'I'll be there, Dr Lily, three o'clock you said.' And with that promise, he leaves our car, mumbling, 'I wanted to make sure you were going in.'

I pull out at high speed.

'Bloody mad man, Mom,' I hurl as I drive off, the back door not secured nor my mother's safety belt intact. I glare at her. 'What was that about? How do you know that man? Is he a patient of yours?' Once I am out of immediate danger, the enormity of the risk registers with me and my mind goes into overdrive.

'Shush for a minute, dear.' She flusters in her handbag. 'I need to make a call.' She spends more time retrieving her cell phone than including me in her space. The seconds tease me, heavy with silence. She dials and waits. I wait. The conversation is one way, a voicemail call. I hear her instruction: 'Frank, we have company today, double trouble.' My head swings towards her. What the! She hangs up and ignores my intuitive stare.

'What is that about, Mom?'

'Frank is a colleague.'

That is not what I meant, company and trouble is the ballpoint area I'm covering but Mom fills in approaching gaps.

'Frank is my IMCA.' Simply put. Short initials for what? If she had texted me this I would be confused.

'Mom, you have to explain. I ... MC what?' I do not take my eyes off the road this time but I hear her intake of breath under my words.

'A for advocate. Frank is an Independent Mental Capacity Advocate.'

The simplicity of her knowledge is not shared by me. I have not heard of an IMCA or Frank before.

'Is Drew a patient of Frank's?'

'No, dear.'

Seconds pass. I force the topic. 'And?'

'Frank's a compassionate advisor dear. He befriended Drew and his partner in her hours of need.'

Compassionate is not a word I know either. My ass slides from left to right in the seat. The battered silver Nissan looks out of place under the majestic tree avenue as it tails us.

'Drew is keeping close tabs on us, Mom.'

'We will be safe in the clinical set-up, dear. Keep going.'

LIAR.

Unspoken fear mutates, a thriving weed system below ground level, sucking energy. We drive in compounded silence as my brain races.

'Why did I not get invited to the soiree?' Hurt glistens in my words. 'Looks like a nice place.'

13

'Oh, you were working, dear.' She sidetracks, 'The house is magnificent, comfortable and relaxing, kindly gifted to the cause of ...' With a slight break, she adds, 'of patients.'

'Charity?' I quiz. Mom is involved in altruistic pastimes.

'Yes, a charity of like-minded individuals.' Her blasé tone does not partner her body language. I'm witness to her agonizing intakes and the continuous shifts of her skinny, skeletal bones offering no relief. Her ankles cross and uncross so many times I lose count of the brittle clicks. The airwaves of R'n'B tunes reach my soul. The passage of time is not being kind to Mom's body. It is hard to watch. There is a chill running down my spine collaborating with the damp autumn dawn dew seeping into us as we drive deeper into its ravine. The protective metal of the car is moistened. The road is monotonous, on it goes, toying with human mortality. It depresses me, this road will be here long after we are gone. I shake myself to lift my mind out of negativity.

'Try not worry, Mom.' Pointless words offend us both.

'Dad was up wandering with the daybreak,' she speaks mournfully.

'The usual then,' I reply. Why we let the diurnal clock animate our time, I don't know. Who made these man-made rules? Dad is hounded by the normality of time. I went to bed with the dawn rays. Rules are made to be broken.

'Did you eat breakfast, Mom? Together?' Alluding to the loving companionship my parents have always brings a smile to my mom's face.

'Yes, dear, we did.' Her chuckle softens my inquisition. 'And I went to the toilet and wiped my bum. I didn't wipe your dad's.'

'Funny, Mom,' I jest in return.

Her merriment transforms the reality but I think my mom looks older almost overnight. Today, she is different from yesterday. I'm observing this extremity. I curse this turn of events. Mom is studying me. We fixate on one another momentarily, mere seconds yet a powerful connection. I see concern spring in the circles of her pupils. Reflected in my mother's sharp, blue eyes, as clear as a mirror, is our fused fear. I look away and view the road. I control the day in as much as I am the driver, the deliverer of the goods, the means to the end. We are the meal on the table for the practitioner, the patient to the doctor. I wonder how my mother, a doctor who becomes the patient, mingles on the other side of medicine. I pay attention to the build of traffic but my mind wanders; whatever my mother is feeling or thinking in this moment, there is no controlling. Worry invades our genetic beauty.

'I need a coffee, do you want one?' Pulling into a Starbucks drive-thru, I note Drew does the same. He is mirroring my car.

'Yes, please, and a doughnut, dear.' She pats her handbag on her knee. 'I have to get you to sign a consent form,' and she starts to rummage. 'Where is my purse? I have it in here,' and the wide gap reveals the contents in her bag. Expertly, she wields a gun. The car swerves and veers by a car exiting. 'I will put this out of sight.'

'Mom,' I shout again.

'Stop the drama, dear. Can't a mother have a piece?'

I almost crash the car. 'You have a gun.' The incredulity floods my voice.

'I've had a gun since before you were born, dear.'

I'm confused. Mom's a pacifist. 'Why are you carrying a gun in your bag on the way to the clinic?'

'Careful, Olive.' She multitasks, the irony of her caring temperament, the gun-wielding doctor. 'To

15

answer your question: In case your dad takes it upon himself to go searching in the bedside drawer,' she summarizes. 'He would think it's a tin opener or something more mundane.'

'Here, give it to me.'

'No, Olive.' Her voice is crisp. 'I have organized a member of the staff to hold onto it for me.' And she firmly replaces the gun in her bag and pulls the zip. Her gnarled fingers are at war with the joining seams. I respectfully look away, but I swivel my head to look at her again after a few seconds.

'Keep an eye on the line-up of cars, Olive,' she instructs. 'It's all arranged, dear.' Still she struggles with the zipper. I reach over and complete the last pull for her.

A huff angers the cavity. A member of the staff is the wrong person to be stashing a gun. But she has not asked my opinion.

Dr Lily progresses tentatively, 'There will be plenty of time to clarify things up in the clinic, dear. I'll fill you in on everything there.' Purposely, she welcomes the weak sunrays shining on her face. 'Today is the day.'

'Two grande, double-shot, soya lattes with two doughnuts, please,' I order into the hatch and sit back. 'Mom? That looks very like your car?'

'Where?' She pushes her chin up which matches her higher octave, her voice is louder.

'Two cars ahead, pulling out into the lane.'

'I can't make it out.'

She's not wearing her glasses I see. 'It is your grey Mercedes.'

'He must be taking it for a test run.' She blows the irregularity away, 'The law of probability,' she mutters, almost to herself. 'This is the local store.'

'It's in for a servicing?'

'Something like that, dear.'

I study the rearview mirror. Drew is right behind us, in line. He gets out of his car and walks to Mom's side window, she presses the open button.

He says nothing. Drew is hovering at the window. He shivers in the t-shirt he is wearing, the heat of the sun not yet strong. A rank smell of sweat reaches me. He trembles with fright, like a runaway animal. Mom passes her jumper to him. 'You will feel cold because you are in shock, Drew.'

'Mom!'

'I have no need for it where I am going, dear.'

Shell shocked pause, Drew is undecided if he will wrap up. 'That will be sixteen dollars total,' says the teller. I pay and pass the first cup over to mom. The safety of my car is my preference but I get out and take the second tray and walk around the front to Drew. I push a warm cup of coffee into his hands, I can reorder. A lost expression clouds his eyes. 'Thanks, I have no money on me. I slept in the car ...' Instinctively, I go to leave, uncertain of his state of mind. This is the first time I have been asked by my mom to be her carer in any form. I'm unnerved by the irregularity and by his company.

I have never had to hang around with her associates.

I never fully understood this confusing day.

'Here, Olive, you take my coffee,' suggests Mom as I get in beside her.

'No,' I say but she puts her cup in my hands.

'I've had a cup with Jim.'

A quirky group, passing around the cups. Mechanically, Drew sips the steaming coffee with no response, oblivious to our kindness. He is lost to himself.

A lone sailor on a solo journey.

How was I to know Drew and I would become kindred spirits this very day? Grief makes lunatics of us.

17

The silence for me is uncomfortable with heaviness. I zoom up the window. He stands there. I drive out the exit.

'Thank you for accompanying me, dear.' I hear a sob in her voice; it mellows her tone. 'It means so much to me, you being with me, more than you realize Olive.' Her eyes mist over. I intervene to lift her mood, words are jewels of history.

'Hear me out. I understand the implications of this day, the final untried medication. Hopefully it will shift the very ground we both tread on,' I console.

My intelligence gnarls my insides; I can feel it before I can digest it, bile rises, the acidity of my stomach is spewing up the one piece of toast I could barely swallow. We will make plans. I will be available to my mother more than I am, if I have to pencil in appointments to protect our intimacy.

'Remember when I took you on the jet ski for your seventieth?' I tease.

'How could I forget that fun?' We giggle.

'You are a daredevil,' my admiration is audible.

'I know, the slightest turn on the accelerator and it gleans the surface,' she laughs. 'I surprised myself.'

'There is always a way, Mom.'

'Yes, dear, there is.'

'The water held your weight and lifted the pain from your muscular frame.'

'Olive, that was a great idea, dear. Thank you'

'Listen up, I have another one. Will we go up in a hot air balloon?' My words elevate with enthusiasm. 'Lifting to the sky and being carried along in the breeze will not cause you any pain. And you will love it. Gliding over treetops and lakes, seeing the world for miles and miles from the sky.' My joy rolls off me. 'The ethereal movement is astonishingly breathtaking. And we can pack a picnic basket.'

18

Mom clutches the armrest and leans towards me, her raspy breath tunes out the radio with a lifelong tune of our own.

'I love you, Olive.'

'I love you, too.'

'I love you three.' She smiles at our ritual.

'I love you four.' My infant steps learning how to count come to play.

Mom made learning fun.

'I love you forever,' she voices to the universe her universal truth.

'I love you more,' I recount my last line.

'I know you do.'

'Ahh,' we simultaneously reply in union. We laugh, just as we did every night when we hugged and voiced this pledge, a childhood memory to see me through to and in adulthood, our nighttime intimacies spilling into every aspect of our life. I want to be her protector, my mother has been mine.

'Almost there. Mom, you know you can talk to me, right? About anything.' My voice is definite and strong, only I feel the lump in my throat or can the doctor notice it? I make a quick turn of my head her way and then focus on the road again.

'Why do you say that, dear?' Mom remains looking ahead. The windscreen opens up the world, slicing us to minimal beings.

'You must be worried about today.' My vision is marked, attentive to the immediate car bumper feet ahead of us.

'No, Olive, I'm not worried for me.' And she smiles and turns to me. 'Quite the opposite, dear.'

'Are you not afraid of doctors? You know how they can be, having been a consultant yourself. Always having to look over your shoulder, isn't that how you put it?'

'We are not monsters, dear, you misunderstood me; it's the system that is horrific, not the doctors.'

'The clash of the clan in revolt then,' I joke.

She looks startled. 'You've no idea how spot on you are, dear.'

I dislike people, no matter how defined their roles. Ordered, numerical systems work for me. Lawsuits and human error are swallowed by the medical arena, which is a minefield. Many a case has upped my payroll, discrepancies offset medical expenditure, it's a given. Compensation is a lucrative business. I gleefully deduct my percentage.

Her phone rings. She registers the caller and does not answer the phone. 'Better to talk to the team in person, and we are just here,' she alludes to my curiosity. 'Today I intend to gain well-deserved peace,' and Mom blesses herself.

'You okay then, Mom?'

We are just there. Deciding to let her arrive quietly, without me prepping her for action, is best. I concentrate on the road sign, directing to a posh-looking avenue.

'I'm okay then.' I note she has purposely repeated my turn of phrase.

We both voice, 'Jim.'

'Poor Dad.'

'Yes, it is pitiful to witness,' and her voice tears up. 'The loss of self.' Mom takes a measured intake of breath, and hastily adds, 'an apt description for the cruelty of Alzheimer's.'

Three little words with mammoth description: loss of self. Both my parents are leaving me as I have known them. I swerve with gathering speed.

'Can you drive a little slower, dear? Please.'

I do drive fast but not now, and being accused unfairly flares my temper. 'Drive carefully, dear Olive.

20

You have a long life ahead of you, treasure it.' Mom's voice, is certain and strong, unlike her aging body. 'I trust you with my very life, dear daughter,' mesmerizes Mom in a citation.

Her mind is sharp, a prized asset in her professional life of medicine. My mind is sharp but I am no match for her. How will she assimilate into the environment as a patient, a little old lady? Will she be an outsider in her elder years? I do not expound the obvious. It is not the time to be right. We exist in different time zones, I can't stand how limp-along my mother's world is. The dilution of my norms heckles me.

'Okay is a bullshit word,' I throw out there. 'It tells one very little and masks a multitude.' I feel her eyes on me but she lets me be. The dread stays close, hanging onto me like a strand of lost hair.

If only, if only, should have … the curse of retrospect. The pulse of dread could have been paid attention to. All would not have been lost.

I drive on in private turmoil. I can talk to my mom but there are brutal areas of intense honesty that I can't open up to. I'm all over the place. Hidden dilemmas I'm still trying to figure out for myself. I'm sure it's the same for all of us, even for my elderly mother; she is in the arena of existing like the rest of us. Is my mom a carrier of the disease? The overwrought worry has me uptight today.

My parents are growing old and I don't know how to handle them or me. We could spend a lifetime talking about it, I suppose, and there would still be issues to clarify that would go beyond my remit. I wish I had tried before Dad faded. My blood boils. Dementia has no conscience. I'm afraid of the loss, my sadness. My selfish little corner of the world where I'm happy for them to exist is narrowing everyday. I'm disheveled by this unpredictable and uncontrollable cycle. The ground

21

is shifting my house. I do want to tell my mom of my fears, but then that is the problem: it's not about me or my. It is about them but it was always about us as a unit. We are a family.

We drive into the grounds of the clinic. Heavy, impressive gates demand respect. Landscaped Floridian royalty of symmetric colours and heights beam a mood of lush serenity.

'Fuckin' new drug better work,' I demand, of the medicine, projecting my voice off the roof. This, our last juncture, Mom has been on every pill available.

'Human nature fixates on details to avoid the problems.' Her professional voice of old is music to my ears. 'Drugs are the new gods in our lives.'

We are all playing with potions, diluting and dissolving the real problem of aging. So we talk in generalizations, about everything except saying the existential essential, the mildew rotting roots of our family tree.

LIAR.

If we do not mention the fungus, it may not spread. I, the accomplished accountant, never totted up this immeasurable disease of lies, a secondary evaluation after the rising medical costs of both my parents. Unnerving, my weakness is alienating me from them. I cannot figure out the length and breadth of fear. Clear logic is my usual forte. The unknowns don't suit me. I forget humans are the gods of the universe these days.

Illogically, I pull over to the sidewalk.

I could have abandoned this day.

Drew's silver car pulls in behind us.

'Olive, I hate being sick too, but there is nothing I can do.'

We both notice reciprocal tears on our flushed cheeks, tears that honor the truth of our situation. I fall to her, a victim of nature too and want to be nurtured in

22

her arms. I can't help myself, she has always wrapped me in her arms.

'You look tired, dear,' notices Mom, the grayish circles under my eyes easily spotted to a knowing eye.

'Touché, Mom,' I reply, we both grin. 'I had to work late, sleep came in the early hours of the morning.'

'You work too hard, dear,' she adds, nodding her head in dismay.

Her fingers brush my hair. It nearly trips off my tongue that my erotic hobby had played a big part in a late night but some things I do not tell my mom. 'Yeah, Mom, I know.' I smile. The realization that mothers do not disclose certain details to their offspring did not register with me until now. I notice Drew has stayed in his car, small graces.

She gently pats my back. 'It will all pan out, dear. These things have a way of working themselves out.' Silence responds to her. I'm not ready. 'Let's move on with this day, dear.' The words reverberate the sounds of agreement as I confirm with a shake of my head.

More talk without saying much.

The details are lagging on the journey. 'And you are hurting my shoulders,' she squeezes out in a soft yet sorrowful lush.

'Jeepers, Mom, I'm sorry.'

Every touch now inflicts injury. Her handbag is digging into my stomach too. I lift up and situate to grasp the steering wheel.

We're intimately close but there is an intrusion in the cavity of my little vehicle. Dread is lodged between us. Unknowingly, this emotion breaks our connection, an invasion of shell shock paralysis, and stuns me from reacting to her humility, yet this is the very day for such gallantry.

Emotional upheaval gets lost in practicalities.

Words churn around and around. My head hurts.

23

Humans have always been in motion. On cue, I turn the ignition.

Mom gets out the words. 'Stop pulling against me,' she pleads. 'Please.' I hear her anguish, yet I am oblivious to her distress and swallow up her words undigested. 'Work with me, dear.'

Her cell phone demands attention.

I see frenzied ambition in her darting eyes. She texts, the larger letters allows me to read: **Alert - Drew in grounds.**

Who is she texting?

Would she have told me? Her voice, calm and collected, hypnotized him too, Drew threw me a curve ball, just as my mother had. The orchestration continued, and I continued.

She catches me glancing at her phone screen. I react and look away. Then she places the gun on her lap.

'Mom, I'm not happy with that carry on. Give the gun here.'

'No, don't touch it. I don't want your fingerprints on the gun.' I feel the quiver in my diaphragm. 'I don't want you to be implicated.'

'Implicated?'

'My patients are my patients.'

LIAR.

Mom reserves anonymity, I assumed to protect me, not her. This juncture is where I regret not stalling myself, not letting Drew speak up. He could have prevented it.

Indecision.

'Fuckin' idiot,' I swear to the rearview mirror. I see him tailing us.

'The poor man is beside himself with grief. His young bride died, she was a lovely girl. Client of mine.' And Mom drifts into a silent recalling. Softly, I hear her murmur, 'riddled with cancer ... Poor Drew.'

'Poor girl,' I empathize.

'No hope,' Mom replies, 'til we gave her hope.'

White knuckles glare at me, the wheel can suspend my pent up frustration and take the pressure. The skin is taunt on my stressed hands, my six weekly jabs of botox can't offer such elasticity.

'I'll get the team to give him some time today.' Determination masks Mom's eyes. She has the kind of face where the wrinkles recede behind the crystal glint in her eyes. Intelligence abounds in her mind up to her late sixties.

Stupidly, I continued onward. I drive us to the end.

'Okay, doll, let's concentrate on you and show them what you're made of.' I want my Mom to recuperate and gain strength. 'Forget him.'

'That's my gal, how is your work?' Similarly, we have a zealous approach to our careers. I note she continues to text.

'Work is hectic, Mom.' Focusing on the mundane is the survival tactic we've been employing to get us through her ordeal of checking into this clinic.

Mom nods her head again. 'You're a competent woman, Olive. We are very alike, you and I.'

'Yeah, Mom, we are. I have your work ethic. Thanks,' I smirk, although I am so proud. I fill her in. 'I've signed off on a big case just hours ago and I'm happy with that,' I continue, to fill the gap of avoidance. I'm on the edge, almost free falling and it's scaring the shit out of me, rehashing what I know will steady me even as I feel harassed. Almost as if my inner eye was all seeing and trying to shift my ground.

But I let my intellect override my gut. 'I've been offered a job promotion in the London office, but I'm not sure.'

'Why?'

'London was never in the plan.'

'Plans change, Olive.'

'They do Mom.'

25

'Don't let fear stop you, Olive, ever.'

'Will you go over with me for a few days when I sit the interviews next month? My treat. We can do our Thanksgiving gifts.'

Mom becomes agitated. I'm glad I did not tell her the cost of this drug before the trial. I don't think these few precious minutes are the right time to have an offload.

I regret talking shop.

'We can shop at Harrods and visit the palace and the change of guards,' I suggest excitedly.

'I don't need the latest style,' jokes Mom.

Whistling at the Porsche as it glides by, I miss the dismissal of the invitation. 'There is prosperity in medicine. I can see the new building ahead.' Half an hour only has gone by and my life is somersaulting.

'Are we here already?' Distress resounds in her voice. Her frame rises and falls with deepening intakes. 'Olive, you know you don't have to be on top of things all the time.' I shrug my shoulders. 'No, listen to me, please, dear. I understand that now, the privilege of aging wisdom.'

My young ears are closed.

'Go with the flow, Olive. Things have a way of solving themselves. Everything becomes irrelevant eventually, with time.'

'Only an old person can talk like that, Mom.'

'Thanks very much, dear.' A hurtful uplift of tone is obvious in her endearment but her smile is strangely tart.

'Sorry ... I don't mean to add insult to injury.'

'I know you mean me no harm dear.'

LIAR.

Why had I stopped talking at the opportune cusp of time? Afraid to add limitless offense to her character, she has achieved this herself. This day was an ordinary day, but it is extraordinary.

26

I leave the philosophy to her as I navigate the steady flow of arriving traffic, humanity at its meanest. We journey in companionable silence. Mom is quieter than usual. I figure she has to be a little scared. We make quite a pair. The link between us may need maintenance at times but we are a duo to be reckoned with. I build up to the disclosure, the guilt is choking me. I cough croakily. But then the job is done for me because my phone rings.

'Hello?'

'Hi, Olive, it's Pam.'

Wow my P.A. is contacting me at 7.30am. Impressive.

'You're on loud speaker.'

The hint goes way over her head. The disclosure lands. 'I've set the meeting for 2pm today, a late lunch as you instructed.'

Mom's eyebrows arch.

I bite my lip. Holding my breath, I hang up without further ado, the words tripping out of me. I rake my fingers through my hair, a sure telltale sign I'm under pressure.

'I'll have to leave you for two hours and go into work later, Mom.' The mood changes instantly, the hollow tin car the perfect setting for my shallowness. 'I have a meeting with the client I was telling you about, she has to sign off on her account. I need her signature.'

'I need your signature too.' Mom says nothing more. I'm confused. The friction crackles. I'm grinding my teeth. The engine handles my enforced pressure on the pedals, logistic stunts I can employ as we speed up the avenue. We are here and we are barely talking. Aware I'm backtracking on the deal, we had our arrangement, I mesh the details.

'I'm the next of kin, to be present at the clinic at all times, if you have a reaction to the medication or something today. Can you stall the trial until I come

27

back in?' That must be the consent form she wants me to sign. Mom still remains silent.

'I'll hurry back to you,' I fluster rapidly, to avoid the hardened stance. My nails tear my scalp.

'I would prefer if you re-schedule your appointments, Olive and assist me in my business at hand today.' And she shuffles angrily and too fast, I hear her wince in pain. 'I thought we had an agreement. I had your word.'

'I know Mom but for fuck's sake, it's only a couple of hours.'

'That is all it takes for me too, Olive.'

I glare out the windscreen.

We all have deadlines. I do not want to argue. I continue cautiously, the air laden with stress by two determined women journeying en masse. 'If the meeting runs over time, I will wind up, I promise.'

'Do as you please, Olive. We all have to do what we have to do.'

My breathing shortens. Was my mom saying it was okay for me to do my stuff today?

'In my professional experience, it is always family that lets a person down. Nothing changes much.'

Having to drive the car is getting in the way. I can't give her my full attention, the conversation is disjointed. I want to throttle her. I've killed before. I'm a twin, was a twin. Karma. I sucked the life from the weaker one and was born the victor. I thrive on competition to this day. Darwinism accompanies my every step. I should tell her I'm giving her my time, right now. Ungrateful mother!

'I was hoping my case would be different,' she adds softly, talking to herself.

She is right about universal norm of family. Any funeral I attend, there are more friends upset than family presently suffering. I bite my lip, egging myself to stay calm. We have done fine so far, we are almost there. The claustrophobic tightness is sucking us both inward.

LIAR.

A three dimensional hologram, Mom sits rigid, I sit rigid, and the truth of the matter sits rigid. The grotesque draped over us, the ironic prop of journeying.

I fume.

Does she forget I'm a grown-up with a life of my own? I cannot be at her beck and call. The voice in my head is in full conversation with me. How the elderly forget they were once young and free to live their lives. Now I could murder again. I can't tell her I had myself tested for MND, ALS as the New Yorkers termed it. Mom is not to be made feel I'm marking her gene pool for a downgrading.

'Hmm,' the neurologist blew an opening in her lips. 'Tiredness is a universal norm.'

The symptom I presented to the paperwork.

'No rise in a ceratine kinase in the bloods,' she reads stats on a sheet, clipped to a board. 'Do you stumble?' she asked.

'When I'm drunk, I wobble.'

She was not amused. The whizzing around I daily push my body to excel has the doctor's frown deepening.

'Maxing the body is an opinion on a formation of the disease.' She scowls.

'Then the human race will end up forming it,' I say. 'Burn out is an epidemic.'

'The cause of the disease is a mystery.' The intellect opens a can of worms.

On the pretense of a girl's weekend in New York, I presented my genes to the best centre in Manhattan. And it's still a fuckin' mystery why my mom is sick. I pat her shoulder. Will I tell her I tested negative? Maybe

29

another day. For now I keep screening her physical demise. I don't mean to measure her on a scoreboard.

'We are regurgitating similar experiences, Mom.'

'I hope not, Olive.' She sends the wish out into the universe.

'You were a strict timekeeper in your day, Mom.'

'In my day … Ah, I get it, Olive.'

The day will become our day.

'Mom, life is strict, we both live out the same routine, drudge our way through landmarks, women are not that different of bygone eras. How come you can't identify with me? Why can't you recall how you had to chop up time?'

I try to explain how, to her, my time is in demand. Mom sits rigid. 'I'm entitled to a personal day off for a death. I told HR I'm going to a funeral today. Imagine my gall.' I break to draw in air, my face is flushed and sweaty. 'There is the expectation I can get some papers finalized, like after the fake refreshments of my fake funeral. That's all. I won't be gone long, Mom.' I mumble useless words. 'I'm so pumped to have landed this client, Mom, I will hurry.'

A stone cold silence continues.

I'm the young one, I assume my business is more important. How condescending of me. The competitor is the more able bodied. My life is more extreme and taxing than my elderly mother's.

I dare say this to her.

I utilize the silence. The extra paperwork from my parent's aging is frustrating and is mind boggling, with the insurance and medical forms mounting. My mind ticks over the logistics. Deceit was never in the picture I painted. I convince myself to keep quiet. A clinic is not for private intimate matters. Mom always said the medical world is not to be trusted with a person's personal affairs.

30

I was trying my best to stay ahead of the game, in a personal and professional capacity. The itinerary is tight. Can I not give her this one day just for her?

'I can manage by myself.' Her pointed voice of silver steel hardness flattens me.

I met her support team.

'Thanks, Mom, I know you can but I will be there.' I smile, she is frustratingly forgivable. Message alerts twinkle from her cell phone, she engages with her business, dulling me effectively.

The radio saves us from off-loading on one another our pent up nerves. The music facilitates my slipping in the obvious but I can't help myself and finish with a norm.

'Circumstances change, Mom. You know this, for heavens sake.' She sits passively, the disciplinarian of my past. Conformity breeds contempt, I could slap her. Intensely, I grip the wheel. Half of me wants to ask her to hail a taxi, I can gladly go to the office earlier than planned. Does a child have to obey a parent forever? Does a man have a predestined life of obedience when he becomes a husband? Such as my father, Jim, does he fall inline with my mother verbatim? Even my one sister, Missy, conveniently missing, a blur in the family mug shot, will keep in contact with our mother before me. I'm the youngest daughter, who gladly walked in mother's shadow. I muse in the frosty silence, I usher to the universe, I can't wait for this day to be over and done with.

'Let's hurry this shit along then.' Silence greets me again. I can't wait for this day to end.

Anger burns in my chest. It's not for me, playing second fiddle to the master fiddler. Mom is the composer, always has been and always will be. It maddens me at times. But I would not want to live without our melody; our music lifts my spirits to soar

31

beyond the sphere of comprehension because it's the very essence of my soul, although our loyalty within the family confounds me at times. Officialdom will save the landslide. I change tack.

'I'll sign the form before I head off.' Collaboration to lead us along.

'Yes, Olive,' she replies. 'There is one form in particular I must hand over to the team today.' In her hand a crisp singular sheet is waved at me. 'I have signed it already, last night. And with your dad, his signature is on the form too. And Missy's.'

'Oh …' I focus on the road even as my intelligence jumps ahead with this news. Mom is not always a step in front of the processes. All the documents are vetted by me usually. Dad's dementia knocks him out of the ballpark, nullifying the legality of his signature. But I quiz her. 'Missy too? Why are all our signatures necessary?'

'I will go through it in detail with you when I'm checked in and the procedures commence.' She grips the bag tightly. 'Keep going dear.'

We sit side-by-side, a million miles apart. Taking orders is reverting me back to my childhood. It does not sit well with me. 'Mom, a grown woman can't be treated like a child.'

'I know that dear.' The car drives on.

The avenue pulled us along, like a conveyor belt.

L I L Y

Oh no! How is the car journey over? We are here. I can't go into the clinic yet. Olive; I need more time with her before the team come on board and start to direct our day. I'm ready, calm even, I've made up my mind. My concern is for my child. Elements of my life flourished but motherhood is the core of who I am. My children gave me more, more than I ever gave them. I have to say thank you.

Red tares from the thorns twine a pattern on what little flesh hangs on my fingers. Leaving Jim's warm embrace, I tiptoed into the garden in the middle of the night, adorned in a floral-nightie overcoat. Digging in the midst of the rose bushes, I selected the burnt orange blossom, five head bloom, of tangerine perfume.

It will stun Olive in the summer. All will be forgiven by then.

I must remind her, she will have to be careful of the thorns, the stark branches, like a witch's broom. I had to unravel the knotted roots, physically and mentally. The urge came in a flash, the removal from the heavy soil took hours. There are no buds yet for Olive to see, but the power lies within. I hope she minds my favourite rose bush.

Drew has robbed me of my peace of mind, the opportunity to engage our intellectualism. Olive is a tough negotiator.

The cold air salutes my self journey's personal plans, the chill before the freeze. I wish to share my inner thoughts, the very workings of my soul because then Olive will understand me and what I am about.

I'm afraid of my own body, a tragedy for a doctor to confront; the chronic pain taunts the onslaught of the muscular revolt the motor neuron disease releases on me daily. Eventual shutdown I have to look forward to. For now, twisting in the car unravels me. Simple movements incur torturous rips of pain along my legs and in my hands. Prolonged healing, a tidy description for constant aggravation, the doctor in me knows the drill. And families do not always agree on the treatments, I'm certain of that fact too.

Olive looks annoyed with me, she is impatiently tapping the wheel. Wait until the day moves along and then she will reel with anger. Kids, what you think they can do, and what they do, are two different realities. But I love her with every inch of my being. She is a blessing, pure joy. I'm full of gratitude and pride, she is a great daughter.

Why have I left telling Olive so late?

She has proven her worth, her metal, and is a young woman of stamina I'm in awe of. With her capable mind, she could have easily done medicine. Doctors develop a coping mechanism, I have. Olive's emotional intelligence I'm unsure of; up to today, I've never measured the character of my little one. We always glided magnificently together through the years.

But no two people think the same way.

No regrets, I will not entertain regret, I tell myself. My brain instructs, but my heartbeat is racing, my soul is searching and my treacherous limbs are torturing.

My heart is breaking. I stepped over the threshold of my home at the start of my marriage, and again this morning, at the end of my marriage. Jim does not comprehend the farewell kiss I planted on his cheek as he lay asleep. I'm glad he does not know how to worry anymore, dementia's only grace. I've said my goodbyes. I do wish a final visit to my birthplace had come about, so I'm like the ordinary Irish-American on that score; the pace of my degeneration is speedy, denying me my freedom.

Those close to me have reeled in their reactions and have been supportive to my cause. As a consultant, I'm aware of the statistics. There is always a negative. In every family, there is one who will disagree and oppose the decision. Olive is going to be my one. I know it. I've always known it because she is my champion. If she feels strongly about something, she will ignite a divergence to a plan. 'Very like her mother,' I hear Jim renounce.

Olive would be proud of my fun of late. I went up to a stranger on the street yesterday, and said, 'Here you are,' and handed her a hundred dollar bill, a regular occurrence of mine recently. 'Did you win the lotto?' the middle aged lady wondered with a delusional gasp. 'Something like that. Let's say I got my wish,' I threw in, the sheer delight she expressed was empowering. It's only money, but we crave it so. The well wishes and thankfulness I gleaned from strangers was true humanity as it should be. 'I'm a secret millionaire,' became my out clause to prevent me having to explain myself as I went up to people. I have millions, wealthy clients insisted on donating to my medical work. I understand their generosity now, because I too have no need for money, I can't take it with me.

Spread it around is the motto. And I do have a secret. So I'm telling small, white lies. I wish the philanthropist in me had expressed itself earlier in my life, before the winter of my days. The last month has been a laugh. Walmart's car park was a hoot.

Staging my proposal, I parked very near the trolleys. I left the car with the keys in the ignition and a home made sign saying, 'FREE CAR' on the dashboard, with a note sellotaped to the windscreen: 'Myself and my husband can't drive anymore - doctor's orders - please accept this gift of a car. Ownership details in the glove compartment.'

The comedy of it, Olive would have loved to have been with me. As fast as I could, limping along, I took cover and hid behind a people carrier a few spaces up and watched customer's reactions. They stopped, read the sign, looked around, some people did full turns, like ballerinas, but on they went on their merry ways and left the car alone. I almost gave up, but the trickery of spying became addictive. I was enjoying myself.

Holding in a cough, I saw him walk up. Dark haired, loose top and trainers, the young man was the perfect candidate. He lay on the ground and looked under the car, before opening the door and sat in. Reading my note, his head bent to empty the glove compartment. I made it over to him. 'Hi,' I beamed. Like a gymnast, he sprang.

'Lady, I meant no harm,' he said.

'That's okay.' He squarely stared at me. 'This is my car, but I won't be driving it anymore.'

He studied me, then said. 'Am I being punked?'

My hand held my chest. 'No.' He asked if this was a candid camera set-up. I filled with laughter. 'Me, me, a little old lady, presenting a TV show. I'm flattered.'

What a laugh, I told him I can't drive anymore, which was partly the truth. No need to frighten folk, I fudged the dreary details. His kind words helped me more than the old car ever could have. He needed a car, he worked night shifts and not waiting for public transport will cut his sleepless hours and get him home to bed as the world ticks over. I waved him off and hailed a taxi.

He had the decency to call me, via the insurance company making the call, for which I paid the next year up, to thank me again and ask if I had gotten his big bunch of sunflowers. Olive would have got a kick out of the fun. Chronic pain destroys joy. Random acts of kindness have propped me up and kept me strong as this day neared. The color of those last happy days have had an aura to them I've missed. I got into this line of work I practice because of such promise - work with what one has, make a call on it, in the context of now, with no falsehood of wide compromises. This is the way to go, as far as I'm concerned, in the vast medical arena. But the moneyed machine demands continuity.

My marker to this very day in medicine - sometimes the right way to go about business is the considered, wrong, unconventional approach. As a pioneer of choice, I was a success, looking after my own, raising my two fine girls with Jim, working doctor's midnight shifts, refusing to let the glass ceiling exist, and I did it, the ceiling became my floor. I've overcome professional obstacles. Red tape I've never paid homage to, even as the monster of a building towers majestically over us. Impressive décor does not rock my world in the new age clinic, it's the heartbeat of the team I reserve respect for. My team is super, they have treated me with respect.

'Here we are, Mom,' she says. I know she is coaxing me to move. The speed of my existence, my daughter finds alien, just as I find it a nightmare.

'Give me a minute to catch my breath, Olive.' I have mishandled this journey, my daughter, oh, my poor, adorable daughter.

'I should move on, this area is an allocated parking zone,' she says.

'For the love of god, dear, stop rushing on,' I cry out.

'Wow,' she replies. 'Chill.'

I stall.

'Cool place to work in.' She views a modern architectural wonder of crisp lines, light and chrome. The cold sunlight beams off the clinic's structural surfaces, the mean machine sparkles. A long whistle toots from her lips. I smile. I will miss her whistling, the little things hurt the most, not the loss of my house. I'm not morose, because I am true to myself. I have been with all my clients, against the odds, right up to the end.

Though I'm not proud of how I have sidelined Olive. I'm only human.

'She's a beauty, bet this place is costing you a fortune.' Her lilting voice I want to listen to for as long as this day allows. We are snug in the car, our intimacy is guiding me.

'I'm bored out of my mind. I want to get moving, Mom.'

'I have to change the music, dear.' Reaching over, with sheer concentration, the pressing of the buttons to classical hurt my finger's joints. Silencing the R'n'B beats, swirling violinists perform. 'Real music,' I say.

'No appreciation for the young,' her light tone teases.

'Will I hear music in the next life?' My voice trails, a sob clutches my vocal chords.

Olive is unsure how to answer me.

I don't blame her. Who is to know the realm of the unknown? God, why have I left Olive in the dark? Why did I think taking her by the hand, showing her the clinic was the best way? We would not be in this mess today. Missy kept forcing the issue, to tell Olive, bring her up to speed, when I was putting it off and off, Missy had to stay away from her little sister to avoid a reveal

38

of the real situation. Cancelling the morning papers because Jim does not read anymore. Releasing a fund to pay the care agency for Jim. Bringing the cats to a new owner, paying the bills, servicing the boiler, having the insurance sorted. I have been busy. The list was pages long. I ticked off the list, all except for Olive. Olive was top of that list.

And yet here we are, on different pages of the same story.

An awkward silence descends. I smile. Olive relies on her trusted humor. 'Jeepers, how terrible not to have the jammin tunes,' she says.

'Those latest lyrics you favour are very rude, Olive,' I say but there is no point in trying to influence her musical tastes at this late stage.

'Yeah, aren't they fab,' she jests. 'I love their raw content.'

'I suppose, every era to their own. My generation has many needless restraints.' I swallow a lump in my throat. Bravery was never a problem for me, I'm too intelligent to conform. But it's my marvelous mind that has directed me to abandon ship. I have been drawing Olive in too minutely, dissecting her loss, sharing solutions, over thinking. To bring Olive on board, I have to try and make her understand. 'Olive if you were to drive out of here today, without me.' She glares. 'Stranger things happen. What would you miss about us the most?'

'Darn, Mom, what are you going on about?' Her eyebrows spread as her voice widens. 'Why are you asking me such questions?'

'Please, Olive.' I take her hand, 'I have to know.'

Confusion is etched on her face.

'Say what comes to your mind,' I help her, in a precise tone.

'I could not imagine never seeing you, Mom.'

39

'But we do not see that much of one another.' My reply causes her face to crumble. 'I'm not complaining, dear,' I say, rubbing her hand caressingly. 'It's normal for you to have your life without me hogging your time.' I rush on. 'Your job is demanding, and rightfully so, you are good at it. Go for gold. Make the buck. I can't be asking you to come over when the office is open.' She goes to interrupt but I wave my finger. 'And in the evenings, I don't want to go out.'

'I thought you liked the movies and dinners.'

I have to tell the truth. 'Sure do, but only a few times.' Recognition is not dawning on her face. 'I prefer sitting in with your father.' We smile. 'Guys should be with you on dates, not your mother.' Now I see her face making some sense of my point. 'When you find love, you will be your true self and want to be with him, become a unique entity, as you should do.' Her eyes see me. 'I would be a filler act.' I'm losing her again, my strong woman does not believe me on the power of a woman and man's love. 'Rightfully so, your mother is not to hang out or stop you reaching your full potential.'

She hits the steering wheel, 'Why do you not listen to me when I tell you I may never marry?'

'I never said marriage, I said love.'

'Mom, but I'm happy doing my own thing.'

We are on the same track. 'You know I condone such a privilege. But us two, the treats of going places, doing things like the water sports are a once off, with the order of life, I'm aging,' I go for the norm first. 'I won't be able to do them, dear.' She nods, I continue, 'With the curse of my condition ...' but Olive interrupts me.

'I can harness you to me or a big hunk when we jump out of a plane.' She tries to overcome our reality.

'Nope,' I shake my head. 'That's not for me, dear.'

Both of us do not speak. But I do not have the luxury of time today. 'We can't holiday together anymore.

Memories of sand and sea, are in our past, not meant to be in the present, or the future, Olive.' I use every card in the pack. 'You love to ski. And the cruises, four countries in four days, I could never ...'

'The south of France,' she pounces. 'What about Monaco? I want to take you there, I know you would love it.'

'I'm only human.' My smile fades in private thoughts. I would have loved to travel more. I do not tell Olive this wish. They say you regret what you did not do, not what you did. I agree. 'I wish I could just fly away.' She hears my remorse and comes to my aid.

'What I would miss the most is our chats, Mom.' A tear rolls down on the cheek of my brave, straight talking girl. Gathering air in my tired airways before I speak is painfully crippling my frame, but I must keep explaining. 'Yes, me too, dear,' and we are both tearing up. Continue on course, the doctor in me instructs. 'I understand, Olive, I do.' I must try. 'Nobody is around forever.' Go with your beliefs, I instigate. 'I hear the voices of loved ones. Everyday I listen, to loved ones who have passed on.'

Olive is switching off.

We have very different opinions. I can see her bored expression when we talk of anything to do with talk of an afterlife. Time is running out, I will fail in my task. The team will be here, waiting. I have let Olive down. Tears drop from my chin, Olive hands me a tissue.

'Press record on your cell system.' She stares at me like I'm mad. 'You can hear my voice anytime then, dear.' I have left a letter for Olive but if this is one of the thorns of her grief, I will try to help.

'No, Mom. Stop playing with my head.'

'For me, dear?'

Olive presses record.

'I love you Olive ...'

OLIVE

'If you are ready, Mom?' I say again. She says nothing. Why does she not want to leave the car? I'm getting nervous. Is there something wrong?

'Are you worried?' I ask. I assumed she was on top of the medical itinerary. My work commitments will go AWOL if the time moves this slowly this morning. Please let her not be having a relapse, her colour is very pale. Fuck, it's her legs, they must have given in on her completely, she warned me this is coming. 'Mom, will I get help?'

'No, Olive. Just leave this precious short time with you and I, dear.' She senses my confusing frustration, explaining, 'Please, I'm a little worried.'

'Try not worry, Mom.' If only my heart was as strong as my voice. Use my intelligence, I order myself. There must be solutions to her dilemmas. 'I would love to learn how to fly.' My private wishes bring a smile to her tired face. 'A helicopter first,' my energy zings with the outline.

'Really?' she quizzes. 'Why a helicopter?

'So I could pick you up and drop you anywhere you wanted to go and to hell with your future disablements. We can outsmart the use of your legs, Mom.'

Pure pride mixed with utter sorrow flashes across her eyes. I see love and sadness at the same time. It frightens me. Maybe I should not have mentioned her going to be a cripple. Hurriedly, I lighten the future picture with shining strokes of soft hues. 'I will take light aircraft lessons.' I wipe a tear away from her cheek. 'You can come up in the sky on every class, with the instructor and I. We will see the marvelous world from our private vantage point.' I catch my sadness and bury it. 'I will lift you on board, Mom.'

'That sounds fantastic, dear,' a teariness sounds in her voice.

'Imagine the fun, we would love it.' The more I think of it, the more I'm on course to find a way to help her. 'The glorious colours of the sun rising, Mom. Floating clouds, picturesque landscape of green fields, little houses and little people, with little problems.' I sweep her clinging hair from her damp eyes. 'Our big problems will become little ones.'

'You are my best friend, daughter,' she cries.

'It's okay.' I try to interpret her distress, 'Mom, you won't need your legs.' I continue with fragmented handling of her medical situation. 'Can I help you? Let me know what I can do. I will drop you here. Sit on the bench over there, then you will not have to walk far. I will go park the car?' Order keeps me on track.

'I won't have to go far, dear Olive, they are lovely, helpful suggestions.' Long exhalations droop my shoulders downward. There has to be a way around the nightmare of her reality. I sit and wait. What is keeping her so long? Not understanding the effort her limbs have to force themselves through to work is the probable reason, I mindfully converse with myself, Mom is at her full potential. I sit and stare out the window. I'm looking at a squirrel. The tail is spectacularly full and fluffed, it has to get in the way of

43

running up the tree. No, there it goes, out of sight, the branches hide the body. My mother should get in my way but she doesn't, we synchronize. I have to be doing something, I can't just sit.

'Wait until you see the Greece trip, Mom.' Loving showing Mom my new car, I tap the monitor to the screen image and open my file. The latest file viewed pops up. My man of the month is there in all his glory with his fine three-piece-set.

'Olive,' she swipes my arm. 'Please don't tell me you have a nude automated reply of your bits and pieces.'

Laughing, I reply, 'No, Mom.'

She nods relief. 'I am a masterpiece,' she giggles, a twinkle sparkles in her eyes. 'But I was for your dad's eyes only.'

'Really?'

'Your father had this notion to paint me.'

'Never!'

'It was a year after we married. He could have had a worse hobby,' she winks at me.

'Sweet, Mom.' I pat her arm with pride.

'There is more to me than you understand, dear.'

'You're never a nudist?'

'No, but I've no problem with skin art.' Olive smirks. 'The aging demographic are a strong lobbying group in their own right, Olive.'

Images of folds of wrinkling skin cross my mind. On cue she exposes further insights.

'Olive, when I pass you will not be left a body, there will be no body for you to deal with,' shoots out of her mouth.

A quizzed frown lop-sides the perfect cubic building before me.

I turn to her with a gasp. 'No body?'

'I've donated my body to medical science,' she adds. 'That department will be handed over my body.'

'Fuckin' hell, Mom.' The crippling emotional overload my mother has just heaped on me is undeniable in my voice. 'What will I use in the funeral?' Then I stop, calling time-out. 'We are getting ahead of ourselves.' A car, an instrument of caution, is an accelerator of time and an annihilator of time, vicious in its capability as a time machine.

'There will be no traditional funeral as such.' My parent has wiped out an existential connection in seconds. In an instant my life has changed axis, I envy the solid building of concrete and steel. 'Yes, I have relinquished the rights of my dead body to medical research. You won't be left with a body.'

I flinch and recoil away from the steering wheel. 'Why are we talking of dead bodies, Mom? How creepy.' I squirm. 'You want to be pulled apart after death? I had no idea.'

'What's the difference? I am pulled apart in life, Olive.'

Her body has actually shrunk in the car seat.

'Missy had a coffee with me yesterday.' Bitter sibling rivalry joined the cold morning. 'She is the executor of my requests. Our family legal team, Alistair Winthorp and Co., have a copy of my medical wishes dear.'

My tone carries a jarring measure. 'Missy is the executor.'

'Yes, the appointed person to see that my last wishes are played out.'

'Why did you not select me?'

'You are busy enough, Olive.'

'Your medical wishes? A copy?' My voice grates. Mom always had a file of paperwork kept under lock and key in her study, growing up, the mysterious un-opening closet plagued me. 'If it's all wrapped up then, what do you need me for today? Ah yes, I'm the donkey, towing you here, carrying your baggage.'

'Try to understand me,' her voice is as angular as her skeletal frame. 'You are the loved one with me today. I don't think you truly understand me, Olive. I had the choice to select you to be with me.'

I hear a worry in her tone. She continues, as if we have all the time in the world. I'm thinking, why are we not going in? How long is she going to sit in the damn car? I stop my fingers tapping on the steering wheel and count to ten.

'I'm very unhappy with my lot, dear. This prolonged misery is too much to bear, I don't wish to be resuscitated if the urge to survive kicks in.'

Human weakness is not my forte. I'm speechless.

'You have to know these details, dear. The doctors will ask you to sign off on me.'

I am listening but my internal screeching is louder, tuning her out. Every fiber of my body is reacting. 'No resuscitation. You're sure of this, Mom?' I try to add an interpretative note as I pull my hair.

'I'm certain of my plan, dear.' The sterility of her tone befits the doctor on board. The clinic has made my mom clinical. There is a coldness to her.

Nodding to respect the duty of obedience, the rational side of my brain commences to try and surge ahead of my emotions, but I am reversing in maturity. In my mind's eye, I can just see death. And soon I would smell it due to our proximity to its coordinates. My intuition keeps me on my guard, eluding respite.

Mom makes a tight reply. 'Please be sensitive to my issues, Olive.'

LIAR.

I could not register the explanation in the car, in mere minutes. What is that word? Now it hounds me. The word swims in me. I hear it roar in my bloodstream, swishing rapids of issues. Mom's subtle approach.

'All I need is a loving death,' she slips in.

46

My anxiety interrupts my senses.

If I could move, my fists are punching.

What a harsh thing to imply to me, I will love my mother until my last breath.

'Of course, I will mind you and love you up till the very end. Anyway, death! Why are you mentioning it, here of all places?' Under duress, loving people act crazily.

'Olive, I have to talk to you of dying.'

'What?' I yelp. 'Now?'

The vehicle is no protector. Dying is normal to a doctor in this barren building. I never wanted to see where my mother works. I don't mean to be a figure of ridicule, or dishonor the esteemed doctor still thriving in my mother's genes, but I can't think of a worse place to hang out, sickly death for company. I just can't meet it with invigoration. I rest my eyes on her. I see the old lady in her, masticated crumbs of toast stick on my mother's coat. I ignore her oversight, I don't want to embarrass her. Menacing noises barge in. A firing ambulance spins radiantly past us, in our destination of paradoxes.

She's pulling at her finger.

'I want to give you this, dear, before I go ... inside,' her voice falters but recovers defensively, irony drips, 'and you might not make it back in time from your important meeting.'

Mom is holding her emerald engagement ring in the palm of her hand.

My body recoils.

I have never seen this ring off my mother's finger.

It appears too strange to comprehend yet the fact is right before my eyes. Actions speak louder than words. The ring has no finger, its bare appearance obscene in its nudity.

Where is her wedding band, that's gone too?

47

'Mom,' I shudder. 'Put your ring back on you,' I shriek. For fifty years Mom has worn and treasured this ring.

'No, Olive dear. I want you to take the ring.' Her voice does not quiver. 'This is my choice.'

I shake a negative. 'No thanks.'

'Do you think I have not thought this through? I wish to pass my ring to you, Olive. Respect my wishes, daughter.'

My mind explodes with realism. I want no promise ring. 'Of course you can take ownership of such decisions, Mom.'

'Then do what I ask of you, especially today, dear.'

What is she on about now? Will she be robbed in this place? Is that why she does not trust the environment with her precious keepsakes?

Yet I have to trust my precious mother to this clinic. A look of sheer determination emanates from her. As usual, mother knows best, she always takes the lead.

'Right then.' I place the ring on a non-wedding finger, the implication of a sealed deal I do not comprehend repulses me. But she is the reason I truly embrace life. The dotted friction is due to how alike we are, strong, insistent females. At times I almost hate her.

'Can we get a move on now?'

'Shortly.'

My patience is wearing thin.

'All will be revealed in good time. Without time we do not exist. Time gives legitimacy of existence, gives proof to matter,' she says.

I hate her and love her intensely.

Car horns join my private tango.

'Let the dudes wait,' the rebellious nuance audible in my tone.

There's a tailback of vehicles in the driveway because the doctor will not let us enter the clinic.

'Just because I'm getting old does not mean I don't know what I want, dear.' Then she smirks. 'You wear it well, dear.' She sees me playing with the ring.

'Don't push it, Mom. Or me.' I am clutching at any strands of control I still possess. The car has been our cocoon to carry the load, we have to exit this transient safety. I'm still at the wheel. The responsibility weighs me down, for a few hours I have to guard this treasure. 'You're a bitch, Mom.'

'I know that, dear.' She speaks gently, not wanting to offend.

'Don't think this means anything,' I insist.

Mom replies, 'It means everything. The clinic is new age.'

'How did you select this clinic to work in and to check-in to? That is, if we ever go inside.'

She ignores my hint. 'Innovation, dear. I know some of the consultants from my mentoring days. They sat in on my tutorials, I trained them in. We kept in touch,' she divulges. 'They have their practices here, are instigators of change. I have come full circle, I wanted to work with them again.' Casualness vapours from her. 'Ground breaking initiatives come with a price. I promise to fill you in on everything when I get settled. You will witness the expertise of the consultants for yourself.'

'Everything comes with a price,' the accountant in me jests, welcoming comedy in this tragedy. With my big mouth, I spring, 'Will it not be weird for you, the master lagging behind the students?'

'No, dear, it won't be like that, and I'm honoured to witness the fruition of my lifelong work.' Mom looks satisfied. 'I will pay top dollar for the best care willingly.'

My vision was of rotting fruit bowls, leftovers that taint fresh produce. Next door to the beds of fresh cotton sheets and fluffed up pillows are flat-lined dead bodies in recliners with stale, soiled covers of sheets. Both entities co-exist in the clinic and in my mind. The co-inhabitants breed peculiar sorrow. I have to hand Mom over.

I'm itching to move, yet rigid with fear.

I feel like a rubber figurine. Pull one way and I conjoin with the force. Pull another way and I have no choice but to go in that direction too. There is a danger with such compliance, the fatality of duplication means I could tear and rip. I'm being pulled in all directions. When do I know when I'm about to tear? I feel like I'm coming apart.

Commotion drills deep in my head. Pounding pulses, throbbing blood bangs against my internal canals. The crescendo continues within the space between the two of us.

Then I feel it before I see it, her hand reaching over from her side of the car to my side, as it lies and rests on my commandeering one. Both our hands on the driving wheel now, steering our entwined destinies together. Her touch anchors me. My hand is not complete without her guidance. She is my directing post. 'I'm ready, Olive.' The cragged wrinkles are ugly to view and almost obliterate the beautiful entity beneath the aged, cracked skin. But I see her beauty. Guilt swells in the pit of my stomach. In agreement with the sway of the crowd, the onset of the aging process dispels belief to any of its advantages. I don't find growing old personally appealing. There is no strength in her hands.

'About time,' I joke, because this is about damage limitation today.

I understand my mother is pro-active, we are alike in this welcoming attitude to new procedures. Tummy tucks, botox, lipo and tweaks to my twelve year-old breast enhancements are the clinical procedures for me next, the dates are set. I make my own decisions too. And I don't need my mother to hold my hand.

'Let's get me sorted,' she confirms. A fleeting glance of shared lineage locks our intent to do this together. She is way smarter than me. Mom knows that underneath my persona I would want to be here for her today. 'Please stay strong, Olive dear … for me.' Her eyes beseech my very soul.

'I will, Mom. I will stay strong.'

I'm jumpy though. Searching the rearview mirror constantly, I can't see Drew's car. Cars have been overtaking us in a steady line. Where is he? I would gladly keep driving out of here, our companionship trumps loneliness. 'I like being with you, Mom, just you and me.'

'I like it too, dear.' Mom sounds sad.

We lean in, our foreheads tipping. Her calmness is the magic of my childhood and can still catch me off guard in my adulthood. A pause encapsulates us, perfection in its unity of love. Sitting, doing nothing, a perfect pastime because we are together.

Time stood still. I feel my mom is happy being with me. It feels like the longest of time we only gave mere minutes to.

'Do you know why I called you Olive, dear?' she adds as I undo her safety belt.

'No, Mom, I don't.' I love my name, I have never met another woman called Olive.

'Tuscany. The serenity of the landscape evoked my senses during my honeymoon. The abundant olive tree, self sufficient to survive the dry climate, and thrive to generations of empowerment. The minute I held you in my arms, I just knew it was your name. Promise me you will visit Italy.'

'Then I will have to visit Tuscany,' resounds my hearty reply.

51

'And make love in the tree's shade,' she giggles. I giggle in return.

A release of sort balances our equilibrium, I breathe easily as I have always done in her presence.

'For now, I've stayed closer to home. Dial this cell number on Skype for me.'

She fumbles with her cell phone and calls out a number, she starts to put her hand in her pocket.

'Another delay, Mom? Great.'

She ignores me.

I set up the panel system.

'Hi, George,' she greets. 'I emailed you.'

'Hi, Dr Tully. Yep I got it.'

'George, hold up the brochure to the camera.'

A glossy colour beachfront tower image fills the screen, glorious sunshine, soft sand and the blue Atlantic Ocean ripped.

'Thank you,' she says, then looking at me, she hands me a key. 'With love.'

'No way, you and Dad bought a condo on the coast,' I beam.

She laughs with merriment. 'Yes, we closed a deal, but on a penthouse, and the real estate is for you, dear.' My daze makes her continue, in slow syllables she outlines, 'You own the penthouse, Olive.'

George gets in on the excitement, 'Daytona beach, one hour's drive from your office, a perfect weekend pad.'

I'm thrilled, my body jumps up and down, then I frown, confused 'A penthouse for me? Why, Mom?'

'Why not? I've more money than I need. And why wait to share it with you? We both, Dad and I, want to give you this gift.'

'You bought me my first car, but that's when I was sixteen ...' I'm grasping for sense. 'I never expected this, Mom.'

'You're a sun babe dear, it's your private solar panel for your wellbeing,' and she pauses. 'Having good times will balance the hard times.'

'Forever the doctor,' I tease, doling out the meds.

'Forever your mother,' she adds.

'Wow. I'm thrilled, Mom, don't get me wrong, I'm so surprised but this needs more attention. I will go over the figures and details, were you given a fair price?'

'Oh, Olive, forever the financial expert.'

I'm not sure what to make of this. 'Why not enjoy your rightful inheritance dear, when you are young? Beats me why people stash their loot until a recipient is past maxing it. You're in the party mode years, enjoy,' and she kisses me.

I'm not prepared. Is it only me that is pivoting?

'Don't put limits on us, dear. Let's face the music together.'

We grasp hands. I trust Mom.

LIAR.

I should have known she was mentally rewiring. I try and decipher the secret code of motherhood, it eludes me. I recall the car. Why is the car hounding my recall? Because I was the driver, driving her to hell.

I decide to let my mother lead, it's pointless to object the norm, like my full rack of shoes, most of which I can't walk in. What's the point in living if you are not learning? Mom can have her glorious leadership spot.

She is beaming with the gift surprise. I try and share in this moment. Everyone eats and drinks but few savour the flavor. It is not my turn to demand her attention; she needs mine. Damn it, she is talking of inheritance. The coin has flipped. My luck has run out. It's the law of averages. No one can estimate how long the world will seemingly revolve around them before it leaves them behind. And if I didn't like it, tough, I could do the numbers perfectly. The bets are all off now. And

I know it. Mom is old and is sick. Dad is old and is sick. Fuck!

Obeying the sunshine, I have to omit the shaded areas. The day looks full of promise, a sun of breathtaking colorful. Wanting out of here is not an option, I do not want Mom to feel alone.

LIAR.

How am I here? I'm too young for this shit! Nobody told me about this time lark, how it vanishes into thin air, how we waste it if we don't face it.

How can two certainties be so sharp in existence at the one time? I love my mom, full stop. She needs me today. I don't understand how the decisions I usually make are baffling now. The rules in life I strive to and adhere to rigidly, are not adding up for me at this moment. How long is fear present for? What percentage of my life will it take up? I sought release by my neat little digits, they usually do the trick. I liked making outlines, tightly cordoning off predicaments and solutions. Work is contacting me. 'I'll just answer this email. The office have sent three.' Order is dissolving and this loss of control is tilting me, I lose myself in work details. The strategist in me craves the rules. Reading my emails stabilizes me.

No one would want to talk of this dull, incurable pain of growing up, of acceptance. And for the first time in my life, I am a naïve observer, with no choice or decisions to make. Mom is in charge. Medical appointments of my nearest and dearest had no place in my itinerary. I always said some people don't know how to live, my mother always maintained that some people don't know how to die. I halt my mind and concentrate on the return email.

'I'm sorry to be taking up your time, dear.'

'It's fine. Okay. Ready. The car park is nowhere near the reception. Typical,' I spit. The problem we complain about is never the real problem. How come I did not see that my mom had reached this juncture? Inheritance of a penthouse! Nothing in the world compares to her when I really think about it. I want to be calm but I could easily explode.

Mom remains quiet.

As if for a first time I take account of my aging parent. Why had I not put her as a top priority on my list of figures? Make a mint, travel, these are my life factors. The elevating numbers of my bank account had my full attention, not the rising numbers of my parent's passing years. Disbelief. How was I so stupid?

I gulp fresh air as I open my window. Light whispers flit across the cocoon of the car.

'Life is never black or white, dear. I don't want to be a burden to you.'

'You're not, Mom,' I lie.

We both lied.

'I am sorry, Olive.'

The magnitude is eternal but I cannot see beyond a few feet. The angst co-joined to my body cannot be removed, her heartfelt words pass by. A heavy heart might describe the symptom. The bright sky does not take my blues away, the sun shines, the bright and dark tones of life infuse around me. The light bounces off the car as we sit with our dark emotions.

'I can sit on the bench,' offers Mom helpfully. My shoulders tighten.

'When in terrible pain, you make decisions.'
'Eventually you are ready to get out of the car?' I tease. To my horror, we have only been on the road for forty minutes and the day is snailing along. She takes minutes to join the handles of her handbag. 'The bench is positioned well by the entrance.'

A Disney-like landscape of circular 3D bushes and strong color schemes of regimented floral design greets the eye on manicured borders by the bench. Such order, if only all life could be lined up in definite patterns.

'There is a story to that bench, dear. Drop me first, I'll tell you when you come back after parking.' Mom sounds more upbeat and capable.

'The expense of the landscaping fee alone,' I huff to myself.

'Plenty of time,' issues Mom, almost talking to herself. A burst of loyalty joins our company. When my mom makes up her mind, she is not for turning. 'Cost is irrelevant; the end results are what matter,' resounds the doctor. Befitting possibly, we are in hiding from one another, no medical discussions are forthcoming in the car which was unusual; Mom, the doctor always had an outline of procedures.

LIAR.

I'm paying the ultimate price.

I do not want to drop off, like a taxi with first class geriatric care. This is not the exceptional care I signed up for today.

I was not prepared for a trade off.

We are a winning team and on cue we turn to one another simultaneously and smile in sync. A good team is a good team, as Dad would say. Alzheimer's - another side to aging nobody told me about either. Mom is poised.

Her graciousness is astoundingly unique. 'I'm too long a withering to be upset with the mundane dear.'

Momentarily, her attitude halts the noise in my head. Then my frantic, organizing nature kicks in louder again to block out my mother's truth. 'The avenue is pretty but far too long,' I calculate. 'And the car park is a good few minutes walk away, Mom,' maps my brain, as I study the road signs to turn off in the opposite direction. 'No respect for the elderly, these hip architects.'

Beep! An impatient horn shrills behind the car. 'For fuck's sake,' I howl. 'I'm going to cause a crash. Well, we're in good vicinity to have one,' I joke and we both understand the merriment. The duality of managing my mom and me and the encroaching medical world is etching cracks into my shaky reserves. 'Ok then, I can trust you to the big bad medical world,' I joke. I give her the thumbs up sign. Privately, I cry. How is it possible for a person to express feelings completely different on the outside from how they feel on the inside? The proof is external, the evidence is illusionary. All my exposed physical parts harmoniously link but my mind is a tangled mess.

More angry horns join along with the rhythm of my chaotic mental orchestra. I'm stopped in the designated shuttle parking area. We were just sitting there. Maybe Mom needed to keep the normality. She understood the uniqueness of that time together. I am fuming, and I'm supposed to be creating a mood of serenity. But when I am charged, I'm charged. There seems to be no space in my brain to think and drive. I am more of a danger behind the wheel than I realized. A nervous laugh escapes from my dry lips. I look in the rearview mirror again. Drew has disappeared out of sight. I'm relieved.

'Ok, Mom, I will bring you over to the seat. It's a nice morning and I will be back in-'

'A few minutes,' she completes, ruefully acknowledging my necessity of calculating all things in every aspect of my life. Mom, by choice, never wore her watch this morning. 'I won't be gone before you return to me.'

She easily jested.

Mom sways in the passenger seat, gathering up her belongings.

'Olive?'

'Yes, Mom?'

'Olive ... I entrust you with my life.'

'I know that,' I reply staring at her worried face. Is she fearful of the shuttle almost touching our bumper? 'Jeepers,' I yelp as the reinforced mobile muscles over us. 'The size of that vehicle.'

'The clinic offers a complimentary shuttle service, dear.'

I turn to her, 'Really? How much are you paying for that free service?' I shake my head. 'I will have to look over the paperwork when I have time. You could have told me there is a shuttle.'

The tapping on the window is no longer justifiable. 'The rude buck!' I jump out and square up to the security guard.

'You cannot leave the car here lady.'

Thinking fast, I kneel down and put my ear to the front wheel. 'Do you hear that?' I ask him.

'What?'

'That hissing sound.'

'I've heard all the excuses under the sun,' he salutes me. 'Move the car along.'

'Here,' I motion. Never one to be cornered, I twist the value open, ever so slightly, and release the air. 'Bend down and you'll hear it, I think I have a puncture.'

Unpleasant puffs camouflage his difficult appendage as he tries to bend over his overly large girth.

'I'll be damned,' he says as whooshing air reaches his ear.

'I have a manual pump in the trunk. I'll manage, thanks,' and I smile a beam of pleasantness. He walks away. 'Can this day get any more complicated?' Before I straighten up, the tranquility of the resting place is blasted by gunshots. Two deafening blasts zing in my ears, the disturbance is near, the invading bangs in the airwaves only feet away. A man is being wrestled to the ground by security. An alarm is shrilling from the

58

building. 'It's Drew!' My visibility is unhindered, the pathway clears, people are running left and right, gorging a see-through tunnel.

'Oh no, Drew,' gasps Mom.

'Call the cops.'

Drew is roaring at the top of his voice. 'I want the cops to come to this hellhole.'

A second security man comes running, to assist his obese co-worker, now sitting on Drew. Handcuffs are put on Drew and he is pushed into the clinic. The cops' siren is trailing a blazing echo. Cop cars speed up the avenue, skid to a halt. Two officers remain on the sidewalk.

'Get back in your vehicle, miss,' I'm instructed, the officer signals to the crowd to do the same.

Reluctantly, I slide back in. 'Darn Drew,' I snarl. 'I'm imprisoned in the car yet again, the moron.'

Destiny tried to prevent me entering the clinic.

Mom's cell phone buzzes. She starts to text someone.

Leaving her to her business, I get a buzz when a CNN van arrives and parks parallel to me. A camera crew and a reporter hop out. How did they get here so quickly? The revelation hits, its Mom's world that has a different setting - a geriatric pace.

And I'm in its time warp.

FRANK

The earpiece tells me to move. 'Three. Two. One. Enter.' With a spring in my step, I walk. Security men, either side of me, guard me against the swarming followers. The one man show is on the road.

Showtime.

The fragrant scent fills the air and mingles with the applause and screams. 'Welcome, Frank,' the crowds call. 'Thank god.'

Fans pull my arms, I shake their hands, flaying in multiples toward me. 'Hello Frank's fellowship,' I answer. I only make it down the walkway a few feet. 'Frank,' they call. I stop by the young man on my right.

'I'm Shaun,' he squeals, nervous and thrilled that I have singled him out. 'I joined the fellowship three years ago.' He is squeezing the blood flow out of my fingers.

I nod to security and they enact a release. The no touching rule is hard to impose at these big forums. 'Glad to meet you, Shaun,' I respond. 'Thank god. What profession do you work in?'

'I adore you, Frank,' he gushes and snaps a selfie of the two of us. I smile the smile.

'You are my idol Frank.'

Again, I smile a smile that does not reach my eyes. Another one. The fanatics are the cause of me having a twenty-four hour bodyguard, the downside to my escalated status.

'I'm going to quit my job as a teacher and follow you.' He goes to leap into my arms for a hug. The security men step in, I step out. 'Volunteering my services is the vocation for me, thank god,' his face smoothes into a delirium spasm.

'Thank god,' I reply and walk the ten feet to the front row. I climb the eight steps to the stage. The podium I ignore, there is freedom to pace the stage and walk with the earpiece microphone. The applause builds and descends. I feel the empowerment my followers shower on me. The law of attraction has attracted these kind people to me. Busloads arrived, hours ago. Crowds sit and eat the sandwiches I sell them and drink the coffee I charge them for. The cash keeps flowing in.

Dream big, Dr Lily advised me. If she were only here to see this.

I've arrived. A Ted talk is the nearest description to this seminar I am giving. The audience settles, become quiet as mice, munching on their snacks, ready, for me, Frank. I look out to them. As far as the eye can see, fields of lavender bloom in the acres of land the foundation purchased.

I've conquered the masses. Round Wood is one of many holdings the fellowship owns. I give praise. The open air auditorium is professionally set up. I start.

'Frank's fellowship ...' I have to pause, the roars blockout my words. I talk louder, shouting to the community. 'Frank's fellowship believes in you.' The crowd roars and claps again. A group of V.I.P followers are led on stage. The crowd erupts. Music to my ears. The laying of hands on the reserved group always reels in the believers. My mind is always astonished by the loneliness epidemic of modern living that drives these people to my door. Yuck, the hugs, the reaching out to me, patting me on the back. I shrug with distaste, I detest being physically touched but they need leadership and something to invest in, the dollars are flying in, the billboard illuminated on the right of the stage calculates the donations. I can't bear it but I grin, the show is going live, we are on daytime TV, a prime spot on a popular channel.

The PR team is prepped; they plant a hummer, the followers follow, the humming builds to a crescendo, all the audience hums. I raise my arms to conduct them, I downstream their volume as I raise my vocals. I hum a solo piece. At the top of the platform, I lead.

Then I hear a bang. I cower under my arms. 'Gun shots, Frank.' I come back to the present moment when I bend over my lap. Mr P. is dripping salvia on my earlobe. A second gun shot rings loud and clear, reverberating in the airwaves, then I hear shouting, 'Call the cops, I want the cops to come to this hellhole.' I sit up and look out the window. The shuttle is stopped and pulled up behind a car, parked in the shuttle zone. By the clinic's reception doors, two security men are taking down a guy.

It's Drew. He better not screw this day up for me.

Today is the day I step into her shoes.

I will take over the team.

OLIVE

'Don't talk to the media,' Mom instructs me as a reporter walks up to our car. The reception area is cordoned off. I'm a sitting duck again.

'Did you see the gunman?' the reporter shouts in the window. She is persistent, 'Is he white or black?'

'I want them to go away, Olive.' Mom sounds desperate.

'Do we have a hostage situation here?' the news representative shouts, angling for a scoop.

Instinctively I shield my mom. 'Don't worry, Mom.'

Her cell phone buzzes consistently. 'They are going to tarnish the reputation of our good clinic.' She gives an imperceptible shake of her head. Checking the incomer's number, she answers the call and talks pointedly. 'Dr Doran.' She fidgets with her slacks. 'Yes, I'm here at the clinic.' Mutterings respond in a muffle by her ear, in reach of my hearing. 'I'm in the car, by the door. We were sitting a while, me and Olive.' More disjointed conversation. 'We've seen the spectacle,' she pauses. 'No,' her body twists away from me. 'I will be keeping my appointment today.'

I take a deep breath, I can feel my face reddening. I'm eavesdropping on her call.

'The heat is undesirable, I agree.' She sneaks a side view peak to me. 'It was Drew.' Pausing to listen, she returns, 'No, Doctor, I'm not for changing my mind today.' Her face softens. 'Fine. The officers will exit out the back doors, good, then I will check in.'

I can't sit any longer. 'Hold on here, Mom,' strategically I sneak my input to her, over the call. Leaving the car and herself to the phone call with her doctor, I approach the shuttle and signal to the driver to let me onboard. With widening eyes, the handsome face of warm Indian skin tone, he looks alarmed to be adding another person to his load. The journalist has chanced her angle of a story with him too. The door opens. I step in.

'Thanks,' I smile.

'I think we have to remain in the vehicles.' He is confused by my law breaking attitude, but before I can engage with the good looking driver, a front-seated rotund passenger addresses me, or I think he is talking to me. The large man can be clearly heard in the confinement. Why do people speak so loud? I have no choice but to listen to him.

'You are in safe hands,' rejoices the tall, robust passenger with a black fashion addiction, dressed head-to-toe, a block of black. His pale, plump cheeks do not match his dark outfit. His words sound like a sermon reaching the masses on the transport system. Looking left and right of me, I wonder, is he addressing me? There's no need for any one in particular to converse with a reply. The preacher man nods to me and continues with his knack of adding tidbits to a vacant space. 'Thank god.'

He is weird, I think, making the void impressionable. Then he drops a dot of lavender oil into his right palm. Solemnly, he clasps his hands, massaging them reverently. Sequentially he anoints the hands of his neighbour, an old, feeble man in a wheelchair, almost as if a ritual, with a tremendous tenderness. A showman, the dark enigma, for all to see and partake of, my instinct of spying on him perturbs me. The intuition of who the baddie is flashes in my mind as if I'm in a Bond movie. What is his game? I'm glued to the duet, but the heavier man holds prime position. The compound of the shuttle is now imbued with the aromatic lavender aura of his fetish ways.

'Will you stop stinking the vehicle out, Frank, please,' issues the driver mannerly.

'Is the stench of soiled bandages a more appealing aroma?' the authoritative passenger enquires. The driver concedes defeat, graciously. 'As you wish, Frank, as usual.'

What an odd man Frank is, but a smart one. I agree with his aromatic prognosis. The shuttle stinks with putrid body parts and lavender buds. I know which smell I would opt for.

'Apologies, I'm parked in your assigned area, the shuttle space,' I intercept honestly to the driver. He is so cute. Mellow brown eyes complement his soft smile. I can't help but smile a huge wide beam back to him. 'The cops are leaving with the deranged fool of a man by the back doors. Can you give me a little more time, please? I'm assisting my mother to the door because the avenue is so long. I didn't realize you were available to help me with this service.' I lick my lips and wonder what else he can provide? I rattle on to the handsome driver and my annoyance melts into the perfumed air.

'Take as long as you like,' his gentle voice attributing sincerity to his mellowness.

My heart gladdens, he is gorgeous. There is no intimidation towards me, only respect.

'When the circus is over, if you give me a few minutes, the car will be gone.'

'Sure.'

Not used to altruism, I continue to explain myself. 'My mother cannot walk far, so I pulled up by the entrance, not realizing it is your designated spot.'

'Good call,' he agrees with me. To relieve my distress, he cajoles, 'But Frank here will be giving out the last rites if we are packed together for much longer,' the driver smirks.

What a nice manner. He's a beacon of hope. I could easily be distracted from my task. Sexy and fit scans the outline of my antennae. I pinch my finger to stop reacting in my knickers, but he looks like a good kisser, his lips are dreamy, full and soft. My own mouth puckers up in response.

The gazing audience puts a stop to the carry on, the energy on the shuttle is flat, a non-committal atmosphere respected by passengers, sharing the same space with its physical confines, on the same journey.

'Thanks,' I smile to the inclusive gloomy gathering.

The dark-clothed passenger interjects. 'Thank god.'

The driver turns his head to acknowledge his regular passenger. 'Yep,' the driver replies to him then turns back around and winks.

The converging conversation catches my attention. 'Mr Patterson,' flows the greeting from the oil-dispensing, darkly decked out man to his old fellow passenger. 'Glad you made it to our door. Thank god.'

'Yes, Frank, I am glad,' replies the jaundiced wheelchaired passenger.

'The ministry is ongoing. Thank god.'

'Thank god.'

The driver grins again at me. 'Don't take too long, please.'

'Lingering death is the path we are all on,' I hear. The jaundiced neighbour devours every word. 'Let me assist you on your way,' administers the dark one in a lilting

66

melody. 'I am an able bodied man at your service, thank god.'

'Yes, Frank, you can assist me,' commits the elder, 'thank god. We will walk the way together. Thank god.'

Perplexed, I shake my head to dispel them.

'Thank god,' others onboard repeat.

The resonance of the conversation vibrates within me, jarring my composure. Get me away from their zone. I found it hard to bring my mother here, I could not fathom how this Frank guy could mingle so readily with malady.

The media troop run to their CNN van. 'They must have been tipped off,' I say. We see the officers driving away, Drew is in the back seat of the third cop car that falls in with the row. I swing around and exit the shuttle. The driver keeps me in his line of vision, following my movements. Running around the car, I open the trunk, retrieve my umbrella; floating cotton swells of cumulus clouds threaten a shower. Hurriedly, I go to her side of my car.

In complete contrast to the frantic pace, adjusting to a gentleness that could not escape my awaiting observer, I lovingly guide Mom. She slowly walks the excruciating steps. Her legs are not giving in, this time. We lean in to one another in mutual support; one helping the other. We blend, the cold seat creaks as Mom settles along the beams. I run the few steps back to the car and take out a rug. I rush to her, pack the sides of the cover tightly around my care. Autumnal moisture sparkles in her silver hair. I kiss her forehead. Two women with our own entity, co-joined, paused, a unique time capsule capturing us.

This pace is slow, I'm aware of this. I see the driver check his watch. Time is ticking on. No one has all day.

Medics walk past, not one comes to my aide. They rattle me as a tremor passes through me. My eyes impel him to understand as I sneak a look the driver's way. Straightening up, my startled eyes of chestnut brown lock with his equal mahogany colour brown eyes. I de-ice his stance, my instinctive peacemaking wave does it, as it undoes him. The United Nations could have learnt an important technique from my authentic manner; I imply I'm doing my best under the circumstances. He returns a wave, an innocent connection by natural reflex.

My instincts spiral. Stopped in my tracks, I give the impression of being still but my libido is doing a flaring Latino-zumba. To hell with computerizations, I could do with the real McCoy. A good bonk to release this pent up frustration pestering me this morning would do the trick. The porn never sated my appetite. Fat chance of a shag here of all places, I grin. If he had any idea of my dirty thoughts. I grin. Dutifully, I go back to get the bag from the trunk. He is still watching me. I can feel his eyes on my body. They draw out a force of sexiness in me, tantalizing my reserves.

Bending over my booty, to empty the trunk, I hoist her overnight bag, this takes on a whole new meaning as my ass is in the air in all its glory. A laugh escapes from my lips; who would think lugging luggage would be so much fun? Seconds pass, yet an eternity plays. Time has no power.

The power is mine for the taking. Momentarily, I am more sensual than physical. I sway my ass, pause, lift her medical bag, elongate my fine figure and bang the trunk closed with force.

Personally, I welcome this playful intrusion. Survival, under extreme duress, searches out laughter. The dilution of my fear is necessary. The notion of a war bride makes perfect sense to me, the entity, extreme, then over; before her life started, she could be a widow.

I'm glad I played with time, a little fun, a little of me.

Vibrancy enthralls just as sure as sickness stalls. Everything can wait. This juncture in the clock is for no one else but us. I sneak a grin his way. The rules of norms are defunct. It is like a parallel universe where only the two of us exist. If I have no relief, I will disintegrate. This innocent guy has no idea how he is saving a little bit of my soul. I can smell the hormones emanating from my pores, my vagina's dampness a joy in this joyless morning. Aware my mother is nearby, it could have been on a different planet.

His reciprocal observance entices, lures my interest to him, I twist his way, turning my enlarged lips, flushed face and full frontal armour to him.

'Bravo,' he mimes.

I get his drift. 'Yes,' I mouth back. 'Thank you.' I take a bow, my breasts swell from this angle. My stressed physique is magnetic. We have brought the busy morning traffic to a standstill. My peaking arousal, a lovely divergence, throbs in my veins, an intimate capsule forms.

'Olive,' calls Mom nervously. 'Will you get off the road? Why are you standing in the middle of the avenue?' She flusters. 'You will get yourself killed.' The all-seeing eye of the parent never closes. 'And why are you eyeing up that driver like a wanton hussy?'

Blushing blooms colour my cheeks.

'Because I can,' I laugh.

The concern in my mother's voice breaks through my sexual prowess. I turn away from him.

'Sorry,' I say without including that I had not meant to forget about her. 'I did not mean to worry you, Mom, the shuttle driver is hot.'

My sharp arousal is strong, emanating a powerful surge. The moment makes perfect sense somehow. I enjoy the feeling, the feeling of being fully alive. But our time is over, gone. My rippling sexual residue ebbs to a

69

slow pulse, I direct my energy to the task at hand: my mother. We teeter on the periphery of a new destination. We are both exposed.

'Do not insult my intelligence, Olive. What are you at today?'

LIAR.

What are you at today, Mom?

I swear, to admit my fear of her death, my ultimate fear of my mother dying, is hard. How could I worry my mom with that fact? What child is ready for such inevitability? A second nipping worry ranks high on my mind so I distract her. 'I'm spending quicker than I'm earning the dollars, Mom. Lately,' how could I put this to my Mom? 'I'm constantly seeking out avenues of sexual release to handle stress,' and a life matter is discussed with the doctor.

My mother has an amazing grasp on the finest intricacies of human ways. 'You've seen me flirting with the driver just now.' There is no need for bland platitudes. 'That's a doddle,' I continue. 'It's the hard core stuff I have to get a handle on.' I take a deep breath and go for the truth. 'I'm addicted to porn.' My fingers run through my hair, tousling it like I am tousling my insides, trying to untangle my compulsion. 'There, that's the first time I have said it out aloud. You are the first and only person I will tell and that's what has me frazzled. I was up for most of the night watching porn, my hard earned cash is burning up in the heat of the show. That's why I'm overly anxious this morning. And why I have to go to the business meeting. I can't afford to lose a client. I'm sorry.'

Now I feel better. This is a hell of a lot easier to admit than the harsh reality of Mom fading before my very eyes. We are all diminishing our true selves; little chinks of our life slide away everyday. I'm tired of grasping the slippery ropes. We ski at our peril. The alpine's beauty can cause destruction. Mom is about to respond when we hear bellowing.

'Ah, the Madonna,' reverences the large, dark, towering man. He is hovering above my head, his presence preventing Mom from responding to me. Startled by the nearness of his voice, I jump. Did he hear what I have just said? I thought I was conversing privately. Why is he so near to us, invading our space? He is a horse of man, still, yet poised to react in one stance, with his overly long eyelashes. I'm afraid of horses. Frank is like a rare breed, he unnerves me too. He stinks of dense lavender.

'Frank,' greets Mom.

He ignores me.

Fine by me.

I do not interest him in the slightest.

'Hello, Lily.' He extends his right hand while he holds his belongings of a black overcoat, prayer book and brief case to his left side. Everything stinks of lavender.

'I thought you were inside, Frank,' salutes Mom.

I'm pissed off; my mother is ignoring my personal divulgence because of him. It's unfair. Who the hell is this fucker? Mom is side stepping me. There and then, I distinctly dislike him.

'There was a slight delay,' he throws me a dismissive glance before excluding me.

Slithery man.

'Imagine, gunshots in our space of sacredness. We've all arrived safely,' expounds Frank. 'Thank god.'

An elderly man in a wheelchair is nearby. Frank pushes him nearer. Old people all look the same to me, but I see it's the jaundiced passenger from the shuttle. Lavender wafts from him too.

'Nice to see you Mr P.' Mom touches his arm in a supportive manner. So they are familiar to one another.

Mom looks like her old self of medicinal wonder, her natural attentiveness to the fore.

'Good to see you too, Dr Lily,' he pants the words with difficulty. 'It was Drew.'

'Yes, it was Drew,' she reinforces the facts and they drop heads in the positive yes. 'We have to work a strategy out for him,' she says.

I am the only one at a loss. They are a community of regulars to the clinic whose paths have crossed. I am the one out of step.

'I've seen you two guys.'

They freeze.

'You're the guy stinking out the shuttle,' I whiff, purposely scrunching my nose at Frank. He stands regally. My eyes sketch his imposing frame. 'And you are part of, or in on the act of embalmment, too.' I include Mr P., age is no barometer of engagement.

Mom clutches her bag defensively. There are no introductions offered to me. I've a part in a silent black and white movie. If you could measure my eyes, you'd see they have widened and doubled their volume. My mouth could blow a perfect gum balloon before I remember to shut it. My miming is far from indifferent, I'm ready to pounce if I need to.

'Uplifting lavender oil Olive,' inhales Frank, like he can read my thoughts. 'Inhaling activates the hypothalamus region of the brain,' he sermons. The others nod positively and breathe deeply with him in unison.

He knows my name, it rails my temper. I refuse to inhale with them.

Frank is not to be stopped. 'This sends messages to other parts of the body to work as one, a holistic approach to serenity.'

'Thank god,' they unanimously chant.

I abdicate from the group.

Mom can read my indifference and speaks up. 'You apply drops to pulse points on the body, dear, like you do with your perfume,' she addresses me. 'I would like you, dear, to anoint me later when I'm settled in,' suggests Mom to me, relying on my humane gene.

LIAR.

You drip fed me in your environs of the clinic.

'We will be fine together, Dr Lily. We venture down the hard road today,' the phlegm-filled old man Mr P. consoles Mom.

'We will accompany one another today,' adds Frank looking at me. 'Thank god.'

Mom becomes agitated and darts a warning shot to the old man.

But he rambles on.

'You have your daughter with you today just as you wished, Dr Lily, thank god.' His mucus words are barely audible.

'I'm glad I could be here,' I lie but offer the usual pleasantries.

Only Mom can tell of my falsehood. I am running my fingers through my hair, as I do when I'm dueling with intent. I have not walked through the door to the other side and the doom and gloom is prevailing. The demon gin still in my system from the early hours fuses on my taste buds. I could do with a drink now. I wonder if there is a bar in this fancy clinic. Thoughts of insanity bark as loud as my heartbeat.

Can the hangers-on hear it?

'You should keep a gratitude diary, daughter dear,' laces Mom with satire. 'You don't know how lucky you are until it is too late.'

'Yeah, yeah,' I answer back.

'Hey! Wat time you leavn at, man?' shouts over a young guy, smoking by a nearby tree. Laundry bags sit on the ground at his feet.

We react and I notice the driver of the shuttle beside us, he must have walked up behind me too.

'Just on my break,' answers the driver to pacify the would-be customer. 'Next drop is in a few minutes.'

What are a few more minutes in this longest of hours.

I had a few minutes to play.

'Ave to take a wiz,' adds the unknown guy between puffs of his ciggie. 'Don't you go without me, ye hear,' he utters. 'Damn avenue is too long.'

The driver nods in agreement.

'Destiny awaits, thank god,' sermons Frank.

'Thank god,' Mom and Mr P. repeat.

Standing on the outside when we should be getting inside eggs me on. I feel a little at a loss, surrounded by these odd characters. My mother is the core reason I am hanging about. The driver has an immense pull on my attention, but I concentrate. 'Mom, I'll hurry back, ok. Are you sure you are warm enough?'

Before she can reply, I take off my jacket and wrap it over my mother's shoulders. The air is warming up but cool. I have to do something to quell my unease at not being in control.

I could ignore the others.

They have no interest in me either. But the height of Frank is difficult to evade.

He casts a shadow.

'I will be fine with my kind friends, dear.' My mother is inviting them in.

LIAR.

You are not fine with your friends, Mom.

'There is safety in numbers,' she adds.

Is she playing with me? We always tit-for-tat with numbers, it's our thing. I'm the brainy child of the family.

74

Distractingly, the driver moves around me and sits down in the vacant space beside Mom. A spasm shoots through my nipples, I feel them strain against my lacy bra. I give him ten out of ten for cuteness. What about me? Self esteem can be a zero sum game or it can blow the digits off the scales. I like high stakes and partake greedily.

'It's me.' His tone caresses my sensitized skin.

Nice ... Can the others hear the hum of my musical joie de vivre.

'So I see,' I reply cheekily, immediately wishing I had said something intelligent. My brain had been rewinding seeing him earlier, then voiced the exact thought. Stupid mouth, I chastise, but I want to see every inch of his fine physique. When you fancy someone, you just do. There is no explaining the finer details, there is only the experiencing of them. Hallelujah, now I worship.

There is no malice in his tone. I am drawn to him. As natural as my breath, I understand the attraction. I'm so sure of myself, my body not letting me down. And it feels fantastic. The clarity of how I'm wired is crystal clear.

It would be a sure way to release this turmoil raging through me. Instant gratification, it works for me big time. I will get his number and hook up. I can tell he is interested because he is here. I could reach out and touch him, and the vixen in me does just that.

'Thanks for earlier.' I brush fingers over his arm. I will make the most of being here in this dreary place. The modern, successful woman I am has no details of compassionate ground. Time is collateral.

'Look, Mom, it's the kind shuttle driver I mentioned to you.' I lift my touch from him.

'Yes, Olive, I can see him for myself.' The doctor includes. 'And I can see you have a problem,' she winks.

'We were talking. You are better in the flesh,' I tease and Mom laughs aloud. 'I mean, up close and personal.'

'Much better in the flesh, dear, every time,' Mom cajoles.

The other hangers-on do not join in the joviality. Frank perfectly huffs. 'We should go into the clinic,' he interrupts frankly. 'I will take you, Lily.' His command is precise. 'Thank god.'

He irks me. Who the hell is this guy? Why does he think he should accompany my mom? Already, he has a wheelchaired man to push. He must be on a power trip. I shoot a look at Mom.

She ignores my inquisitive look.

We had not passed over the threshold. I never wanted to come to this clinic today. How I wish I had listened to myself ... Like when a passenger does not get on a flight and the plane crashes.

Frank is in his element and continues unhindered. 'Let me walk the steps with you, Lily,' he offers. 'Thank god.'

My skin crawls at the imposing fucker, Frank, his block of physical mass weakening my sexual arousal, souring the moment. The nerve of the man; a cock blocker for sure.

Sounds become audible, the swish of the revolving doors swing in the background and rush of shoes tap on the pavement.

'I will take my Mom,' I insist. 'The hell with the car,' my temper flares. 'And who the hell are you?'

Mom sneaks a glance at the others.

There is a short pause.

Then it fills with giant ramifications. I notice she flusters around Frank. 'Let me wait for Olive,' she requests of him and gives him a gentle smile. 'I will see you inside, Frank.' Mom disseminates information for me as I study him. 'Frank is the leader of the pastoral team in the clinic Olive, I told you about this kind man already.'

'As you wish, Lily,' agrees Frank with a compassionate manner towards Mom.

My mom ponders a second before replying. 'Yes, Frank, I will be on the other side of that door with you later today. I'm ready for my trials and tribulations.'

The driver senses my distress and intervenes. 'This bench is of great craftsmanship, a perfect resting place,' propositions the peacemaker. 'I love to relax here. I'm on a break, I could sit here with this lady while you park your car?'

'Thanks,' I bluff.

I don't like taking orders; being told what to do is not one of my strengths.

I'm in foul form, the disturbance to my libido by a pain in the ass, Frank, dilutes my coursing blood.

I have lost my verve. My rational brain has kicked in, much to my dismay.

'Cos here comes the security guard to clamp your car.' The driver infers further, 'After the high risk, gun shots,' he exasperates, 'they will not tolerate any irregularities.'

I expound in a colorful expletive. 'Another fuckin' problem.'

The rush of life takes over my day again, overtaking the rush of hormones.

Same dilemma.

Dull routine commences.

Frank nods an affirmation to Mom.

Eventually he includes the driver and me in the communication.

'How nice to add more diversity to our little group,' his smarmy smile matching the ironic twist to his voice. 'Thank god.'

My eyes turn to slits, I fly darts of anger his way.

77

'Oh, I'm not interested in becoming a groupie,' smiles the driver in my direction, latching me on to him. My eyes open wide. 'I'm more a one-on-one type of guy.'

A wet patch glides in my pants.

Frank continues disagreeably, over-riding the point of view. 'Inclusion is limitless, thank god.'

Wow, Frank likes the sound of his own voice. And we all stand listening to him - how maddening. How will I shut him up?

'There is more reward in giving than receiving, thank god.'

'That's for sure,' the driver puckers his lips.

My lips mirror his flirting action.

Mom is chuckling on the bench.

'What a pity you will not join us.' I hear no sincerity in Frank's voice. 'We have a cozy community, thank god.'

Unhappy with the innuendoes building around the bench, too light for his demeanor, he switches his full attention to the old guy. 'I'm not forgetting you Mr P.'

'I know you would not leave me hanging, Frank,' affirms the quiet patient, in a low manner that warms him to me. I'm fidgety, demanding control of the situation making me want to scratch my prickly skin. Let me think, I plot. The shuttle driver could sit with Mom.

'Okay.' I stand my ground. 'I can handle this.' The creepy Frank reverses a few feet. His taint of lavender lingers, my senses, alert and hyperactive flood with adrenaline. 'I agree to his plan,' and I wink at the driver.

'As you wish, Lily,' Frank says. 'Come with me Mr P. Thank god.' He leaves as silently as he arrived, pushing the unassuming Mr P.

What an odd man. Quivering, I've been spooked by the dark strange one, on the eve of Halloween season. Is he a moral, righteous demon of a man?

Gauging Mom, I am about to ask her questions about Frank but she aptly turns the tide of events by turning to regard her seated companion inquisitively. 'That's very kind of you, young man.'

'Thank you, I appreciate the company.' He pauses and looks at me continuing, 'it's very lonely sitting behind the wheel all day.'

I give in to my warring instincts, deciding not to analyze the crap happening around me. Taking time out on a bench is not on my list of priorities today. But it is a lovely surprise. This is like the start of a new time for me, overlapping the time as I had understood it.

Time was never as real as this new timeline is. The physics of time are altering. I should get moving but I am stayed. The opposite of time running on is in play. Time is slowed and is not rushing by. My existence is now. I'm enthralled. I welcome him into my private space. He had already imploded into my physical arena.

Mom looks content, she sits back, allowing the sequence of events to play out.

'I should …' I voice, almost a whisper.

They smile at me in unison. The contagious disease of consent in the air.

'I'm Dr Lily Tully,' she offers warmly. 'Pleased to meet you.' She extends her hand.

'I'm Mike Leman. Pleased to meet you too.'

Mike holds her hand gently, taking care not to squeeze too tightly after observing the gnarling of her fingers. I like his respectful demeanor all the more for it.

'He has the same brown eyes as you, dear.'

'Is it you or the fiery lady chaperoning you who is going to the doctors today?' he teases Mom.

Giggles rasp from my mom. One is never too old to giggle, I muse. Privately I applaud our companion's easy way about him. The irony of his remark is not lost on me.

'Just me,' mom jokes and adds, 'this time.'

We all laugh. 'Thanks Mom.'

'You have a calling laugh,' issues Mike. 'It invites one to laugh along with you.'

'Thank you, young man. I have never heard that turn of phrase.' She accepts his difference, I can tell.

'Mike, this is Olive.' Mom lets the adjoining names align, rejoicing in the reciprocal introduction to follow.

Well done, Mom, I coyly smirk her way, ravishing the moment. I have a name; now to get his number, I privately jest as I tilt my head her way in gratitude, she is a game player.

She is happy with herself.

Mike smiles and stands up, his head only just above mine, his body closer now and his hand reaches out to me.

'Olive,' he caresses my name with a lyrical accent.

'Mike,' I respond and place my hand in his. We shake on it.

A person may shake a million hands but may only remember one. This is my one-in-a-million, a strong intense hold, there is no escaping the intimacy. We hold one another's hand for longer than we need to.

'Excuse me?' enquires Mike as I start to chuckle. Comedy is close to tragedy. I don't have time for this today but Mom is playing matchmaker, forcing life to come through the other side of pain.

'My Mom is acting the matchmaker.'

We all laugh. I'm so proud of my mother and her strength of character. Mom recoils in agony nanoseconds after her escape of laughter. 'Oh, it's good to laugh, even if it is too painful. I'm accustomed to the agony.' She halts, 'I'm scared.'

Two words of simple meaning, simply spoken, speak volumes.

80

'I would be too,' offered Mike.

'Me too Mom.' And for the first time, the horror of her world registers with me. I am more afraid for her than for myself. Maybe this is why my instincts are screeching this morning.

'Do not worry for me, Olive, I worry for you, I'm acclimatized to death, it has no hold over me.' Mom transfers a glance of concern onto me. 'I'm scared for you dear.'

Why is she scared for me? Unaware, I stumble further.

'Well, go on then,' Mom instructs.

'Mom, don't direct me,' I snipe.

'We all need a helping hand,' Mom replies and she goes to twist her ring by habit. But now I wear it.

Already she misreads the way of the land she is irrigating. Her bare wedding ring finger misses its loyal companions.

Mom, don't tell me what to do, I privately seethe. Let me be my own person.

The tune of the singing birds goes unheard in the fractious place.

'I'm scared of the health system,' Mom utters, almost to herself, relinquishing old fears in her olden years. 'Autonomy has no standing among the multiple.'

The notion strikes me … How strange a fellow doctor does not trust her comrades' workplace.

'The clinic is a vicious business.' Mom shakes her head with regret. 'Such times we live in. To take away a person's freedom of choice is an atrocity, a denial of human rights. Cost is the determining factor these days. Imagine cost over care,' she mutters.

Rubbing her fingers along the knots of the wood, Mom adds, 'Olive, this bench has an inscription in my honor.'

'What, Mom?' I strain to see. 'No way. Where?'

81

'Here' and she lifts her frame up slightly from the backrest. 'A retirement gift of sorts. I requested they place a resting seat outside the doors - a stopping point, to ponder and assist the ailing, weary soul that needs a place to rest.'

'You never said, Mom.'

'I know, you are right, but there was no need for a fuss. You never came to the clinic with me before today because of your demanding job. This is the first opportunity I have to show you all of this, dear.'

I bend over her shoulder and in the middle of the backrest is a brass plate inscribed with:

Gratitude To The Visionary Medical Campaign
Of Dr Lily Tully

Mom, you are full of surprises.

LILY

'Do you have to go back home to your country for funerals, Mike?' I ask him.

'What a spot-on, intriguing question, Lily.' He measures my correct discernment with a respectful tone. 'It was my accent that gave me away.' I smile and he continues, 'yes I do,' and he puffs, 'it's costing me a fortune.'

'I'm sure,' I agree, 'but I'm aware the rite of passage is highly respected in Hinduism. My daughter thinks my day is moving at a snail's pace. The mourning period of thirteen days, attended by family members, sitting and praying with the disembodied spirit of the deceased, as it awaits to obtain a new body for reincarnation is very special.'

'You are a knowledgeable lady, then,' he compliments me in his sweet tone.

'We use lavender essential oil, you have two elements of embalmment.'
He offers the answer. 'Sandalwood is applied to the forehead of a man and turmeric to a woman.'

'In the world of medicine, I have been honored to meet individuals of diverse beliefs and faiths.' I pat his hand. 'We all die a death; there should be tolerance of traditions and rituals dissimilar to one's norm.' My slip of the tongue adds, 'I wonder will I come back, to reincarnate? It will be an eventful journey to find out.'

'I'm glad you think that way, Lily.' He shakes his head, whether in disbelief or wonder, I'm not sure.

'Oh, I do, Mike, I certainly do. I wish folk were not afraid of a different way.' Before I can help it, I'm philosophizing. Recuperating from the stress, in the brief absence as Olive parks the car, the offload to this stranger is a blessing. 'The law of polarity gleams you are right and I am right, when we stand on polar sides of a perception, belief, and opinion.' I chuckle as I listen to myself lecture. 'You poor man, I do not mean to bend your ear,' I add. 'I give talks in seminars and conferences, on the field of medicine adapting to life's diverging sociological patterns.'

'On the contrary, Doctor, you are most interesting.' He sits up straighter. 'All day I listen to customers complain I am in the wrong, when the shuttle is running behind time, because the timetable is right, so they are right. So I am in the wrong then.'

'I don't recommend small mindedness,' I say.

I can feel his eyes on me. I have to stir my resting bones, the hard bench is hurting me, but I won't complain, there is no point. 'I've always wanted to go to India,' a sigh slips from my frame. 'Sharing the little time I have left with an Indian is befitting.'

He does not know how to respond, I can tell. Closing my eyes, I try to block out the pain. The sun is warm. He has a nice manner; he doesn't have to talk incessantly and allows me to rest. I'm not going to tell him about the cremation service at the house. We had a private service with only a handful of guests after we carried her ashes from the crematory. Drew's wife wanted to be cremated. Shelley was not a Hindu, but it was her thing, placed, second among her three final wishes. Drew allowed the ceremony to go ahead, eventually; he doused the initial ignited timbers with a bucket of water in the crematory, he was so distraught, her passing came over him badly. Newlyweds robbed of history in the making, is tragic. Shelley was dying; her body rejected the heart transplant. Life is cruel, the perfect match of organ tissue, a successful operation and at the last hurdle, her body, the host, would not accept the new heart.

Drew has frightened me today. He is unstable. We, the team, eased his wife's release. Who is going to care for Drew? I've left emails for colleagues to enlist him on their reference list. I placed Olive's name on that list. She will have questions. Whose grave has he opened? Shelley's ashes were scattered in the ocean, as she wanted. I've seen the service because we were there, on the shoreline of the house.

My mind is fragmenting with all of this emotional commotion. I wanted only to have Olive in my heart today. The morning has not gone to plan. Maybe Round Wood was the better option; the house is a holistic, home from home. They did suggest the house for the final rest. 'You old cat,' Missy tut totted and placed a second marshmallow on the stick. 'Please don't burn the goods this time,' irony laces off my cheeky tongue, the twist toward the log fire is too difficult for my body, I smell the old wood, curling a wave of smoke. The peace of the mature wooden gardens, shielding us, is heaven on earth. Evening dusk mists a spell over us. We sit on rocking chairs. Jim has a soft lounger with Frank. Missy can barely bend over her swelling belly. She is in good form after the threatened miscarriage.

Now I evaluate the companionship, it registers.

Olive may have fared better without sole responsibility for me at the clinic. But I had made up my mind, and put the plan in place.

Shelley, the time before her send off, was happy. 'Welcome friends,' Frank called, 'thank god,' when Drew and she, joined the group. They had been walking on the waters edge. 'I love this house,' Shelley gushed, and she reached in and robbed the sweet, sticky treat. 'Hey!' I pretended offence. 'That was mine.' My mouth waters, I can almost taste the sugar. 'Frank owns this house,' I said aloud. 'Wow,' bellowed Missy. 'I never would have guessed.' Frank looked nonplussed. He was having none of the earthly glory. 'This resting place of souls is for the foundation,' Frank shot me a raised eyebrow and adds, 'Thank god.' 'Thank god,' we all replied.

We had to register as a foundation, the deluge of donations and gifts was mounting. Nurse Jean oversees the handling of all goods to the administration.

'Speak the truth now, Frank.' I turned to Missy. 'Frank was gifted this house,' her eyebrows arched, 'by a retired wealthy banker, a gentleman,' I add and recall in silent memory.

I never forget a client.

The log fire burnt fiercely, flames of heat lapped around our bodies. Evenings in Florida are warm and balmy, but the coolness accompanies in the late evening after the summer. We were snug and I continued. 'Frank lives here, but, in a kind sweeping act, he placed the deeds into the joint ownership of the foundation.'

Missy scowled at the account of the turn of events. 'Why?' she rudely asked him.

'Because the troops gather at a base.' Frank's mode of sermon perplexed her, the look on her face was incredulous.

It brings a smile to my face even now.

Frank likes the masses around him, he does not want to be alone. Round Wood is a perfect base, I've spent many a contented time there, but Olive, forever the strategist, would want a state-of-the-art medical arena to meet the demands. I'm certain of that.

There was no need for a compromise. I'm proud of my work, I attend to it in the clinic.

The clinic it is.

OLIVE

Unhindered, we lean on one another and walk the polished floors. I'm looking over my shoulder, rattled by the violent gun scene we witnessed. 'I still think we should go home, after the gun ordeal.' I try to dissuade Mom from the plan of today.

'Gunshot wounds are an everyday occurrence to a doctor, dear.' She dismisses the drama. 'I will only be a few hours, dear. We should stay now we are here. Could you take another day off work tomorrow, if we go home?'

LIAR.

Work - you threatened the work card.

That tenet of the conversation keeps us on this path. There was no way I could take more time from the office. 'Is there a psychotherapy department in this clinic, Mom?'

'No dear, why?'

'Oh, just with the loony bin carry on, I expect to see Drew again.' Distrust cloaks my shoulders.

Moms not as bothered by the event as me. She moves at an actual leisurely pace. But then she is walking through the corridors of her world. I want to get in and get out. The pace is killing me. I've only spent just over an hour with her but it feels like ages. I think she is purposely slowing down the day, our time together. Bless her, I smile to myself. Our reflections slither by on the marble sheen. A quantum leap of possibility resides in these ultra sleek quarters.

My expectations are high.

The modern décor alludes to excellence of care.

The core of the building with skyline levels is a hive of activity. Glass balconies rise above our heads with the allure of five star accommodation. Leafy plants in ultra modern chrome planters give the Floridian theme one loves to get lost in, of possibility, where dreams come true.

'A full-time botanist must be employed to restrain this forestry. Add to the bill,' I tot up and admonish her tastes.

'It's only money, health is more important than wealth, dear.'

'You're right, Mom,' I confirm. 'But I will take both.'

'Wouldn't we all?'

A Centrum designer waterfall lushly cascades. A zombie zone; slower, bored inmates patter by. We pass a café. The coffee does not smell great, no enticing aroma soothes my nerves.

I don't want to be here. I wish this day over.

I wished this.

Be careful what you wish for.

We are signed in, there is no escaping, the administrative details have been approved in the office. We were given premium attention, up to the point of signing the insurance clauses, then we were dismissed to find our own way to our quarters. The staff takes no notice of Mom, occupant of room thirteen as we slip in to her quarters.

A serene pulse occupies the confines of the dull green cube. I'm surprised with the seamless floor-to-ceiling finish within our box, there are no grouted tile lines anywhere. No bumps or lumps in the material world.

'Why are there no skirting boards?' What a weird thing for my mind to be focusing on.

Mom throws her head back and laughs. 'Gee, Olive, I forget you are such a novice in these surrounds. Bacteria harbors in the dirt, there are no nooks or crannies to allow the room to be hosed down after each resident.'

'Wow, this clinic is sleek.'

'The clinic is ultra efficient, Olive,' and she lifts her fingers to carry out a dust test and shows me the result. They are nude, no dust. I can't believe it. 'No print of any occupancy is left behind in the room after a patient exits.'

'I need this look in my apartment.'

'They take air samples now.'

Mom is an expert compared to me. I envy this advantage, I applaud her expertise. She envelops the room in a dignified manner. I the daughter do not possess such dignity.

'You're in your comfort zone here, Mom. I had no idea the place was so futuristic.'

'Futuristic, yes,' her lip quivers. 'My future self has no setting here.'

Oh no, have I upset her?

Medical advances progress at a fast pace, Mom's health obstacles have polarized her in the opposite direction.

'This must be hard for you,' I add although not fully understanding her anguish, because I've never given my future self any consideration.

Her shoulders resign in a downward agreement. 'The bizarre disconnect between what I feel and the collective attitude of my peers is hard on me at times, dear. But I feel honored to have you with me, and to have had residency with my family up to the seventh decade of my life.' Mom smiles but I can see pain behind her façade. 'Thank god.'

That term, thank god, jars in me, and what a strange term residency is? I'm not signing her over. With a compulsion to claw my arm, I egg myself on, take care of Mom, keep my hands busy, so I lift her bag onto the armchair and open it to help with the unpacking. 'Well, Mom, you're not taking up residency here. You will be home tonight.'

A wan smile crosses her face. 'I never wanted to become senile, Olive, time up is time up.'

This statement catches me off guard. I stall taking her wash bag to the sink. To be honest, to me, my mother is ancient but astute. Very little gets past her, this was always the case in our relationship. But I can't answer with a lie. I can't promise agility, of mind and body, for her lifetime, in the best of health, no one can, we know her prognosis of motor neuron failure. 'I know, Mom.' I continue with futile activities of placing tissues and her cell phone on the bedside cabinet.

By letting the day unfold, I let her direct me. My way of paying homage to her, I'm here.

'Daughter, I'm glad we have the opportunity of this day, to share my heartfelt wishes with you, my dear, loved one.' Her heavy sigh saddens me, unsettles me. My mom is not a defeatist. Her strong voice reaches out to me. 'It is my time of telling.' Mom pats her chest gently. 'But I'm so nervous. This reminds me of taking you on your first day to the school door and hoping you will go.' We both smile at the recall of my obstinate ways.

'You were more fun than the teacher, Mom.' I nearly add, 'back then.' Rapidly, in my solo years of education, I didn't need her as much. We lived alongside for decades, fixed on an out-of-date version of daughterhood, right up to this very moment. Mom does not need me here, she needs a doctor. But I want to be here. I cannot get enough of my mom, on some existential level. Is there anything new to learn from the other? I'm not sure.

In marches a hefty nurse. I'm taken aback by the sudden entry. 'Have you told Olive?' she addresses Mom, in an Irish accent.

'No, Jean.' Mom closes her eyes.

'Have you told Jim?'

'Yes.'

'Right, I will leave you to it. The clock is ticking, Lily,' she directs to Mom and reaches over and shakes my hand. 'Hi, I'm Nurse Jean. See you later.'

She leaves us.

I'm replaying the confusing conversation.

In collaboration, I add, 'Told me what? Does Dad understand you having to come here today?'

'I don't know, Olive. I hope he will recall our conversation from last night. I did outline the events of the day, I've told Jim everything. We had a lovely evening together in preparation for me leaving him today.' Her eyes dart over me.

'That's good, Mom.' I place her wrap over the chair, half listening as I sort her items.

'I can't go on with the pain, Olive,' she quickly throws out.

'What?' I stop sorting her bag.

'I can't. I treasure the glimpses of my old Jim, but they are far and few in between our reality. I treasure my past. There is no treasuring my future.' She brings her hands together in a prayer action of homage.

I pause and watch her. She walks gingerly around the room, touching the surfaces with her fingertips, an old colleague back among her world. I can tell she is thinking.

92

The lunacy of striving and coming so far, to be bluntly stopped in our tracks, is potent for me in this environment.

There is very little for one to do but wait. The sick bed makes me take stock. Mom was the expert, now she is the patient. It has to be difficult for her. To me, it is a twilight zone. The norms of the outside world, have no place in this setting. Speed does not exist, everything moves at a snail's pace; check in, settle in, hang around. We are waiting for the consultant. Waiting. I'm not familiar with that concept.

LIAR.

The normality lulled a mode of complacency.

My cell phone blinds, I ignore answering it with all my might; if I take a call I could be dragged into a scenario that takes my attention. I see her take in the room as it enraptures her. She is fading as I know her before my very eyes. These four walls close off my reality. I want to scream, enact energy. But there is no option but to fall in line with the mind boring trivia.

'Some doctor should invent an app to self test at home, to stop all this paraphernalia of clinical visits.'

'You're a forward-thinking young woman, Olive. They will do some day, but not in my day.'

'Sure you'll live to a hundred, Mom, to spite me.' I don't sound brave.

'I'm proud of you, Olive. I hope you can be proud of me - always.'

'I am, Mom.' I stilled and listened. 'I am.'

Mom continues sharing her private thoughts.

'Last night unsettled me, Olive. I blessed your Dad's memory loss for the first time because if Jim does not remember details, then maybe he won't grieve for me in every detail, like I have been grieving for him, Alzheimer's pulsating, death of self, in the land of the living.'

93

I cannot speak. Mom misses my dad, the life they had shared, deleted by the corrosive erosion of dementia. I miss him too.

'I detest feeling helpless, for Dad,' she cries, 'and it is ahead for me, when my bodily control deserts me.'

I walk around the bed and take her in my arms. I feel her recoil in agony; I can't even comfort her. I wish I could obliterate her agonized existence of physical and mental pain. Wonder Woman was my favourite heroine, great hair and fab boobs, with her powerful memory erasure, a rap of rope, once roped in, she vamoosed recall. Mom could be hypnotized to forget her diagnosis. Fantasy over reality ... No wonder I'm addicted to erotica. I must discuss this with her later, who would want to have their mom cry? I wish I could do a twirl and fix our life, like the TV character. Mom continues to steer the course of action, our queen, in our household.

'Dad truly loves you, Mom, even in his limitations, he loves you with his whole heart, just as I do.' I place a soft kiss on her cheek.

'We need to talk too, dear.' Her voice holds a soft command, the determined request hangs in the air.

Here we go.

I can't take much more upheaval, my patience is running thin.

I hear my mother but purposely I go over to the sink to pick up the vase. Prompted by my line of thought, Mom loves roses, yellow petals will be of comfort when I have to leave her alone and go to the work meeting. I read somewhere, that people regret what they did not say, more than what they said. I understand that right here and now.

I have all this clarity in my head but I cannot voice the words to the meaning. I'm having a silent conversation with my mother. I'm walking to her, looking right at her. I can hear my voice, I think I'm communicating with her because my head is full of her.

A perfect room in a doll's house, we are clean and primed, the roses the perfect added touch. But I live in a real world, the girl has grown up, I had loved playing with my doll's house. Now I do real. The air is heavy with unspoken truths. Spinning rings of frenzy begin to charge within me.

I feel a little nauseous. 'I feel woozy.' Still, I move, I lift the roses over to her bedside locker.

'You should eat, dear, the day will be long. I'm always telling you not to skip breakfast.'

'Not yet, Mom, I'm not hungry. Later.'

'Later,' Mom repeats my assertion.

I choose to ignore her smart return. I lift the bed pillows and spruce them up, the wasteful dribble of time, the luxury of time, the preserve of the young. Plenty of time to talk after, I pacify my quaking self. I have to calm my tangling emotions. Not allowing my mind to think further than turning on the tap on, I wash my hands, to control the antiseptic environs with mindfulness. I feel yuck in here, a climate of sickness, the flowing water soothes my senses, the coolness relaxes me, my hands rest in the immersion.

Tick, tock. Time is intricate,

I know I'm unable to stop the invasion. I want to be brave.

I curse under my breath, I wish I were on the beach dipping my toes in the ocean, fully immersing in vitality. Somehow the time is never right to let go. Critical deadlines determine the clock, yet they are obsolete in the realm of the medical timeframe, the world is another planet.

'Mom, do you feel like the world in here is a different universe, parallel, to the world out there?' I look out the window.

She laughs, 'Yes, you are perceptive, Olive. You may well figure out the ways of this clinic all by yourself.'

The room is too small for avoidance, maybe this is why I'm being curtailed by my mother in this place? The plusses and subtractions that make up a life in the clinic are of a different discipline from my neat professionalism of accountancy. The rules are different. My mother knows me too well. I'm here at her request, minimizing my life. Nowhere is as taxing as here, I feel useless. I should sit and wait it out, but that makes me feel redundant. Instead, I busy myself, the endless activity, whizzing me about her.

Mom sits still. I'm uneasy in her calmness. She is too calm.

I don't want to chance my luck. This is manageable if the parameters are kept tight. We are a symmetric umbrella, ready to be put up in the storm; if even one spoke comes apart, the perfect shape is undone. Electric static stings my fingers when they touch the chrome bed rail, making me stop in my tracks, my overwrought energy affecting me. I pull back and rest my hands for the first time that morning.

Then a new beat restarts. Flip, flop, flip, flop.

A pair of slippers taps on the floor in our room, overtaking us. Mom and I stare at one another. Freeze frame, we watch this little old lady get into the unoccupied bed. The silver-haired thief pours herself a glass of water and sips. She is in a world of her own, typical of this place. I exhume a puff of anger. No company expected, but we have a guest.

'The cost of this place and you have to share a bed,' I joke.

'Olive, why are you so negative?'

Mom turns to the visitor, who assumes we are staff and says, 'No milk and two sugars, please.'

I start laughing.

We look at one another, mystified at what to do next.

'Mom, she thinks you are the service lady.'

Mom's tender words flow to the patient.

'Can I help you?' she asks.

'Two sugars,' is the reply.

'No way, today is my day off,' teases Mom. 'I will not be putting on the kettle again, domesticity no more, a great addition to today.' She falters.

'What did you just say, Mom?'

There is a quick knock on the door. A young nurse pokes a sallow face around the frame.

'Be in, in a little while.' A mellow Filipino dialect fills the room, with a beaming smile.

Seconds later, she retreats, into thin air, a magic trick, a regular stunt in this illusionary world.

'Fuckin' hell, Mom. Do they lose patients in this place? No one has come looking for the wanderer yet.' The see-saw of my emotions sway. The nurse had retreated so quickly. Minutes are passing unaided. We are left to our own devices. I can't be still. I walk to the door, put my head out, but the corridor is empty. No missing person alert. My anxiety flourishes. Would Mom be looked after in this place? I pace the floor. Mom is sitting and chatting to the helpless patient.

'It's pointless. That old one is delusional. Drugged-up patients.'

'Olive,' Mom says, displeased by my disrespect. 'This little lady is managing, her way, like the rest of us.'

'Do we look like we are holding a coffee pot?'

'Where's my coffee?' the intruder intrudes.

'I'd love a cup of coffee,' enjoins Mom in harmony.

'I'd murder a coffee too.'

We smile.

'Yes, you are jumpy. Must be the withdrawal symptoms,' surmises the doctor.

'Very funny, Mom.'

The comedy of the dilemma, suffering damsels in need of coffee.

Mom thought she was getting a break from living with confusion.

Life is confusing really.

The age-defying medicine of laughter naturally lifts our mood. We giggle, as piles and bedwetting disclosures abound from the little robber, her intimate disclosures teeter on a fine line of embarrassment. 'What is worse, not knowing how to evict the guest or how to stop her divulging more details?' I ask Mom.

'This clinic is liberal but I'm not volunteering as a bouncer,' jokes Mom, trying to flex her fading muscles and enact a strong arm pose. Her tired limbs are not able to join along in the game, her mind is stronger than her traitorous body.

'I will buzz the nurse back in, Mom.'

'Leave them be, they must be occupied,' instructs Mom. 'Time enough for me to be in that bed, we won't unduly distress this little lady.'

'Okay, Mom.' I don't contradict, she has a more accepting manner that I did not inherit. And she is not rattled in these surrounds.

Sunlight shines through the large window, masterminding a slant in the cloud. How come I never noticed the light in this room? It gives a new karma to our confines. But we are still left waiting. I can't sit, I open the window. The natural air is more inviting than the stale recycled air.

Looking out, when I have to be in, is a queer form of prison. Being here hems me in, draws out the wild animal in me, instinctively having to find a way to escape. Positive thoughts are purposely sought for in my head and heart. I want to be here for my mother, I love her. Mom will have exceptional care, she has said so herself. I must remember to tell the nurse to go easy

98

on the medication, there is no need to drug my mother. I must ask the consultant about the side effects. The swell of emotions build in my stomach, my lists medicate me. My cell phone is buzzing, probably the office. Another message is left in the voicemail, I hear the chink of a reminder toll. I could distract myself from life and play with the cell phone. That would be the easy route. My mind is full, it runs from one dilemma of my mother to another. Is this a competent clinic? The present invader taking up my time derails my trust in the system.

'Mom, don't take extra tablets in here.' It's my turn to instruct. 'They are always on the look out for suckers to try new drugs.' I motion a pendulum swing with my head, extending to an exaggerated no. 'Even if they promise the meds will make you live forever. You know better.'

'Yes, Olive dear, I do know better.'

'And please don't sign any more forms I haven't checked.'

'Don't treat me like a child, Olive,' her voice sounds haughty. 'I will sign whatever I see fit to.'

'Mom, I didn't mean to offend.' I twist my hair and walk over to her. 'I don't like that the staff have not noticed the missing body yet. Poor auld doll is not aware of her disorientation but the clinic has a duty of care, and they are none the wiser. It's a tad worrying.'

'Jeepers!' Mom nudges her elbow into my side. 'I'm not in here because I'm going gaga.' The unspoken worry over the future of Dad's depth of deprivation sneaks into our mind. Internally I cry, I'm the more harassed of the three ladies present.

'Please, Mom, be careful today, the mind altering effects of medication are unclear.'

'Maybe you should have a go of my bed, too, your turn next,' she replies tartly. 'You need to chill out, Olive.' She is not jesting, she gauges me adeptly.

Okay, chill, I instruct myself, Mom has enough on her plate today. We observe the busy bed Mom gladly shares, but there is no division for me, I don't share her attribute of kindness.

Mom cannot turf out the socializing little lady, this is my mother's way. 'Adapt dear, life takes us by surprise, always, thank god.'

'Sure Mom,' I don't sound convinced. 'I'm not as humane as you, my training is in definite facts, your field is in the potential.'

'Maybe, dear, in my experience, when the facts are fully accounted for, the only outcome is the humane.' Her voice is strained. 'Let her be.'

'We're so different, Mom.'

'I think we are very alike, Olive – you and I achieve what we set out to. Did you get Mike's cell number?'

'Yes, I did,' my smile beams.

'Good. Your private world is your domain, daughter,' concludes Mom. 'Your child does not have to converse with you on details, a parent knows this, their child is the adult and has to stand on their own two feet.' She takes a long inhale. 'Olive, just because I'm aging, dwindling in years, please don't turn this day on its head. I'm proud of my autonomy.'

'I won't disrespect or offend you, Mom.'

She lifts my hair out of my eyes, an eternal parental tick. 'I respect your mind, respect mine.'

I'm thinking of Mike's full lips. I concentrate to answer. 'You were always a formidable parent, a force to be reckoned with.'

'Were?' A nark of tone responds, 'I still am, dear.'

I give her the thumbs up sign but this signage causes a frown. 'Just because you've become an adult, that part of my entity, a formidable parent, does not change.' She turns her shoulder away from me, our intimate leaning, separated. 'Child, you will never outgrow my standing.

100

I will always be the parent. Some things are just not open to discussion. Your sexual forte is your business; I have a nuance that is my business,' she raises her voice. 'I can understand why you find porn addictive; your personality is all go. Enjoy your sexuality, lucky you,' her eyes roll.

'Mom!' I howl.

'Yep,' she winks. 'There are sides to me you don't have privy to. Me and Dad still cuddle,' her tone is a blasé approach to the physical.

'Mom,' I yelp. 'Enough,' I expound but laugh in merriment. I wake up our sleeping guest. 'I love you, we know one another intimately, but there has to be room for intrigue.'

'I suppose so, dear. I'm going off course a bit,' she bites her lower lip. Mom does this when she is concentrating. 'Never relinquish on your choices, dear.' Wow, mind games are the dish of the day. 'I won't ever give up my freedom of choice, my body is closing down, not my mind,' she sounds full of conviction. 'Stay in charge of your life, Olive, at all times, that's the advice I gladly give because I believe it.' Her sermonizing astonishes me. My mother is not a woman who sets herself on high authority, lording herself over me, ever. Opinionated maybe, but dictatorship was not her style. 'Thank god,' she adds robotically.

The side kick hits a mark, annoying me, her impassioned voice reverberates around the cube, the air crackles. The hairs on my arms stand on guard. My body stiffens.

That turn of phrase makes my blood boil.

Is it a mantra with the team in this clinic?

I never want to hear it again.

'I condone your openness to exploration. Well done, girl, I've brought you up fine,' she applauds, her hands tip off one another in the slightest of touches to avoid pain. But her eyes are alight with vigorous energy. 'Life is too narrow-minded for so many. What a pity.'

I become quiet. Is she discussing sexual appetite? Was I in control? The ferocity of how I fancied the ass off this shuttle driver had knocked me off course. Losing control was more apt a picture.

'I hope you will always respect my decisions, Olive. I respect yours.' And she takes my hand. 'Let's shake hands on acceptance.' Her grip is full of determination.

'If you can stop thinking I should have a husband. I'm contentedly single.' I smugly call her out on one of her misconceptions.

'Boring,' Mom replies and throws her hands up. 'Girl, you have no idea of the rollercoaster you are missing. No one holds a mirror up to you like a partner.'

'I do my own soul searching,' I scowl. My defensive manner surprises me.

'But you go a step further, more than you ever thought possible, for your significant other.'

'I think if I had a significant other that would prevent me from seeking out new ventures.' Our debating mentalities come to the fore.

'Really?' A smug tone comes from Mom. 'I think because of the other, you go the extra mile.'

'I prefer multiples,' I jest. 'I'm very good with numbers.'

'Yes, you are.'

'Pristine books that all add up, tick my box.' I tilt my head toward her.

'A life all sewed up intact, or so you think,' she lowers her eyes and shakes her head. Another deep inhale of breath and she continues. 'Life is a balancing act, Olive, we all walk the tightrope.'

I can't imagine my mother walking a tightrope, but I dare not say, she is volatile if I digress her intellect with any mention of old age.

'I thrive with challenges, Mom. Marriage would be boring to me. Domesticity, yuck,' my face scrunches up. 'Bring on the modern era. I hit and quit. It suits me.'

'Yet the young ones are bored these days,' she adds and takes me on. 'You say you are bored. Marriage is the most challenging event you will ever find, dear.'

'Don't hold your breath.' I pause.

Is there any point in this discussion? She has made her choices. Such as this clinical world. I'm on her territory. She would gladly sit with patients. I'm itching to turf the thief and be on my way.

Brain deadening waiting.

This medical morning is too long. I wonder can I leave sooner than I hoped, call an earlier meeting?

LIAR.

Mom had me imprisoned in capsules of restriction: the car, the clinic, time.

'I would not trade my identity for a safety net,' I catch my voice from sounding condescending. How do I voice my opinion to my matriarchal, conservative mother?

'I only want what's best for you, dear.'

She cups my cheek in the palm of her hand. 'I'm telling you there are other ways than what you know.' We agree to disagree, I nod my head. 'Live your life your way, decision making is the ultimate challenge. I have found this to be so in every area of life, marriage, parenting and in my line of work.'

Never wanting to come across as a critic of my Mom's choices in her life, I had held my own private court over the years. She hinted for a wedding date; Mom settled too young in my opinion. Guest lecturing, mentoring and tutorial part-time work never could compete with the success of a full time career. Yet she preoccupies herself. 'Do you still volunteer on community health days, Mom?'

'Yes, dear, I do. You are right in your estimations, in every aspect of a person's life and the decisions they make, there are plusses and minuses.'

'Do you regret not succeeding to the top of your game, Mom, not becoming the Master Professor in your field?'

'I did succeed, dear. I have you, I have my family, and I did all I could do in my work.'

'I mean professionally?'

'When I took time out from the institution, I stood back,' and her frame squares, she stands taller, 'and contradictorily, I became more of a doctor. I saw the whole picture, not the small patch I stood on everyday I worked.' She sweeps her arms up. 'The goal is bigger. I realized I was climbing up the career ladder but I was leaning the ladder on the wrong building.'

'Wrong building! Did you want to change career?' I feel my jaw drop.

'No dear, I wanted to be a better physician. I will get you onboard today.'

LIAR.

Mom you should have tried harder.

'Before I became a mother, I'd never known pure acceptance. In medical college, the human race is clumped into mass form. Differentiation is a cause of alarm in medical circles. Well, we are all different, you kids showed me that, each person is unique. How could I regret such wonder? You gave me my enlightenment. I had no right to cut an individual into segments that suit medicine. Work with, suit the patient, then the doctor, became my motto.'

'You've always been a devoted doctor, Mom.'

'Yes, I'm loyal to my patients, right to the very end. Olive …' Mom hesitates and sounds distressed. 'The words evade me, in my hour of need.' Mom looks frantic.

104

'Are you alright?'

'I'll be fine. Give me space to express myself. And you're right, dear.'

'Oh, about what? This may be a first.'

'Stop it,' she pleads of my teasing. 'I do enjoy social media. It's an unrivaled forum for exchanging information and ideas. Thank you for insisting I move with the times, that's why I have made up my mind to -'

'Doris,' chirps the overweight Irish-American nurse, far from a picture of health, raspy and out of breath, bellowing, to match the masse of physical volume. 'That's where you've gotten to.' And before the intruder answers, she is whipped up. 'Let's get you back to your own bed.' No room for maneuvering or obstruction with the ninja nurse, I privately surmise. 'Have you told Olive by now?' she asks Mom.

'I'm getting there, Nurse Jean,' says Mom.

'See you shortly,' replies the firm handler. I am not given a second to make any demands. She is too brisk for my liking. No one returns to freshen up the soiled sheets or replace the used glass.

'You're right too, Mom. The clinic will want to avoid individualism, herd the patients together. Your cup of coffee will be served when they decide, not when you want it. What do you have to do around here to get some service? Everyone has to assimilate into the group within this institution.'

I barely catch my breath and go into full flow again. 'They will slip you tablets at every opportunity, Mom, morning and evening. The pills will be used to confine you by sedation. Brainwash you to comply, it's the system's way of controlling the chaos. Patients are dulled by the medical world.'

'I agree, Olive. The individual can get lost in the system. A patient should have a personal plan in the whole scheme of things. I have one.'

A knocking is on the door. I think, time for the doctor. My face falls, Frank is at the door. Mom confronts him. 'Well?'

'The cops are here, I've seen them snooping around.' They do not look away from one another. 'They will want to talk to you about your patient's grave that was tampered with.' Her eyes never blink.

'No way,' I gasp.

'All in a day's work,' dismisses Mom. 'And Drew?'

'Still at the station, thank god.'

'They must be aware of the restraining order.'

'Yes.' Frank is very solemn.

'Right so. Lie low Frank. It's a necessity for your protection. Thanks, Frank, see you later, I'm wrapping up here.'

'Yes, Dr Lily.' He leaves quietly.

I'm stupefied by her ruling demeanor. Breathing deeply, the stench enters my nostrils, filling my lungs, unstoppable. A cloud darkens the skyline, leaves signal farewell as they blow away. This place makes me feel morose.

The state of Frank perplexes me.

Move on, forget him, I mentor my distress. I know the consultant, Dr Doran, will not make me happier. Tests. The big 'T' attaching itself to every aging person has edged its way into Mom's diary and subsequently mine. It is only one day, just like every other day, it vanishes, I keep telling myself, consoling the rawness.

And yet I feel like I'm peeling, after a burn.

'My life is full of precious moments not confined to any one day,' she utters into the space. 'Funny how you go backwards, when you are old, you think of your young self. Olive, will you Skype my big brother Dan for me?'

'Sure,' I check my watch. 'It's lunch time in Dublin.' We dial up uncle Dan.

The tone rings and rings. 'Probably asleep, having a nap, how old is he now, eighty?'

'Try again, one more time for good luck.'

This time, he picks up. 'Howdy dolls,' his Irish accent takes the piss. 'Ahem,' he coughs. 'Ladies, I have to be politically correct with you yanks.'

'You better be, bro,' joins in Mom, laughing, her Irish twang long lost to her American years lived in the States.

I love seeing her happy, her smile is huge.

'I can still take you on, big brother,' she fist pumps him.

'Yeah, yeah, want to bet?' croaks Dan, his voice breaking. 'I'll throw you over my shoulders like a bag of spuds and take you down,' he finishes on an exaggerated American drawl.

I grin.

'With all my medical studies,' Mom becomes lost in time, 'I still can't figure out how you could wrestle and tumble me in the air, then catch me so softly. Honestly, Olive, he was an ape of a thing, he threw me about the place, and I never got hurt.'

'I'm the man.'

'Those were the days. You made a warrior out of me, dear brother, thanks.'

'You're welcome, sis.'

'Hi, uncle Dan.'

'Olive, look at you, all grown up.'

'Yep.'

'Sorry I could not make it over to you, Lily, I appreciate the invite,'

He wipes a tear from his cheek.

My heart swells and lifts like a bubble.

'I understand, Dan, I do. Don't worry yourself, pet.' Her endearments swoon to him, their Irish connection re-connected.

'Take care, little sister. I wish you well on your journeys, god speed.' His voice seizes up. 'I posted my rosary beads to you, sis.'

Mom blows him a kiss and touches the screen. 'I have them here with me, big brother.'

When he recovers, he says, 'Olive, you come over for a visit. None of those polite empty promises. Work will always be there. Can't beat the Irish, pure breed, I'll find ye a fell, your ma says you can't get one.'

'I would love that,' I offer politely while I grimace at Mom. How does he know about my private life? Within minutes they hang up, Mom tells him she is busy with the business at hand.

Sitting on a bed? I muse. That's her busy. The nothing happening is killing me. I pace the floor.

'Sit down, Olive, please. Have a cup of coffee with me,' my mother bosses me, as the trolley lady places a tray at the end of the bed.

'Thanks,' we both reply. She must not speak good English, she just smiles, head bent. I'm not used to sitting this long. I think I will go down to the café. Mom can text me if she needs me. Before a decision is made, we hear, a clang of a tool bang our door from the corridor. A ladder peeps in.

'Now, in here next, this room next.'

In bristles Nurse Jean. Behind her is a two man team carrying a tool bag and the peeping ladder. 'How long do you expect to be?' she asks them. 'Ten minutes tops,' the electrician raps off with practice. I want to put on the stopwatch app. I wonder what's going on. I enquire. 'No alarm bells,' the nurse quibbles and winks at Mom. 'Everyone is calling this little box there a fire alarm,' she explains, pointing to the corner of the ceiling. 'It's a CCTV camera,' adds the techie younger man. 'This is a safety check.' The step-ladder is adjusted and up he goes to the electrics. A red light flashes, he presses a button and resets with a steadfast command. 'All in order. Good service.' Nurse Jean, and ticks off the paper work. 'Sign this here after my initials.'

'Unusual how the power source in this new build is playing havoc,' the younger one adds.

'I wouldn't know,' says the nurse. 'Be careful of the patient, please.'

'Can't have the patient conk unnoticed.' The words are out, his bad taste of jokes. His partner falls in, 'Yeah, can't have stiffs taking up the beds, they never pay their bills.' They both chaff away.

Nurse Jean barges past them.

'On you get then. I have work to do.' Approaching the bedside with a wheelie apparatus, the nurse blots out the fixture and the show. She expertly wraps a blood pressure monitoring strap to Mom's arm and without warning promptly puts a thermometer into her mouth. The patient cannot talk, bliss in this surround.

It is easier to work with a patient, when they can't speak. Of course, Doctor, this is how it works.

I note the swift action. I sit in silence, not interrupting procedures. Figures are recorded on the health file. No dialogue or how do you do to me? Nothing.

'See you in a little while, Lily, I'll leave you to get on with – things.' She smiles at Mom and walks away.

And no washing of her hands, on entry or exit.

A fancy building is only as good as the team holding it together. Maybe the nurses wash their hands at their stations, I estimate. I hope the professionals are not a health menace. I have read about unhygienic practices. Well, they will be caught on camera, too right. The installation of software is inoffensive to me.

Out of the blue Mom addresses me. 'I have a pad, Olive.'

'Crap, do I have to wipe you?' Has her coffee run through her?

'Don't be crude, of course not. Use your brain.'

'What then? Tell me, how the hell am I supposed to know what goes on in this place?'

Mom has the decency to look contrite as she begins to explain herself. 'A PAD stands for physician - aid - in dying.'

'I don't understand.'

'Help is available at every juncture,' Mom tries to clarify but I'm still unclear. 'This is my individualistic plan.'

Individualistic plan?

The elastic band of time binds us, stretches and then springs back and rips.

'Dying? I've only dropped your bag on the floor, what are you talking about?'

Yet the room has possessed us for what seems an age.

The extremes of The Bermuda Triangle are to be found in the ordinariness. I shake my head in disbelief. We are only feet away from one another, I feel we are emotionally miles apart, on separate destinations on the same ground. Mom, the doctor, can talk so easily of dying. She is contented, having brought her head around to the necessity of having to come here, I'm not. My parent is accepting this path while I, the child, an adult child, am derailing by trying to manoeuvre the road. Somehow the room feels smaller, too tight, my cheeks will be resting on the dull plaster any minute.

'The pinnacle of my career, as a physician, is to aid dying, it is an honor and privilege to assist a fellow human.' She lifts her head high. 'I have been called a doctor of good death.'

I'm stunned. 'Is there such a thing as a good death?'

'Yes, Olive, there is.'

The nitty gritty of her job was never brought home to the dinner table. My mind swishes, the 360 degrees of puke green compounds my unease.

'Doctors, sometimes, do harm,' the criticism is as stark as the room.

'Go on, Mom.'

'Practitioners should talk to their patients about their death,' her tone of opinion is professionally practical. It's the future of medicine.'

'The future of medicine.'

I want to scream, 'STOP!' I don't think of death, my mother's or mine. Am I attending her practice? Her consultation tone and stance is almost official. Mom is coming into her own in the clinic, I'm disintegrating, the routine, is brain deadening.

'I recall a fine doctor announce my very own thoughts on the matter, in a Reith lecture,' she says logically.

She can't help herself, I fume, tightening my hands into fist balls. Shop talk, I'm guilty of it myself.

I pour a cup of coffee and we sip and discuss the present day focus of medicine - riveting. 'A Reith lecture?' I repeat.

'His delivery was superb dear. You can play back his speech.'

It must be old age! I would not be interested in listening to the sequence of death.

I find it hard to follow her, or give her time to get to where she wants to get to. My fingers are itching to check my messages on the vibrating cell phone, this length ignoring my cell phone is unusual.

'The wonders of modern medical science are fascinating, but they blight the reality of the blunders that are occurring.' She considers my attentive span, I look her in the eye, sensing she is studying me, she ups

111

the ante by adding, 'The amount of money wasted is pointless – the result is the same.'

Our eyes fuse. 'Money wasted ho w?' Mom knows finance captures my imagination.

'Way more money and effort goes into extending life expectancy than improving the quality of life.' Mom pours a second cup of coffee.

I will not lose my temper. 'Are we talking about selling the family home?' I joke. 'The markets are not good, we will not get a decent price.'

'This is no laughing matter, daughter. The financial costs will escalate for my treatments. The well-oiled machine of medicine is expensive.'

'I've seen the paperwork, the bills are not astronomical yet.'

'The personal costs are too high a factor for me,' she points out. 'I can't go on, Olive.'

What personal costs is she going on about? Mom has not mentioned them to me before. I try to help, she has spoken those words again, of giving up. She looks irritated. 'We will deal with it, Mom, together. We will manage, don't worry.'

'I do worry, Olive, but not about money.' A magnet of force joins us as we stare at one another. 'Managing is not how I want to proceed,' her voice is rising. 'I witness,' she stops but restarts, 'I assist patients who have succumbed, because of their incurable illness.'

The TV programmes should have prepared me; we are all mortal, not everyone has a happy ending. This is my reality show. I've a lead part, we both do. I'm her hero, just as she is mine.

'Mom, I wish with all my heart that I could make you better.' We hug, spilling the coffee, the least of our problems.

'Me too, dear, me too. Olive, my experiences of dealing with crippling illnesses, I could not tell you of, a mother will not taint their child's world with such turmoil. Your dad, dear, dementia is a disabling illness but he is not disabled,' she pauses to draw her outline. 'My diagnosis is disabling me. The muscular disease is incurable, it is life threatening, one year, five at tops before my time is up.' Her powerful condemnation shudders through her weak frame, she shakes as she speaks. 'I'm not a doctor who falls back on false hope.'

'Mom, I'll take any hope.' My powerful persuasion is no match for her volume.

'We will differ then, dear one.'

She embraces me and holds me tight.

Leaning into one another, we view the lopsided rose stalks of the arrangement, the stems refuse to be marshaled. This is a sterile setting we are making personal.

The illusion of control calms me, right now, I have a purpose, I'm here for my mother even if the space between each second, the gigantic void of unknown, surrounds me.

My life is changing, challenging me.

I dull a pain hurting my insides, I have an ache the doctor cannot cure. The natural ebb of life powerfully pulses in this dormant green room, a harsh quirk of chance, the hue of green collaborates with the moldy process of decay, the fermenting color taunts me, I close my eyes. It is only possible to do so much but I want to do everything. My speed of thought bakes the air around me. I feel too warm. My face is flushed. It is hard to stay still but my mother is resting beside me.

How can the roses look sadder in minutes?

Evident to the naked eye, they wilt in the medicinal world of rejuvenation. The enduring silence of unspoken thoughts prevails.

'Let's talk, Mom, I'm listening.'

I volunteer my services.

113

She picks up my hand, patting it lovingly. 'Olive, I need you to understand where I'm coming from.'

'Ok,' a worried sigh flattens my frame.

Holding hands, we play an old familiar game, entwining our fingers, best friends of thirty-three years.

Love is our compass.

Love will point the way.

'Where have the years gone?' she languishes.

We both smile.

'I cherish you, my perfection personified,' and she lifts my fingers and kisses each tip. 'How do you give voice to such mystery, Olive? I'm at a loss to do so, to this day. I remember your entry into this world, such pure essence, perfect nose, bottom, fingers and toes. So long ago now - but it seems like no time at all.' She pauses. 'The memory of your wonder, is as sharp to me today, as when you first imprinted into my world. I'm a lucky woman to have had a shared lifeline. The solo journey was not for me.'

On that pointer, my fingers trace the lines along Mom's right palm, gently held within my own.

She continues. 'You are a beautiful woman, more than my dreams could have imagined, more than I aspired to.' With the strength Mom could muster, she places both my hands within her own, and curves her frame, bowing to me.

'Thank you, Olive.'

'Oh, Mom,' I gush.

I can tell Mom is not herself today.

She becomes agitated, 'I have the language for love, not for sorrow.' She brings our hands together to form a prayer sign. 'No matter how happy we are, we can't stop the tears from coming. I'm sorry to do this to you, Olive.'

'It's okay, Mom,' I say, pacifying her intensity.

'Hear my words clear, Olive, and remember them,' she grabs my arm. 'My claim to a readiness for death is because I've been given enough in this life, Olive, because of you.' She pulls at my arm. 'I adore you.'

I hold back my tears. I don't want to interrupt, I am so afraid.

'I give gratitude for the first and last time our fingers will link, daughter.'

I swallow hard. Negativity swells in my blood.

'A time capsule,' Mom adds, lowering her head in prayer, a reverent quietness descending.

Jumbled words roar in my head. She needs this medical interference. I have to respect the necessity of being here, while all my instincts repel it, I have to let them use my mother's body in the tests. Mom has enough on her mind without my howling and dumping.

'Do you trust me, Olive?'

'Yes, Mom, I do? And you trust me.'

'I do,' she adds, 'but we are independent of one another.'

What is she on about? I hope she has not invested her life's savings in any sin shares; guns and war are not her thing, even if very profitable. 'Mom, I handle your financial matters while you are tied up and deal with health issues. Are you happy with that arrangement?'

'Yes. All of that is sorted.' And a question poses in her face. 'Thanks. But there is a conundrum that is bothering me.'

'Can I help you with it?' I innocently ask. 'Tell me.'

'Over the years, acting the doctor, I never considered the patient's family as utmost in the matters at hand.' She is plaiting her fingers in and out, her missing engagement ring has left a paler ring of skin on that finger.

I look down at my hand, the disloyal imposter squeezes tightly on my finger. The exchange does not sit

115

well with me, the impulse to give it backfires up. I sit on my hands and listen.

'The patient is the recipient of exceptional care, not the members of the family. Now, in my latter years, in my wisdom, today, of all times,' her voice breaks, 'I wonder about them, the broken-hearted left behind, poor Drew, beside himself with grief. My mind is full of you, Olive.'

'Have a glass of water Mom,' she is working herself into a frenzy.

She sips. 'Do you think a sudden death, the shock, absorbed and assimilated over time, is easier than knowing a certain death is coming down the tracks?'

I can see this issue is bothering Mom, her hands shake. 'I've never thought about that, Mom.' Her eyes search mine for more direction. I add depth to the communication. 'Loss is loss.'

'I've been giving this area of palliative care so much thought of late. Emotional and mental pain are as subjective as physical pain.'

'Both experiences would be dreadful,' I answer.

'I'm so sorry, Olive,' she starts to cry.

I fetch a tissue.

'When it is my time -' she pauses, I nod my head to show her I'm listening. 'I want you, dear Olive, I wish you to be the final one to ...' her voice weakens. I'm sure my mother felt my body stiffen. 'I wish you to be,' and she wipes a tear from her cheek, 'to be the person of my last touch. Please bathe me, and dot me with lavender essential oil as I repose.'

My body jerks, to banish the dire thoughts exploding. My raw reaction lifts me off the bed, I physically take a few steps away from her. My back is to the wall. The small room pens me in.

'Mom, I don't want to talk of ...' My dry mouth restricts my words, I can not voice the painted painful

116

end. My mind fragments. I silently howl. When I can speak, my voice sounds strange. 'Don't talk of that, Mom. You're not going to die yet.' The escaping air shrinks my lungs. 'You're in for tests,' I insist, the logical progression tries to influence the way of the world, like the workings of my mind could manipulate.

'Daughter, I should be talking to you about my death.'

Yes, Mom, you should have told me about your death wish.

I feel like I could get sick, vomit churns, tipping the top of my throat.

Mom looks helplessly lost. 'I'm trained to deliver such information,' she is crying again. 'But I just can't, it's too close to home.'

'You don't have to,' I speak softly and rub her back.

'I do, oh, I really have to. Death is part of life.' She takes a tissue and blows her nose. 'It's our time to have this talk, dear.'

'I don't want to.'

'I want to.'

We eyeball one another. I sense her strength of old. I know Mom has more in her.

'I have made a decision and I request of you to follow it through.' Her words are clear and precise. The world has reversed, being told to obey your mother, territory of a previous dimension, over two decades ago, when my mother was the boss of me. And here I was thinking I had grown up.

'Yes, Mom?' slump my shoulders in resignation.

'Olive,' and she pauses to demand my entire attention before she continues.

My eyes are seeing her.

Mom raises her head high. 'I have made up my mind regarding my final wishes.'

'Your what?' I spit involuntarily.

'This is why I have checked into this clinic. I am of a certain mindset.' And she searches to find the kindest term, noting my building anger.

'What mindset?' Pacing back and forth at the end of her bed, I will not repeat the words - final wishes - aloud, but they swim like champions through the erratic current of my pumping blood.

'Time, Lily,' orders the Irish looking hefty nurse, bursting in on us. 'Are ye set? She feels the tension in the air, 'You told her. Good now we can proceed.'

Has she been there long? I never noticed the nurse come in to our room. Has she heard our private conversation?

'No!' Mom shrieks. 'Is that the time already, Jean?' Losing her elegant pose, mom flusters. 'And I wanted to discuss particulars with you, dear.' She rises off the bed. 'It will have to wait for now, I've waited this long, because Olive, we have to go,' her eyes beseech me.

'Go? To the consultant's office?'

'No,' they both answer me in unison.

'To my support group,' Mom says.

'Ha,' I shuffle. 'I'm fine here. Can't you leave it for today? You said we should be together, talking.'

'We will, but I promised Mr P. that we would be there for him. I won't go back on my word. Please come, it's important to me.' Mom can tell I'm about to explode. 'For me? I scheduled time to be there, for one another, in time of need. We all require care, all of us are patients in our own way dear, even you.'

The doctor's gloves are on to shift my ass.

My freaking, waving arms display my frustration. 'Stop submersing me in your medical arena, Mom.'

Nurse Jean pragmatically does not intervene.

Mom continues on course. 'Frank mentors this group, Olive. You should get to know Frank. He is one of a kind, dear, a just person.'

My moist eyes blur. 'I'm family,' my shrill voice cuts the air. 'I'm kind and just. I'm here, aren't I? Don't lay the guilt trip on me.' Mom does not flinch. 'You never mentioned a support group to me that I should attend.'

Mom has no fitting rebuttal. Her strategy to direct my heightened emotions and put them to use collapses around her.

'Stay out of it then.' Her reverse psychology is put to play. 'Will you get my purse for me? It's in the locker by my bed.'

I open the cabinet and an urn of lavender essential oil stands royally on the top shelf. Three pellet-sized bottles of clear liquid sit on the second self.

Handing the purse to Mom, she immediately unzips the zip and moves articles around.

'Is this what you are searching for, Mom?' I hold the urn before her. Mom says nothing but takes the delicate bottle from my clutch and puts the oil safely in her satchel.

'I will place this standby in the cabinet,' says Nurse Jean.

I see the nurse restocking. 'Wait for me,' She adds, she is twice my girth and holds herself with authority around my mother as if a pecking order is established.

Was I below her?

Events force my hand; nothing happens in this place but there is always someone around Mom. 'I'll come then,' I state.

FRANK

'Thank god,' I chant. Time to prepare, the deed is upon me. At this early hour of the morning, the private rooms of the minister, off the prayer room, are available, but I lock the door, just in case I'm discovered.

Immersing my body in the life giving force of water, the flow of the shower washes the grime clean, dead skin cells shrivel and are sucked into the drain hole. I watch the swirl. I adjust the temperature to my liking of a warmer degree; the minister prefers a cooler shower than I do.

Lifting the organic, lavender shampoo, lovingly handmade in Round Wood, I puddle thick cream clunks into my scooped palms. I pay homage to my mind, the instrument of power, I chant, 'thank god,' for the full to the brim, mysterious way of the calling, cradling my head in my ready hands. The spread of my fingers through my hair, over the span of my scalp, massages my skull. Scales of dandruff ingrain in my nails. Tenderly, I return to a rhythm that respectfully mingles with my heartbeat.

This is a ritual of love. I mentally prepare. I sense a blue light enter through the top of my head and cover me with a hue, from head to toe. I close my eyes and rinse my hair, symbolically I cleanse my conscience. The soapy liquid enters my ears. I pick the right ear and then the left. One last comb of my fingers in my hair and I lift the body cloth.

Foaming the bamboo cotton cloth with Round Wood's homemade lavender soap, I place the first touch, on my body, over my heart, saying, 'thank god.' I breathe out deeply, with gratitude for the force within me to perform my chosen task. The dense, matting hair softens on my chest from the soapy suds. I don't go to the spa to wax or laser, I have no tedious requirements, which the weak culture of the day adorns to; my fixtures are of a higher realm.

I pump my hand and beat a rhythm, six courageous times, over my heart.

Extending my sweep to the strength of my rib cage, inhaling deeply, my lungs fill with the aroma of the oils. I circle, clockwise, and expel any weakness of character. 'Thank god,' I chant the mantra, over and over. 'Thank god.'

My strong shoulders surprise the cherishing touch that covers their muscles. I caress my back, left and right shoulder blades alternatively, denting the pimples housed in my skin. The attention returns to my front. I lift the folds of flesh forming my middle area, too many cakes during the comfort sessions with clients. My stomach of snow peaked hills, awash with foam. I bend and run the length my hand down my right leg, all the way to my foot. Returning in an upward movement, I follow the outline of my body and swipe across my abdomen, and down the left leg and foot.

I bless my feet that carry me to my clients. I pick a stubborn, patch on my toenail. It budges and washes away. I clip my toenails and my fingernails. I close my eyes and breathe in the oil's aroma and feel the aura filling me internally, the splatter of invigorating warm water cascading over my body. I'm spotless, 'thank god.'

The last area to attend to, a pleasurable job.

I fill the moist cloth with fresh streaming water and soap, lift my bum slightly, tilt my body sideways and wipe, lingering ever so slightly. No time to dally, before the minister may show up and catch me in his private quarters.

Re-cleaning the cloth, I lift my right testicle and sweep under and over, then the left testicle. My sack and crack adorned, I whip my manhood into shape. He is ready and waiting, the routine daily journey awakens him. I lather my hands with soap, the lavender seeps into my pores. Up, down, up, down, my right hand moves, I give praise, 'thank god.' Grabbing the bottle, I turn from the falling water and catch my spray, filling the container with my goods, my mighty sperm. I reseal, turning the lid tightly. I place the goods in a plastic bag.

Nurse Jean will have a syringe. Just as I turn off the tap, the locked door handle is turned. 'Frank?' I hear Mr P. call out. 'Are you ready yet?'

'I will be out in five,' I holler to the back of the rest room door.

'Good,' he wisps a wet reply. 'The support group is arriving into the prayer room.'

The morning's delays have set me back, darn Drew. I hurriedly dress in my immaculately clean black shirt and pristinely pressed black trousers. I sip a drink of lavender infused water, purified at Round Wood.

I am complete, cleansed and ready for the cleansing of my followers.

OLIVE

The soft illumination plays with one's mind.

'Final wishes, Mom?' shrieks my recall, muting the background murmurings in the dark meditation room. I'm frightened. I demand answers. 'What final wishes should I know about, Mom?'

Irritated, I choke on the words. I have never bathed my mother, now it is on the top of her list. What list does she have for me?

'Be quiet in here,' whispers Mom.

Flickering candles glimmer with hope, lullabying patients to a state of acceptance.

One snuff and the energy is gone, candles are easily blown out.

I see the harsh reality of sickly bodies filing into the seats, rotting away in an environment of rejuvenation. Old age does not sit comfortably with me. I can handle a decrepit life if it has no direct correlation to me, like I always hand back a baby, glad it is not mine. Maybe that is why I am irritable around my aging parents. They are not doing what they are told. The full circle of role reversal expands. Here I am at a service with my elderly mother I never intended on going to. Spirituality is a cover up for finality.

'I can't believe you come to this carry on,' hisses my agitation like a rattlesnake curving a slithery stake. 'A support group.'

Mom takes off her coat and settles in. 'There is safety in numbers, dear.'

'What are you on about?' My temper strikes, like poisonous venom.

'We are all praying for a blessing, dear,' she adds, conveying that this normal act is natural.

I observe her deeply, she is meditating, the obliging head drops her chin to her chest.

Mom follows no man-made religion. My mother has always been autonomous of the norms of the day. I too refuse to let guilt spiritualize me. I love her strength for going against the tide of her background. I've been raised with such fortitude, Humanists by choice. She senses my inquisitive observations when I scan the room.

'This is a multi-denominational service, dear.'

Will this bring her some peace of mind?

It's nuking me.

My body refuses to still.

The shadows appear like monsters, towering above us to the double height ceiling, the modern building facilitating the blackout of daylight.

'Mom?'

I try to get her attention as she goes into herself. I tip her sleeve with my hand. 'Why are you talking about final-?'

'Shush, Olive,' she insists. 'We can't be overheard discussing them.'

Is she purposely side-stepping issues? We have no privacy in this clinic.

The enforced silence of the room and my mom's insistence of secrecy swell a rebellion in me.

'Mom?'

124

'Please, Olive,' she pleads. 'Ask for a blessing for me today, do this for me, dear. I'm asking you to work with me.'

I flinch.

The realization that my mother is more than my parent has escaped my maturing. I have moved out and on with my life, the concept of my mother with her own interests other than us, is only now, dawning on me.

I glance around, more people are arriving. There is a good sized gathering. Doctors and nurses sit side by side with patients on the same footing. Are they part of Mom's support group? Mom described the group as an inclusive gathering.

Why am I here? Why has she requested me to hang around today? She does not need me to flex her intellectual muscle.

The stillness unhinges me. Reflection does not ground me, it aggravates me. I try to calm myself.

I sit back beside her, our shoulders parallel, posts of equal stance. She murmurs, 'our realities are different. I'm coming to the end of my journey, thank god.'

That flipping turn of phrase again. The mantra is not pacifying my temper.

'You don't believe in a god,' irony strikes.

'Deity is whatever I think it to be.'

'How philosophical,' I sneer. 'Mom, I want to leave.' A clear path of requesting a parent to mind their child flows from me.

'I'm sure you do, Olive dear,' Mom kindly soothes. 'But this is a room of fulfillment. Not in your opinion,' she agrees as I glare, 'but in my opinion. For me, Olive, for me.' My acidic pose neutralizes. 'I can be my true self as I sit here. I'm drawing a full circle, and the center is me.'

Is she brainwashed? I study her face until my eyebrows form a mono line. She is giving such little snippets away at a time. It is frustrating. Her altruistic pitch makes me want to curse, not give gratitude.

The seats fill.

A casket, center of the aisle by the top pews, does not inspire me. Hanging with a corpse, I tweet and flick a photo and share it.

'Olive!' Now she freaks?

The pajamas-clad crowd chills and relaxes with the death scene too. Probably the relaxant drugs masking the harshness. Is Mom taking drugs I don't know about? I study her.

'I can do what you want me to do, or I can do what I want to do.'

She notes my look of horror.

We've swapped roles, she's the insolent pup. 'Try swallowing armfuls of pills three times a day and get back to me.' So she is on a shit load. 'And they don't work, only the side effects are a certainty.' Toxic build-up could be affecting her if she is swamped with meds. 'Olive, this is a thousand daggers pinned against me. Even animal law permits a thoroughbred horse to be put down when the poor creature writhes in pain. Do you want me to be punished unconditionally?'

My hiccups echo off the ceiling. 'How could you think that?'

'I'm serving a life sentence for doing nothing wrong.'

'I know, Mom.'

'No you don't, Olive. I will not be a slave to history.' What does she mean? But I do not interrupt her emotional outburst. Trying to envisage me standing over my mother with a gun to her head, having to pull the trigger because she has asked me to do the humane thing … I can't imagine such atrocity as an execution. My body tremors, I'm shaking on the bench. Mom reflects mere seconds and continues, not noticing my panic attack. 'The consensus and conventional thinking

126

of our time does not have to be right, Olive.' Her eyes shine. 'I'm a respectable doctor but I'm not afraid to rock the boat.'

Before me I see an extinguished medic enclosed in my mother, a two dimensional role model who is carrying a gun in her purse. No way, I scold my very thoughts. Is she a terrorist? No way. But then no one expects a family member to be a murderer.

'I'm not sure what you mean, Mom.' I can barely breathe. I seek explanations and force the words out. There is no respite, no swerving off the discussion. My mother is side-stepping the parenting role toward me in her vivacious testimony.

'We don't always get what we wish in our life or in our death. But we can try. It's the human prerogative to conquer impossibilities.'

Talking like an idealist unhinges me. The world is far from perfect but my mother is the best. Tears drip on the tip of my nose. I'm crying softly. Trying to decipher the pecking order, I ask, 'do you talk to Dad of your unhappiness?' I'm a bit confused and I've my full faculties. How does Dad listen to her? Has old age heightened the defiant streak in her personality? I instantly squirm with the unfairness of using him as a pawn, it puts me to shame. Tears swell and drop on my lap. The sadness of the truth is horrifying. My parents adore each other, but it is not enough to save them from the trappings of ill health. My anxiety increases, a deadly weapon was in their bedside drawer? In all my childhood imaginings, I never for once thought a gun might be in my parents' bedroom. For some reason it horrifies me. Would Dad put a gun to Mom's head? He might not understand the action? Jeepers, this place of geriatrics is playing with my head.

Mom turns purposely to face me and communicates the truth of the matter. 'Your dad will not remember my final wishes. Witnessing his living but not living in this world is pitiful. I had no claim to hinder him further.' The medic proclaims the denial of choice swallowed up in the world of an Alzheimer's victim.

Again a flash of fright crosses my face.

Mom reaches out to me. 'I am praying for us all,' she says lovingly and wipes my nose with her hanky. 'Leave me be, dear.' She closes her eyes to plead her case, then turns to fall inline with the congregation.

I must find something to do to dry up my tears. Reading my emails evades my life musings. My apostasy never offended my mother over the years. I have departed from religion. My mother respects my choice. Why do I find it hard to repay such privilege? I will be quiet by her side. This is her thing. I smell them before I see them. Mr P. is wheeled in beside us. Frank sits next to me. Mom smiles at them. Frank, solemn and dignified, lowers his eyes before me. Weirdo!

This is going to be a long day.

A presiding minister enters from a side door and walks to the front. Enacting the celebrant role, he commences reading the daily psalms. Reverent heads bend down in the act of one-ship. The angst of having to be quiet and dispel my anxiety is almost more than I can bear but I will stay with my mom. I hold her hand, united before the unknown.

'I am counting on you, Olive, my lovely daughter. These are my friends but you are my family.'

My brain is ticking over.

I inject some meaning to the situation my mother has brought me along to. It must take courage to make final decisions. Am I a coward? Mom is orienteering. My cell phone zings and zaps. Flicking down the inbox - girlfriends text re drink locations. I'll see; I'm jaded doing nothing. Five replies later, I'm free to open a porn site.

'And now Dr Doran will say a few words,' introduces the minister.

Mom taps my cell. 'That's my doctor,' she says. A lean, tall, middle-aged doctor walks confidently to the top of the lectern.

'Good morning.' His voice is steady and warm.

'Good morning.' A unified reply fills the room from the eager audience.

I look around, surely all these people are not thinking of their final wishes? I sense no feeling of this demure setting as the likely death row quarter of the clinic. The waiting line. Empathy grows in my heart. Compassion, not competition, rules the way in this low key domain. Here, you would gladly give up your seat to someone who was just as weary.

I tap Mom.

'No, Olive.' Her demand hits hard. 'It is my time, please be receptive to me.' Her silver hair shines like a halo, not another grey haired lady in sight; Mom has guts, confident courage to be herself gracefully. In the intimate room, Dr Lily Tully holds her own. Blackened roots too black, reds too red and blondes too blonde. Curls cascade from an overly curly wigged head opposite me.

I listen to the guest speaker for a maximum of two minutes and then I drift. He started strong but I was not a patient and found it hard to be loyal to his input.

'A patient's instinct is as credible as the qualifications of the expert,' Dr Doran explains. 'A patient knows their own symptoms. Trust your own voice.'

'Too true,' voice the audience.

'Yes, they do, thank god,' Frank calls up.

'Medicine has to be subjective.'

The room explodes with applause.

'The patient is the expert, the physician is the facilitator.'

Concert goers they all become, including Mom. 'Isn't he great?' she adds, the exuberance of the doctor brandished by the crowd. At least the place is rocking. I snap a picture on my cell phone. I zone out and play with the cell. Frank's huge black shoe touches my boot. He knows I'm not paying attention. The fucker.

I twist away from him to block my phone but I can hear his lyrical hum.

My sister Missy implodes in on me with a text. Her majesty Missy has to wait only nanoseconds, I can't ignore incoming texts.

I'm not coming to clinic U take charge - Missy.

That was it. That is all my sister had to offer. No way. Typical of my sister, I swear under my breath. I will sort something out, I ration.

Next message is nicer. My supposedly reverent bent head belies its objective. I scroll, reading Mike's text.

Hi - Can we meet again? How about on my lunch break? R u interested?

I'm tempted. But I have enough on my plate. My brain is frazzled. Her name is so apt, Missy misses everything. I text my sister first.

Mom's acting Strange - Talking about FINAL wishes – You should swing by- I need you

I re-read and then delete the last three words. Tears splash on the screen, the frustration more potent than I realized. I rub them off with my sleeve.

Something is up

I send it. The message should go to her. My red, puffy eyes double the vision, I'm registering M's: Mom; Missy; Mike; Morgue; Me. The letters on the chrome plate register that we are sitting by the holding zombie room. Cold shivers of my nightmare rerun through me. My skin rises off me and goose pimples take over. I could murder a G&T to take the edge off me. It's this clinic. I have no significant other, only my mom and dad. The reality could drive me to ruin. Coming to a place like this should carry a health warning of insanity.

The guest speaking medic finishes his address. More applause.

Maybe I should know what her final wishes are.

I have never given them any thought. Dread deepens in the pit of my stomach. I want to cocoon away from life's tribulations. Usually I would work hard, surround myself with lists of client's demands to block out reality. I could not do that today. The perverted pull of the twenty-four seven online world is available. Surfing the waves of self emersion, my private videos are my redemption.

His waft of lavender assails my nostrils. Is there no way of getting away from him? Frank leans against the arm rest, half sitting and half forward. He rocks in a slow motion. His head rests in his arms. We are all sitting. He grunts for air, moves upright and pats his chest with his right hand. Is he having a fit? Then, he sits up, straight and proud.

Frank continues to hum.

His lyrical behavior cannot be ignored. The environs are too passive for tunes. Bothering me with his solo performance, I wish we were not sitting next to him. I can't concentrate on my screen. The upper part of his body swings, his elbow dances off mine. His musical repertoire goes against the flow of the gathering, drawing attention to him. Frank, our distracted neighbor would not be silent like the rest of us here. He is going against the grain with intent.

'For fuck's sake.'

Mom pats my hand. 'It's time.'

'Time for what?'

'Frank's tuning into himself.'

Her voice sounds too lyrical. 'Time of empowerment.'

131

My eyes twitch. Franks eases his swaying but increases the volume. The crescendo passes over the airwave. The room can hear his heightening tune. Mom starts to hum too. She is humming with Frank. A primal tribe of gatherers across the plain, with one intent to form a formation, irrespective of age, nationality, health or wealth. The volume swells in unison. The hairs on the back of my neck stand up. The musical vibe is strong and constant, the melody flows in the room. Little by little, from every corner, a humming mounts like a swarm of bees. Frank's vocal output still an octave higher, leading, demanding notoriety. At this point, no one is focused on the celebrant minister. I squeeze Mom's hand, she appears content in her song and ignores me.

Frank is to the forefront. Louder and louder, I can hear his recant above the others. The interrupted sermon halts to a stop. Relief floods through me, it's not just me who has noticed the change of events. I am ready to get Mom out of here. The minister steps down and approaches our pew. Frank controls his pendulum motion.

'Frank, do you require medical attention to control yourself?' asks the tired, silver-haired pastor.

No one was paying any attention to prayer.

'I'm focusing,' issues Frank. 'Thank god.'

'Thank god,' others repeat.

'You will have to stop disturbing the ceremony like this every morning, Frank. I can't hear myself in my own service,' implores the celebrant.

Frank peacefully inclines to agree with the minister by lowering his eyes in contrition. 'I do not mean to dishonor you, Sir.' The holy man takes deep breaths, trying to ease his anger at the carry on. The pastor prays aloud for compassion. Placing his pliable hand on Frank's head, the celebrant prays for pardon.

'We all carry the splinters of the cross,' prays the very irate minister, the laying of hands the safest input he can offer. He probably wants to throttle Frank. I notice his flaring nostrils. 'God help me, give me strength.'

A chain of events progresses. Everyone turns to their neighbor, places a hand on a shoulder and prays for strength. Instant links unite. The congregation in on the act, humming lulls of soft waves. Then the voluntary line up, in single fashion to pat Frank, laying a hand on his arm, shoulder or head. I recoil in my seat. I physically cannot be close to him, Frank repels me. My hands fist up and I sit on them to hide my distaste. 'Don't come near me,' I scold in a low voice, as patients offer their companionship to me. They file past. They shake Mr Patterson's shaking hand. They shake Mom's hand.

Frank is elevated with the final attention. The vibrant, curly-wigged woman tips Frank; a hundred dollar bill flaps, he declines but she stuffs the bill in his pocket. She moves on. I watch her with interest. Yes, definitely a wig, the hair is too voluminous to be authentic and it's sliding as she walks.

We are the last few remaining.

Mom's humming blends harmoniously with Franks tone, a low drill below the radar but evident to my ears.

Frank leans to pat Mr P.'s chest, then lifts back the lapel of the elderly man's jacket. A drainage tube of yellowish fluid becomes visible. In one swift move, Frank tugs the line of the oxygen tank and disconnects it. I gasp and look at Mom. Has she seen Frank separate the line?

'Now, now, Mr P.,' pacifies Frank.

'Now, Frank?' asks Mr Patterson.

'We are all one, thank god,' rounds Frank.

The spluttering patient resounds, 'if you're sure, Frank?'

'You requested to sit with me today,' deliberates Frank.

'Move, Mom,' I roar and push her. Panic rises in my throat, a reflux burns my throat. I'm terrified.

'You're hurting me, Olive.' I swear under my breath in this supposed place of zen but continue to push her past the pew and into the door of the morgue.

'Good Lord, man,' I overhear Frank expound as he grabs the wheelchair.

'Yes, Frank, I did,' the poor man acknowledges.

'We have talked at length.' Frank speaks as if to admonish a child. 'We are in agreement … I anointed you as you requested. Thank god.'

That is all I can hear as Frank leads the patient away out of sight.

My heart is thumping wildly against my chest, counteracting the eerily quiet holding room. My haunting echoes follow me. My cheeks flush a raw red, I'm thirsty, dehydrating. Cracked lips tear as I chew on them. We will wait here. I can contain us in here. Egging myself to be brave, I rise to a challenge. And I know dead people cannot move. I have never been in a mortuary. This is a day of differences. I spurn myself on. 'We should be safe now,' a whisper escapes.

'Olive you are over reacting. Are you catching a flu?' She places the back of her hand on my forehead and feels for a temperature. 'Your skin is damp and you are shaking, dear.'

'I'm scared.' Waves of shock pass through me. Why is Mom not perturbed? 'I'm not the sick one in this place. Did you see poor Mr Patterson, he's a helpless old man?'

Mom is motionless. 'What about poor Mr P.?'

Chattering teeth cannot prevent me from expediting my opinion. 'Frank is a bruiser of a man, he is too rough in his handling of a patient in his care.'

'Query your assumptions, Olive. What you see may not be the full facts.'

'I know what I saw.'

I pause but Mom does not impede. 'Tampering with clinical equipment,' I state.

My whispering has a deep, baseline deliverance. 'Frank pulled the drain line apart.'

'Frank is assisting his friend, dear,' she says.

'Flawed assistance,' I persist. Surely it is a criminal act to vandalize equipment? I will check out this guy Frank my mother holds in such high esteem.

'Your generation has to learn how to adjust to fear. Life has been handed to you on a plate.'

I hate it when Mom thinks she knows more than me and trivializes my perceptions.

'You will understand my ways by the end of day, dear.'

She moves to the storage drawers. 'I have a friend in transition I want to say farewell to, as we are here, now is as good a time as any,' and she walks to the holding wall.

'You want to pay a visit here?'

I expected horizontal sheeted bodies lined up in sequence for inspection, like I see on the TV. The surprising sunlight in the room is the first unsettling factor. Large windows let in of natural light. Golden-orange beech tree branches imperially landscape. There are no shadowy corners. My diaphragm locks, not taking in dead air.

'Yes, dear. Open your mind.'

Visibly serene as it should be, my calculating mind sees no gain, and has not registered the transformation period from last breath to last moment with loved ones as a transitioning period.

'Saying goodbye is poignant.' Her fingers tip the clinically clean floor to ceiling chrome sections, finding

135

her way among the mechanical holding drawers. 'Alphabetical dissent.'

How neat and orderly death is handled, like my bookkeeping tabs. I try to stand up straight. I have been burying my emotions this morning. The heaviness of my sadness is too much, I have to sit on the floor. In the silence, I hear my intelligence. I don't think I have ever acknowledged to myself that I'm sad. I could blame this place of malady, blame my mother, blame the season. Everyone and everything is at fault. But it does not alter the fact. I'm sorry for my mother having to be here, I'm sorry for me having to be here. I should have gone into work. What is all the hassle in life about? These people here do not care one iota for all the crap that I can stack up into a day. I almost envy their oblivion.

'Would you like to stay or wait for me outside?' Mom startles me, a voice from the voiceless.

'Don't scare me like that, Mom,' I scream from the floor. 'I will stay,' I collaborate and lift myself.

'Good decision, dear,' condones Mom.

'Yeah, yeah,' I motion, pulling sly faces at my mother.

'You have to acquaint yourself with death, Olive. There is no getting away from the universal norm of dying.' In mode of medical practitioner, the clinical tone replaces my mother's maternal personae.

Internally I scream, 'You are my mommy! Moms don't talk of death.'

'We are all just a bag of bones, with some spices thrown in. Count your blessings, my dear one, sweet was your destiny and not sour!' And she giggles, 'I think my spice was hot chilli.'

'What are you doing?' I ask, tilting my head to her bending stance.

'I'm taking off my shoes, dear.'

'Why?' I kneel at her feet to help her.

'Out of respect and equality dear, thanks.'

I look around my surroundings. A shiver runs down my body. What do stiffs care of us, mere mortals? I've never seen my mother take her shoes off in a public place.

This is a day of difference.

Dazed, I copy my mother and take off my shoes. Two pairs of shoes line side by side with no feet in a morgue backdrop. Taking a snap with my mobile, I send the image on. An autumnal leaf stuck to the sole of my shoe waves at me. 'Ooh, the floor is cold, Mom.'

I hop from one foot to the other.

Mom laughs. 'Reminds one, that you are the living one. These people are entities of their world. I always take my shoes off in their company, as if a meeting point of the physical and the spiritual.'

Incense sticks waft lavender trails into the air conditioning, regurgitating above us. Mom moves along to read the alphabetical names. She stops and pushes a button on the front of a metallic drawer, it moves forward and fully extends within seconds.

I'm spooked.

A white-sheeted ghost, six feet of lifeless form suspends, waiting, privileged or debased. Humans have authority over the dead. The coldness is immediate, like opening a freezer.

I shiver in recall. Maybe I should have waited outside but I'm riveted to the spot.

I've never seen a dead body.

Mom is orchestrating the process, I'm not needed. Reverently she speaks. 'All is as you wish, Charlotte, thank god.' Mom places a kiss on the cold forehead. I gaze in awe at my devout mother. Taking a file from her bag, she does the oddest thing: resetting dead head, she fixes the cushion and puts the file under the pillow, tidying an escaping strand of hair.

Yuck, squirms my skin. Poker stiff, arms held tight by my side, I'm a soldier of the commandeering Chief. Gobsmacked, my fear paralyses me. The exactness of my mother hypnotizes me. She is engrossing.

'Tidying up details,' she says and renders me speechless. I had no idea that within the brief of my Mom's beloved profession, she came and spoke with the deceased. But she never disclosed such areas of the arena in her work over the family dinner table. And my mother is a great advocate of open family discussions. The doctor within her never retires. Mom is much sought after as a guest speaker and regularly attends seminars. Her command brings me back to the detail.

'I will miss you, Charlotte,' speaks Mom eloquently. 'Go in peace.'

The revolt in my stillness makes me move. I peer in. The deep cavity of white silk cloth is as inviting as looking into a mouthful of teeth. 'I never realized you have such peace with death, Mom.'

'How were you to know? I did not take my work home with me. When I was with my family I was Mommy,' and she smiles a sad salute. 'But you have to make amends to the ways of the world or you cannot do the job. There is no right or wrong way, only the way.' This mantra I had heard my mom say in our home.

'You are quite the original piece aren't you, Mom?' It does not take the accountant in me to estimate the loyalty of this practitioner.

LIAR.

'That I am, dear.' Her little frame expands. 'As a young woman starting out in my career, I felt I could save the world, heal the world, even prevent death,' and she shakes her head in defeat. 'What a foolish thing I was.' Trailing quietly, she says prayers, chanting. 'Times are a changing, Olive, for the better. My blog brought Charlotte into my world. We arranged to meet, here.'

138

'In a morgue?' I splurt.

'Not exactly,' Mom stalls.

Sandwiched in between us, Charlotte is the calm mediator, between two live wires. 'We became close in our contentment.'

'Contentment?' My voice lifts, surrounding us. There is nothing becoming about this stiff, pale vessel. She would be outraged by the red rouge and glossy lipstick. 'I don't like her look!' Irony pours out of me, spacing an area for my brain, to register what mom is achieving hanging with stiffs.

'Oh? Nurse Jean liked it.'

I scrunch my face, but do not voice the disrespect. 'Content Charlotte,' I can safely muster.

'Yes, dear, good one. Content Charlotte, I like that endearment,' gushes Mom.

'Wow,' we are on different planets. How can Mom not hear my sarcasm?

'Olive, a person will not tell their group of friends if they are dying, maybe only one or two will be told.'

'What about Facebook?'

'Maybe the last hurrah in the final hour. In my findings, the contentment garnered in the sharing is very intimate. Others, cousins, in-laws, selfish friends, complain of the unkindness of the omission. But they do not understand, the intent is not out of malice, but out of concern. Who would you tell, Olive, if it were you in poor Charlotte's place?'

'You,' was on the very tip of my tongue but it clung on in my heart, refusing to spill, in a coherent manner. I would have sworn my mom. But now? I'm not so sure. Would I rip apart her world? Content Charlotte has a garish grin set on her mouth. Her dead weight separates my mother and myself. Is that a smug smile on my mom's face? My silence is not a surrendering. 'I would ball my eyes out, so you would find out, Mom and I'm

139

sure I would plaster it on my platform; social media in its untouchable forum suits me.'

'You are right, dear, it is easier to off-load online.'

Again, I'm feeling out of my depth. In this surround, Mom sounds so assured.

'Who would you tell first or last, dear?'

'I've never considered such details, Mom.'

'You should have a snapshot of death, Olive. I have. Everyone wants an easy life, and those I've worked with want an easy death.' Her pause fills the room. Why can't I believe I will die?

The doctor in attendance continues in her work. 'Goodbye, my dear friend, Charlotte.' Mom's words, the last sentiment to rest on her being, I don't interrupt. By letting Mom be her true self, I find a little piece of me, her bloodline child. 'How would you like to die, dear?'

'For fuck's sake, Mom!'

'I mean it. I would like to know, Olive.'

She is like an organic energy in comparison to my staleness. 'Gee, Mom, I haven't given it much thought.'

'The folly of youth.' Mom takes the urn from her bag and pours lavender oil onto her fingertip and anointed the forehead of Charlotte. 'Would you like to join me?'

'No, Mom, I couldn't touch her ... Sorry, Charlotte.'

'Tell me, in your own words, what a good death for you would be, dear.'

Instinctively I run my fingers through my hair, the silkiness comforts me.

'Please, dear,' she invites my private disclosure. 'I would like to know.'

And without grief, sureties pour from me. 'Surrounded by loved ones, Mom ... And with music playing ... No melancholic tunes, RnB beats only.'

We smile in sync.

'What about pain management?'

'Fuckin' hell, I don't want to suffer any pain.'

140

The doctor nods, acknowledging the universal norm and she tightens the lid of the urn.

'How long would you like to be dying for?'

My eyebrows furrow. What a strange question. 'Do you not die quickly?'

'No, dear, bless your innocence. The passing can be a very long, drawn-out procedure. Untold misery for all involved. Such unnecessary tragedy.'

'No way do I want that. Quick and sweet for me thanks.'

'Me too,' Mom confirms.

This conversation is easier by nature of our similarities. Resting Charlotte does not impede. Our hands link, in a guard of honor pose. 'We are a dynamic duo, you and I, dear daughter.'

'Yes, Mom, we are.'

'Women are so much stronger than we are given credit for,' adds Mom and I whisper 'adios' to Charlotte. Mom presses the reset button and the drawer recedes quietly until the unit is privately concealed.

The smell of the oils reminds me of him. 'Mom, I'm concerned by what I have seen in the prayer room.'

'Yes, dear?'

How was I to tarnish her friend and colleague? 'This large fellow, Frank.'

'Yes, go on.'

The description of the interlude has me at a loss for words. Did I see him hurt Mr Patterson?

'Frank pulled out a tube from the old man's breathing apparatus.' There I said it.

'What you've seen and what you think you've seen are two entirely different things, dear.' Mom stands strong. 'Frank's movements may appear gruff, because of his size. But I assure you, he is a gentle soul.'

I am as unbending as the stiffs in the morgue. 'I know what I saw, Mom. What I witnessed disturbs me.'

'Frank would only offer his services after a friend-patient requested them.'

'Requested services?'

'We inhabit a pivotal universe, Olive dear.' Sirens and noise alert us to the surviving anomalies of the world. 'I did think my job was to respect life, but over the course of the job I came to understand it is as much, if not more, about respecting death.' And she holds her arms up like an opera singer, bowing out after a performance. 'Hence, I personally take medical calls in the morgue and respect final wishes.'

I know she is leading me away from the topic.

Frank, and a three dimensional aspects of medicine. 'You are an individualistic doctor, Mom. But ...'

'More than you can comprehend, dear.' Her eyes seek mine. 'I'm a fellow navigator, just like Frank. I'm entitled, to view life and death, as I see fit. I have always said to you: We are instigators of our own destiny, Olive.' Her eyes enlarge.

LIAR.

She had the upper hand on a one-sided conversation that keeps replaying - I hear their conversation in my supposedly deep sleep ...

'The unrefrigerated world has no dynamo. Here, I excel.' Mom looks euphoric, this is her utopia. The certainty of death, compels her. The unknown flat-lining, where nothing is guaranteed to be true and where everything is possible, is her addiction. A chill runs down my spine.

'Ok, Mom.' I hear anxiety in my tone, I see a different side of my mother.

'Life, the act of living and dying, is not all about neat equations, Olive, my mathematician.'

'Stop teasing me, Mom, you have advantage over me.' My arms splay. 'This quadrant is your playing field.'

142

'Yes, it is and it invigorated me through some tough times. Olive, do you think I am intelligent?'

What an odd question, I ruminate. I had always thought my mother was intellectually more gifted than me, but now, because she is old, I wouldn't bet on it. My stalling is taken for agreement and prompts my mother to go further along her line of discussion.

'Do you think you are smarter than me, dear?'

How could I answer? In the past this was not the case, but it is now because she is aging.

'I will always be a virulent campaigner, dear.'

I do not doubt her.

'There is no bravery hiding behind institutions,' her voice is impassioned.

Before me, the professional façade of my parent, the esteemed Dr Tully, is unquestionable. I would have liked to have seen my mother at the height of her career. How proud I feel of her journey. But now she is replaceable. To avoid the truth, I shake her hand. The authentic signal baffles Mom, but she meets me half-way. Our joined hands signal our mutual respect. She will always be my mother, but I tread carefully.

'Mom, what about the law of the jungle? Institutions survive way longer than individuals.'

'I will not wait to be chewed up, Olive. There is no room for complacency. I'm too much of a strategist.'

We stand squarely across from one another. 'You are so similar to me, dear. I hope you will always remember my strength.'

Words of wisdom. I am the naïve observer. Perhaps we are too close, there has to be a gap for growth, for individual traits to evolve; are we stifling one another's potential? There is no space for uniqueness, when censorship, agreement in all things, is the norm. Are we smothering each other? Difference is the pulse of life, not similarity; the boredom of repetition will kill all life forms, because change is inevitable. It is the way of life, natural law.

Her words break through my ruminations.

'We have selected the casket your dad wants, dear.' And she walks over to a desk and opens a catalogue of colorful samples, pictures lined up to view.

'For fuck's sake, Mom.'

Revulsion hackles my equilibrium, I almost dry retch. I have not eaten today but I'm not hungry. I have no appetite in this place.

'Well, in this line of work, I get to see the latest models on the market.' My mom laughs, she actually laughs at the look of shock on my face. 'Treat triumph and disaster the same, dear.'

'Yeah, yeah.'

But Mom is in full swing. 'I'm not afraid of death, Olive. Are you?'

'Yes, I am.'

'That is a pity, dear. Then I hope and pray you are surrounded with love, when it's your time.' And Mom blesses herself to protect her request. 'Easiness is not happiness, be aware of the addiction of applause in medicine, dear. The eternal quest of the cure. When there might not be one. It takes a heroine to say it is time to die.' And Mom pauses and looks straight at me.

'What are you saying, Mom?'

'We need our illusions to proceed,' she states.

This is our moment, life is only what is.

Just as the spider majestically hangs on an invisible thread, the courageous suspension draws the eye to the power of the little creature, going beyond the human potential. As a child, swiping the line, snapping the connection and sending the creature to its peril, something that is regrettable in mature years, I can see that now. The adult pays homage to the weightless play with gravity.

Is it my time to grow up?

I could feel in my very bones my mother was passing on, imparting to me, a treasure to behold, intellectually if not materially, just as was my mother's way.

LIAR.

You talked without saying what truly mattered, Mom.

'I think at times, Olive, if anything doctors, unintentionally, are hurting people's lives by prolonging pain, by means of modern medicine and its interventions.'

The art of persuasion rolls over me.

'The advancement of medicine and machinery, is aiding the choking of Mr P. to death. Eventually his lung disease, will overtake the drainage level they can offer him, because his lung's air sacks will tear and get saggy and they will not fully function, even though the machines are forcing them to.'

I quiver with imagery.

'With less oxygen in the blood and a build up of phlegm in his chest, the narrowing blood vessels will choke him. A very unpleasant death.'

'Poor Mr P.'

'Yes, dear, but he does not have a miserable attitude,' she smiles and pats my hand. 'He made up his mind to take control back of his life.'

'But the doctors,' I restart.

Mom nods.

'Yes, until today, they have chosen, with his consent, to imprison him daily in the clinic and let machinery become his lungs. Mr P. will tell you himself, that he has not been living, he is dying, in a protracted manner. There is no dignity in that system, a self-imposed prison. His death would have been easier, years ago and more natural, if the consultant had allowed him be. The doctors will not discuss the advanced care directive with him, because they cannot guarantee it. One day, his money will run out, and another person will be on his machine.'

I do not answer. I'm not sure I am qualified to. Recalling the image of hell as other people swarms in my brain, but doctors aren't evil.

Mom speaks eloquently, 'We, his support group of friends, are here for him. We call such cases 'the waking dead'. What you witnessed, in the prayer room, with my support group, is a celebration of Mr P.'s life in that ceremony.'

'You're frightening me, Mom. I never knew you were so disillusioned with medicine.'

'Yes, I was, Olive, but I never brought my dismay home.'

How could my mom hide, a core facet of her world from me?

'What do your colleagues think of your uptake?'

'What others think of you, is none of your business,' recanted one of Mom's favorite sayings. 'The desire to live longer, is over-populating the world, beyond its means, that is an obvious case against the advancement of medicine.'

Mom starts to convert me. She wants to kick that door off its hinges. 'When you are in terrible pain, you make decisions. And I have witnessed the slow, eroding death of chemo, zapping all time and energy from a person's final days. Who has not?'

'But this is the way for progress, the latest expertise, treatment. I would go searching for if it were me,' I add.

What would Mom do?

I never wondered before today. Jesus, maybe she has cancer?

The doubting of myself restarts, an insistent worry tapping on my shoulder. I intuitively know I am out of sync with my mother in the medical world.

'Mom, do you have cancer?' I grasp at straws.

146

Mom's smile is willing. 'No dear, I don't.' And she pauses to consider her next reply. 'But I have exceptional medical cover in this clinic.'

Now what is she talking about? The nuance of her tone doesn't reveal enough to me.

'Time gives us legitimacy of existence; without time, we do not exist. And my time, as all our times, will be up. It seems life is always about trying to gain time. I had thought when it was my end, I would tick off the bucket list items.' And her shoulders droop slightly. 'I would have liked to visit India,' she sighs. 'But in the end, all I really want, is to be with the ones I love.' She reaches over and takes my hand. 'Give me your finger, Olive.'

Gently Mom joins the tip of her finger to my tip, she passes our fingers over the diffusing wafts of essence, lifts and directs my finger to salute her forehead. The warmth of her skin seeps into my flesh. 'Thank god,' she utters. I'm speechless. 'You are my priestess, Olive. Thank you for anointing me.' Her eyes fill.

'You anoint me.' I shyly smile with these intriguing pointers of adoration. She turns the direction of our fingers.

'Enchanté, my priestess.' I gasp. Mom puts the tip of her finger to my tingling skin, scorching with anticipation. Exhilaration floods my veins. Acting outside the pale infuses me with energy. This is the payback. Permissible, going beyond the remit of a system, breaking the barriers of the hierarchy becomes my mom, becomes me.

'All we are given is a snapshot of life. It goes so quick.' Mom tightens her grip on my finger. 'You buy anything you want online,' and she bows before me. 'But you can't buy time, one of the most precious commodities.' My mom's voice weakens. 'You need critical thinking for leadership. Eventually, I will lose

147

my voice.' I clutch her hand tightly, forgetting myself, herself, her body racked in pain but she etches out the words, 'This is my life.'

'I'm sorry, Mom.'

'And I'm sorry, Olive.'

Not realizing I had held her hand too firmly, she taps my hand to release her. 'Hug me, Olive. You are my charger.' I gently embrace my mother. 'We don't have to say sorry to one another. How will you know what I want, if I do not speak my mind when I can? Especially, when I can still speak.' She whispers, 'I feel like an old married couple with you, dear, almost afraid to speak my mind, afraid to hurt the other by speaking the truth. We always hurt the ones we love.'

'Do we, Mom?' I ask, at a loss having never fallen in love. 'I would never hurt you, Mom.' Immediately, I feel like the child I am to her, with the childish reality of utopia. My grubby younger fingers, spoiling her beautiful silk top. I once scattered hundreds of pearls across her bedroom floor, after accidentally pulling on the string. And the list could go on. I see the recognition in her eyes.

'Yes, Olive, we all cause mishaps and catastrophes, at any age. Families soak up failings, the saturation point will be reached and is irreversible.' Stay cool, concentrate, I coach myself. 'Doctors should initiate the difficult, end-of-life conversations with their patients, just as loved ones should talk about them too.' The perfumed oxygen chokes my airways. 'I want a remembrance ceremony, Olive, out on the ocean. I'm finished doing what is predestined of me.'

'Ok, Mom.' I try to sound strong. Did I have the capacity and ability to hear my mom talk of her fears and her hopes of death? But I did want my mother to impart her essence to me. Why is she studying me? Alternating stares with imparts of information and

148

pauses. Blasts of heat sting my skin, like sunburn, as my natural temperature duals with the chill in the cool morgue. 'Maybe Mom, my era is all about think it, do it. Chance is very much left to the gods.'

'Leave the gods out of this and stick with what we know. People do not want to die alone. That does not bother me, Olive, I know I am loved. If I slip by without you, have no fear.'

Mom sounds like she is giving a poetry recital. 'I don't want to be too long withering. Do you hear me, daughter?'

She shakes me.

'Of course I hear you.'

The goose-pimples on my arms hurt at each and every rising. I rub my released arms.

'Pay attention to me, Olive.'

I fume and she starts pacing the floor, taking a few steps back and forth. 'My ultimate goal is have a dignified death. You never mentioned dignity in your wishes.'

A bubble of thought bursts.

Withering - her word of demise enters the chambers of my heart, then churns out to tip every inch of me. Like a spillage, I wait for the blot to run its course. Eventually the boundaries will be set. I wait for the fear to dilute. I did not hear anything else she was including. That is what I witnessed in my car's journey this morning, my mother's withering. And every day she gives witness to this, I know it and she knows it.

Plants die in my care. They wither, I water them, some reshape only to brown and then die. My mom will never recover. The dread chills my bones, aligning with the cool air of the morgue. I had to get relief. Laugh til you cry or cry til you laugh, two sides of the one coin, as we two women, stood side by side, of the same love.

'What are you doing, Olive?' hails Mom.

149

Positioning myself against the bright steel fridge - the reflective material is the perfect bright background, complimenting my outline in the shot - pouting, I click.

I have had enough talk of death.

I'm in the moment, because I live and declare. 'I'm taking a selfie, Mom.'

'Olive!' horror resonates from her, 'have some decorum of decency, a picture of the two of us, in a morgue?'

'Smile, Mom.'

FRANK

'Take a leap of faith, thank god,' I preach.

'I trust the way,' he says, his words mucused.

'The confessionals ease the burden, thank god.'

I join my hands together solemnly and lower my head toward him. The warmth of the shared air, mingled with the smell of us, in intimacy, we sit side by side, we have our privacy.

'When you are ready Mr P.'

'I'm ready Frank.'

'Thank god.'

Mr P. swallows a gulp of thick saliva and commences his cleansing. 'This has hounded me over the years, Frank.'

'Go on,' I direct.

'From a very young age, four or five years old, as soon as I could climb the tree to the tall branches without my mother ordering me down,' he wipes a drool of spit away from his mouth, 'I would find a spot, strong enough to support me, lean in and pull leaves around me.'

'You were hiding,' I tease out the emotions.

'Yes, Frank,' he latches on to my grasp of the private divulgence.

'You are in safe hands now, thank god.'

'Waiting, Frank, sitting there, for hours at a time, hungry for the sin,' he blesses himself.

'All can be forgiven, thank god,' I administer.

'If a branch blocked my view, I would bend the curve, pull off leaves and scrunch until I could see clearly.'

I nod to confirm I understand his story. Patients take a while to get to the reveal.

'The wait was worth it,' his voice quickens. 'Soft tits.' Mr P.'s face is dreamy with smiles of recall.

I say nothing,

I've never climbed a tree.

'They were the good days, there was many a time I seen nothing,' he looks at me to diminish his sin.

I nod again quietly.

I place my hands on my knee, lower my head and he continues.

'I've been a peeping tom, Frank.'

His pace of talking increases, the top button of his shirt is soaking with dribbles but I do not interrupt the truth. 'The pastime spread from day to night time, any chance I could get away from school and home and my friends. Girls brush their hair a lot, Frank.'

'Do they, Mr P.?' I'm astounded how childhood memories are so exact in the elderly.

'Night time was the darkening of my sin.' He coughs.

'Now we are developing the depth of the soul.' I speak plainly, my pulse quickens, the darker the sin, the more light I can shine.

'The panties would come off Frank.'

'Well the girls were getting ready for bed, Mr P.'

'I mean my pants, Frank.'

My discomfort is masked, 'I am here for you, thank god.' The offer to continue is sincere.

'I would pleasure myself, Frank.'

152

'I see,' my solemn voice returns.

'I still do, Frank, under my blanket.'

The plaid threads of his warmer touch my black pristine trousers, I move my leg away from it, my attire is spotlessly clean. 'Even when a person is pushing your wheelchair, you, pleasure yourself?'

'Yep, sure do, boss.'

'Kindly refrain from that vile carry on when I'm pushing you around, Mr P.' My voice is sharp. 'Or you can motor along on your electric chair by yourself.'

He looks contrite, 'Yes, Frank, I need you today.'

'You do Mr P.' Opening the travelling compact case, I smudge essential oil on my finger tip and dab a dib on his forehead, saying, 'Let me assist you, thank god.'

'Thank god,' he repeats after me.

'The folly of the youth,' I continue with the process.

'Frank, my folly followed me into manhood.'

I lower my head and cross my knees, ready to listen.

'You are a good listener, Frank.'

My silence registers with him to continue.

'You know I ran a guesthouse,' he squirms. 'Eight rooms, a fair sized business.' He clunks a mouthful of reflux, his damaged lungs unable to hold down the fluids. 'I'm not proud of myself.'

'Go on.'

He coughs. 'I drilled peep holes in walls and then hung pictures up, across from the beds.'

I keep my eyes downcast.

'Marked spots on the pictures and poked holes-'

'Yes, I see,' I say, cutting him off.

'Before I go, I have to ask for forgiveness,' Mr P. calls out.

Stopping his emotional divulge before he says too much about his business at hand, I add, 'thank god.' The corridor is game for all, we could be overheard.

'Thank god,' he repeats after me.

153

I thought he was diverted, but he explains, 'If I could send letters of apologies, the old visitors' book had some addresses after their signatures, could you write them for me, Frank? My time is near.'

Not sure if there will be time today, I pause. I only work with one client at a time, but Mr P. has asked the team for a special final wish - a request of inclusion. 'When I have a spare moment, after caring with Dr Lily and there is time, I will do, rest assured.'

Mr P.'s worry vanishes from his face, the frowns relax, he repeats her name, 'Dr Lily.'

I hum, a melody to share, on our shared way.

OLIVE

Frank is exiting the consultant's office as we walk in. They shake hands. Chums? I wonder. Huffing, I estimate the doctor will have oily hands now too. Grateful I do not have to talk with the big enigma, I cut past Frank with the sharp precision of a chef's knife and take a seat. Mom's tracks are not as clear and she wavers before aligning with me.

'Ladies,' Frank calls to us. 'You are in good hands, thank god.' The experienced consultant assimilates my scowling face.

No reference is assigned to the cause, like walking in a shower, half pretending its not raining and you won't get wet.

Ludicrous. I swear under my breath that there is no privacy in this place. We wait for the doctor to take the lead, our eyes fixated on the medic like frightened deer, paralyzed in the glare of oncoming headlights. There it is again - this feeling of the circumstances being taken out of my control. We are here to meet this very man, but the stepping aside for my mother today was knocking me off my perch. I love a challenge but, I never realized before this morning, only if I was taxed on a mental or physical level did I engage coherently.

All logic went astray when my emotional development was being called upon.

'Hello, Dr Tully, good to work with you again.' The doctor confidently strides forward, extending his hand to Mom firstly.

'I'm glad you are handling my case, Dr Doran.' With a huge effort she lifts her right hand out to the doctor. He steps in closer toward her. 'Call me Lily,' she asks of him. I can see her try to unbend her fingers. The slow painful movement demands his attention. Dr Doran waits in a kind, humane manner. The ungiving curvature of her weak grasp opposes the strong, warm smile in her blue eyes as she holds his gaze. My mom is a beautiful looking woman with striking eyes of marine pools. He likes her, I can tell by his leaning-in body language.

'Call me Paul, or Junior, like in the good old days.' They both smile in recognition. 'The team is ready.' Maybe a rarity in these times for a doctor, but there is no threat of consternation emanating from us toward him. He is quite at ease and breathes slow, deep swells, restoring tranquility to the souls in the room. I like him. There are no disagreements yet. He looks familiar to me, where have I seen his face?

I introduce myself as the daughter and surmise his uptake of me not being as pretty but more femininely assured. There is no challenge.

I am a willing informant, here on behalf of my mother. He nods mannerly to both of us but addresses Mom, I note. That's fine with me, if I had to reference to his morning counsel in the prayer room I was in trouble. If I could recall ten percent of his speech I would be lucky. But the conversation never revisits the private prayer time. The doctor looks like a member of an old boy's school. Staunch-like, wiry thin and upright in appearance. On appearances, I would swear he was a conformist, yet his morning reflections in the prayer room had been so pro-active, condoning patient input in their treatment plan.

I reluctantly take a back seat to allow the consultant consult his patient. The odour of lavender is overpowering in the confines. Another imprisoned capsule, my world has shrunk, the boundaries of this office define my life. The borders of this clinic box in my life. He is tall, he makes Mom look tiny, I observe from the sideline. He has nice hands and clean cut nails, important points in my estimation. Somewhere in my mind, I had this list that the doctor had to live up to. He had to be neat, very neat for some reason. Fifty-something I estimate. Might be homosexual. Caring, he enthused around the maternal figure. No wedding ring. Is my mommy going to be safe in these hands? Is he a good doctor? And my brain and heart collaborate. I feel exhausted. I wish I had slept well last night, I need the invigoration of sleep to propel my day. Too late for that wish now. My reserves fully stretched and I am not the patient. Does this man appreciate how important mom is to me? Lily Tully is not just another number, the sum of a digitally printed case code tag attached to her wrist, my internal workings screech.

'I trust our Nurse Jean settled you in,' he comments, calling upon his reliable encounter list.

'Yes, thank you,' replies Mom with sincerity, nodding her head obediently.

I nod in sync too. Should I mention to the doctor that the nurse had not washed her hands? It seems trivial now. I decide not to bring it up. Was it his job to monitor the hygiene, anyway? He did not wash his hands in front of us either. Who would I report it to? I do not know.

'Excellent. Nurse Jean is an expert at her job.'

Mom agrees with his evaluation. 'Yes, she is.'

The second step on his welcoming plan commences, has Mom been fasting and other trivia. And his body softens. His regal stature is respectful of the frail painful figure of Mom. Weighing up the exchange, the balance is favorable. His presence fills the room but he is not suffocating. The expert's focused mind is compiling his patient's file as he witnesses Lily's physical health first hand and jots down observations without pausing, totting up the evidence while addressing the situation. 'And this is Olive, your next of kin?' he affirms and at last looks my way.

'Yes,' offers Mom. 'But Olive has not signed the papers yet.' They both take account of that fact, nodding their heads to one another.

'A glitch in the system,' he pauses momentarily. They do not include me in their private interlude. 'I will leave that to you, Lily. You know the precedence set up by the team. The attending physician must request that the patient notify their next of kin.'

'Yes, Doctor. I will see to it shortly.'

I try to decipher their talk.

The admissions department held us for over half an hour this morning. I curse the bureaucracy of this place. He reaches for his phone on the rich mahogany desk. I personally detest when during a meeting individuals are side-stepped. 'Head of security?' he intones crisply. 'I've emailed the image of Drew's face to your desk. Have that copied and placed at every entrance and exit security post.' Exasperatedly, he repeats, 'every door. Absolutely no entry, this ID protocol is of the utmost importance.'

We sit listening to him in silence.

'Ted, do you know anyone in the unit downtown?' We wait to see the doctor's facial expression, he nods and eases his shoulders. 'Great, can you find out if Drew gets bail?'

Swiftly the phone is replaced and we are back in business.

Knowing not to disturb the doctor with my questions, lining up with reservations surrounding Dr Doran's choice of treatment is a personal test of endurance. Going on the Internet and researching the findings around the drug Embrel had fragmented my peace of mind last night. There were so many side effects. I need to have a word with the doctor. For the moment I am a mute, externally soundless, the noise internally is deafening.

The two of us women, sharing the same genetic make up, copy one another with silent head nodding in agreement to the doctor's pointers. It is like being back in school. On one level I know I could ask questions but also understand that the master would not expect to be questioned. He is the scholar in his field who knows what he was doing. It is very frustrating, just like being in school. Easily led astray.

But I have to ask.

'Can you make my mom feel like her old self?' I twitch, trying to appear knowledgeable by posing a direct professional question on my part.

'I can make Lily comfortable,' is his indirect reply but he shifts his shoulder blades toward me. 'As I have discussed on previous occasions with my patient, Dr Tully. Sorry, Lily.' And he positions himself to none of us now, a mediator of sorts. 'Lily has directed the sequence of treatment we offer in the clinic.'

Anger floods my blood stream as my temper raises its pulse. They are very personable, I only now cop onto. I'm no medical expert, the two graduated and experienced medics in the room are in a different league to me, understandably. But Mom had not talked much about her doctor to me, or the team, only that she had briefly lectured Dr Doran, and doctors, student interns and researchers were attending her guest appearance lectures. Grateful and privileged were the exact words she had conveyed to me regarding her opinion of her practitioner. This is my first time to meet Dr Doran. I find him honorable.

I distinctly feel out of the loop but a working relationship had commenced and was based on the same component of all partnerships, trust. This powerful partnership with its powerful implications had to be trusted. I decided to listen, and to trust.

'You inspire me, Dr Tully.'

'Tut tut, now.' Mom dissolves from this adoration.

To the observer I may come across as the silent type but privately the inner dialogue is on the top dial. Can he help my Mom? The private debate continues. Forget ideology; I want no fakeology. Intelligence rues the day. In the present company I am diligently listening. I am quietly keeping an eye on my mother and the other eye on the doctor. It appears that Dr Doran respects women, he is giving my mom ample room to voice her worries. 'Olive will be with me,' Mom directs.

It is great he's mature. I had wanted somebody who knew what they were doing and not just out of college, which would have been worrying. Still studying, while innovative, would be frightening. Experience was the key. My face softens, I'm secure with him, there is calmness to this doctor, I like it. I never thought of myself as racist but I am so grateful I can understand his accent.

We were going to be demanding clients. The poor man has no idea what he is in for, I resume privately as the mental challenge continues with lists. He looks healthy, a reassuring good point. How could we take health advice from a doctor if he himself looked unhealthy? And on and on goes my running commentary. The doctor is handsome but I have only a little room in my mind to observe the aesthetic as I hone my senses to assimilate whether he is a competent doctor and to listen and record this conversation for dissection later. Everyone becomes an expert in a hospital.

'Settle in and continue putting your belongings and priorities in order,' he continues, outlining the time he will return. What priorities is he talking about? I wonder, but he continues to direct the line of exchange, almost to the point of the exclusion of me.

LIARS.

Perplexed pulses bulge in my veins because of you.

'We will start shortly.'

A standard smile remains on his face. His eyes skim over us to initiate the exit process. We are being dismissed, his relaxing voice never giving any insult. The atmosphere he created misled me and I never noticed his omittance of the finer details.

'Dr Tully.' He lifts a bound document from behind the clipboard and puts it to my mother. 'Can you sign this for me?'

My head creaks inward to catch a glimpse of the document. Her head creaks in my direction. 'What is it?' she asks.

'I would be eternally grateful if you would put your signature on an article you submitted to the Medical Journal. One of your finest research papers in my opinion on the subjectivity of medical advancement.'

Mom flusters around the reply, looking almost relieved.

How taxing she must be finding this exposure. The twist of faith, to re-invent your person when youth and vigor have deserted you decades ago.

'Oh. You want my autograph,' she grins.

'Yes, please,' he adds excitedly, as if in the presence of celebrity. 'A huge fan of your medical blog too.'

161

How sweet, I think, as my mother initials a grand pile of paper, imprinting her signature on the last page. It hits me, I've seen this man in the picture Drew showed me. He was sitting on the lawn of Round Wood.

'I will always keep this progressive paper safe. In fact I will have the paper framed in the office. You are exemplary, Dr Tully.' And he blushes, pops of color landing on his cheeks.

'And my thumb print?' reminds Mom.

'What does the doctor need that for?' I interrupt rudely.

'For a particular reason,' Dr Doran adds. 'As a progressive step to individualization of the patient. I prefer the personal. A case file number is so cold. And repeatable. The numerics back file eventually and duplicate. Lily's mark is distinguishable.'

'I see.'

The pair collaborates with pride as Mom leaves a definite line of her lineage with pristine ink.

The ensuing conclusion is as pleasant as the introduction. He turns from Mom to me, offering a handshake to me too, having included me in the consultation. I had given him no choice in the matter. But his eyes are sharp, their crinkled corners not as soft as his measured smile.

I conclude he was welcoming but commanding at the same time. I felt he could be a stubborn man but then, who wasn't a tad opinionated, I concede as I'm scouting the shared space to evaluate the level of care Mom would be receiving. The energy is apprehensive. My head is bursting with forced concentration by this stage. I had to know.

'How long will it be before my Mom loses all mobility?' I ask the doctor, my voice unrecognizable to me.

The room swirls around me for the second time this morning, like it exists on its own pivotal axis. I feel faint as I lay bare my very soul to this stranger, to myself and to my mom. I had not intended on such bravery. I acted before I had reasoned the event, like a reflex. Survival is a reflex occurrence and I was trying to keep my head above water in a storm I was sure was brewing. A moist drop travelled along my upper lip.

'The progression of motor neuron disease is unpredictable,' he states plainly, his medical training at ease with my distress - I will tackle what I know, a diagnosis - but then he adds further, in a monotone, direct accent, 'There is no known cure.'

Our eyes search one another, inviting answers. I will not look away and he does not either. 'What will that mean for my mother?' I am rationalizing my grief, externally.

'I have discussed the implications with Lily,' the doctor says, referring to the client-patient confidentiality clause. 'As a fellow colleague in the field, Dr Tully is fully briefed with the situation. I will leave the two of you to work out the finer issues.' Then he addresses Mom only. 'I'm glad our paths crossed, Dr Lily Tully.'

'Me too, Paul.'

I look at them, the fact registering with me that, within the trio, the false pretense of getting acquainted, these two are comrades. I have no claim to a relationship with this professional. It is tiring, this involvement in life's games and politics. Dr Doran has a long day ahead of him, I am sure of that fact and I had no right to hold him any longer. But I have a beguiling strength of character and conclude the meeting.

'Run every test possible. Cost is no factor.' I fight for options.

My mom has an opposing opinion on such matter. 'I will not be paying any large medical fees,' she states

163

factually. 'The executives of this clinic have an excellent remuneration package without emptying out dry my savings fund.' The clear tone of her voice is undeniable. 'The plan we have discussed and outlined together Dr Doran is the way forward, thank you. We will proceed.'

'As you wish, Dr Tully,' the medic confirms.

I am aghast. I might as well not be here, I think. We are not in agreement on how to proceed. This is a moment when I know something is wrong, but I do not act, I pause, my emotional intelligence is not directing my physical capabilities. I'm a print of myself that is out of focus.

He conceals his personal attitude, making a note of varying markers and putting my name in red at the top of Mom's chart. I am steely quiet. Natural fears, anxieties I expected, it is my unpredictable emotions that throw me, even after my years in business. My intelligence latches on to the fact that a deal has been done, my heart crowns the human head on my shoulders.

I sense a prickly disposition emanating from him now.

Arbitration is expensive. Is he a good man? The run of my ranting mind continues. The trust issue cracks open. His smile is a tad too smug, like this courtesy call to me is wasting his time. But it is the most crucial time for my mom and for me, I want to scream. Wanting to physically wrap my arms around my mother is imparting my fears, but I contend with standing close by like a bodyguard.

I recognize her perseverance. She demands respect, from the doctor and from me.

Still mesmerized by the expensive Italian pinstriped suit, his refined persona almost threw me but my intelligence wants answers, as my humanity wants compassion. It occurs to me that the man is not a deity,

164

yet I was treating him as god-like. He had to be able to fix my problems.

The room was full of reverence towards the doctor. But doctors can be wrong; my mother had always accepted human error in her line of work.

I want him to work miracles.

But I understand he is only a man.

With heartache I understand all my rumination would not change the course of events. What a terrible waste of energy. But how do I stop myself from charging my mind?

We leave his office as graciously as we had entered.

I was frightened of him when he was there and now we are on our own and he is gone, I am more frightened.

Mom looks exhausted. Her body has shrunk with the enormity of the meeting. We are both fatigued. The hospital surroundings are leeching our lifelines. The long, hard day is only beginning. I worry. How do I cope with her? Such unfathomable reality.

We are both suffering at a destination of healing.

Mom does not complain, the silence is more difficult to cope with. I am churning. She suggests the café as our next port of call.

'Why the hell didn't you tell the doctor you're in terrible pain, Mom?' I demand, as the daughter trying not to give orders, wanting to help yet wanting to hide my annoyance at the same time.

'I didn't want to bother the man with information he's already aware of, dear.' Mom's words are barely audible, her voice weak as she tries to catch her breath between the spasms of pain. 'It is what it is.'

I heave a sigh of defiance. I have to remain calm. I am here to help. It is my own unease to which I am losing my temper and not my mother I am angry with. The personal truth is I do not know how to handle the

165

change of roles emerging and taking over our lives. My mother has a strong mind; her traitorous body is the deserter. She is my hero. My mother had not needed me really; I needed her. I have been busy and I have not spent quality time with her lately. I thought she would need me more and more, in the future. I was saving up units of my time. How had that day become today? I question the normality of time. How is it autumn already? Grey mass of hovering cloud as far as my eye could see. Where had my summer gone? We never shared an ice cream.

The kickings of my intelligence are brutishly on target. The axis is turning. The alignment is new. The parent now asks the child for guidance, to drive and accompany on a certain day. Mom has a role for me here today. Mom directs the path, I am to fall instep.

'Mom, the man's a doctor, he's supposed to be told about the pain. That's his job!' I stop myself from ranting on. It is not helping her to state the obvious, even if it is helping me to relieve my tension. I cherish my mother. I love our life journey together. I'm not ready for the destination to reach full circle yet. How do I widen the circumference? How can I defy time and space and aging?

When faced with the inevitable I wish for the impossible.

Rain starts to trickle down the window pane. Where has the sun disappeared to? It had been such a glorious morning. The corridor darkens. There is no turning back the clock. I could no longer be the child. It is time to be the adult in the situation. But my mommy would always be my mommy. That would never ever change. The emotional pain is crippling; I do not want to give up the prized position on the podium. But my mom was not to comfort me - I was to comfort my mom. The world is not as I knew it anymore.

Life is becoming stranger by the minute.

Neither doctor has not put my mind at ease, and Dr Doran knows how to charge the big bucks. Funny how the cost of the medicines is not bothering mom. But then I'm the accountant of the group, the expert of the numbers game.

FRANK

'Dr Doran?' I stop him when he crosses our path, an idea springs to my mind. We are walking the corridors, calling into friends Mr P. wants to visit, lonely patients too, glad of a visitor.

'Frank, Mr P.' Dr Doran stops impatiently. 'What can I do for you two?' he asks but he continues to read a chart.

The student medics, four young, eager intellects, line up and wait, like soldiers.

'My iPad is dead, I forgot to bring the charger.' I shrug a silly me.

Mr P. throws me a quizzed frown. 'Can I use the computer in your office?' Dr Doran's body language is defensive.

He raises his free arm. 'I will be using it, Frank,' he expels, 'Tell the floor manager, I have given you implicit instructions to use the computer at her station,'

And he is walking past us before he has finished his sentence.

The soldiers marching behind him.

I wink at Mr P. 'Good job, thank god,' I say. I pat the top of Mr P.'s head. 'That is exactly what I wanted the doctor to advise me to do.'

We move along. I want no trace back, to me and my private computer, should there ever be an audit on the activities of the clinic. I wheel Mr P. to the manager's desk. The wing has the latest technology, impressive desk and flashy leather swivel armchair. I push in his wheelchair and make myself comfortable.

'Will we be long at the computer?' Mr P. wheezes.

'Not too long,' I answer him as I tap the keys.

'Good,' he coughs up snot and mucus.

I hand him a sanitizing wipe.

He blows a hornful sound, trying to clear the secretions from his vocal chords. His airways will be flooding by now.

'You will enjoy helping me with this job, Mr P.,' I say, to bring joy to his testing day 'Thank god.'

'If you say so, Frank.'

He coughs up a load of gunk, I hand him double wipes. 'It's just that there are a few more people I would like to see.'

'We will hurry then.'

I pat his head and turn to the screen. I type in the Google bar: Volunteers. The images and information upload. I read and aloud, comment, 'We don't need African charities.'

'Africa, Frank?' Wet words painfully spill from Mr P.'s lips.

'Wait,' I retry, type the clinic's webpage.

Bingo.

I type a search for medical volunteers, and select the open page forum. I blog the words, Recruits Needed, ask for their feedback on what they can bring to the table of the sick and needy and wait.

I swivel to Mr P. 'Did you donate your house to the foundation?' I ask him.

He can't muster the reply, a single word is beyond his reach.

Greenish reflux fills his mouth. My good deed of the day is taking hold of him, thank god. I'm here for him.

Mr P nods a yes and chokes out the word, 'Yes.'

'Good man, thank god.' I swivel to the screen, flashing with people on-line.

I investigate their profile faces, scroll down and select my candidates. Doctors, nurses, students, and unemployed eager surfers, offering to sit with patients, house mind, walk dogs and get in groceries, they fill the answers to my questions.

I know I'm getting ahead of myself, ahead of the game plan today, but Dr Lily believes in me.

I have bigger and better plans to release to the universe.

'We will need a recruitment room, a private dwelling, it will not attract unwanted attention to our foundation.' Mr P. nods a confirmation.

'Only the vetted candidates will visit Round Wood,' I sermon. 'Thank god.' I place my hands together, they form an arrow symbol. 'There will never be another Dr Lily, but I am here, ready and willing to continue the good work, thank god.'

OLIVE

'Rest up, Mom, take it easy.' I place a cushion along the back of the canteen chair to pad her soft body against the frame. 'This modern furniture is uncomfortable,' I curse the innocent item.

I hug my mother very gently, whispering soothing endearments against the side of her hair that smells of lavender.

'Rest, Mom. I will get you a cup of coffee. I'm in no rush.' And for once this is the truth. It is only mid-morning, my business meeting is for the afternoon. I have plenty of time on my hands. The enforcement of the medical day was supposed to be liberating, freeing me up from the drudgery. 'No rest for the wicked,' I wink at her. This is the first private day I had taken in the nine years since I had qualified and worked for the company. I kiss the top of her head.

A card stand by the cash register drew me in. I share Mom's love of the arts; poetry magnifies our lives. Reading a card, the title, Heredity, a poignant term of phrase. My Mom must be thinking of her mortality. I select her this card imprinted with the poem by Thomas Hardy. I read it as I queue.

I look over at Mom; her eyes are closed.

But as happens, the moment of rest is often disturbed in hospital. The cafe becomes busy and disturbs her peace. Moving her cell phone out of the way, and an A4 envelope, I have not seen before, I set down our tray.

'The iPad is in your bag, Mom. I have one for you. We can Skype later.'

I lift the envelope up.

'That's for you, Olive,' she says.

'What's this, Mom?'

'It's my will.'

Three little words.

Filling up with bile, the room spins, as my head spins.

The outline of Frank's tallness blocks the doorway as surely as it blocks further discussion with my mom.

Nurse Jean flaps by Frank's side.

I then notice the wheelchaired patient, Mr P. with them.

'Hello, Frank,' adds Mom, instigating the get-together, her mental capacity outdoing her physical prowess. 'How are you getting along, Mr P.?' she asks the other frail man, she studies his permanent illness with a knowing eye, while her own brittle body etches a painful curve toward him.

His corrosive sounds of breathing, banging off his oxygen mask, reply, the telltale sign of a person unable to survive unaided, similar to my mom.

Her support group members, mirroring her demise, that link keeping open the line of communication I was not privy to.

'I was just handing over my will to Olive,' mom nods to Frank.

'And I'm not taking it,' I spit.

'Let me put that paperwork in a safe place for you both, in your file.' In flies Nurse Jean, very nifty on her feet for a big-boned girl.

'Grow up, Olive. We all will face a will in our day,' cross-fires Mom.

'I'm allergic to victim discourse,' sermons Frank. They all nod in agreement with him. It perturbs me that Mom has acquaintances in this place and that she wants to hang out with them. I wanted to contain our private situation. There is a will on the table, the horror. I want to stamp my feet like a spoilt child. Flip coffee with them. Timing is everything. I have no choice. My body floods with heat, a surge of flames reddening my cheeks. Pounding the air from my lungs, short sharp breaths rasp from my mouth. Stepping back and forth, a way of controlling the panic attack, the others say nothing to limit me further. No one gives word to my distress. My botoxed armpits are safe from visual wet patches. I sit down opposite mom. The truth of Mom's will can make everything a lie. That is the power a will wields -The truth of the matter catches up on us all. Sooner or later, my mother's disease will spread to me, I will be her mouthpiece. Her progressive neurological condition is attacking her motor neurons, the nerves in her brain. Her messages will gradually stop reaching her muscles. Eventually, Mom will stop speaking. The loss of such liberty is underrated by the outspoken. I could not imagine a worse infliction.

In silence, we all sit.

'Will you push Mr P. in a little tighter?' Frank directs me. And he withdraws his command of the wheelchair, as if releasing a chain from his grasp. 'I will give my services to all, including your mom. Let me assist you, Lily,' he lavishes over my mom, towering protection over my little mother. 'Thank god.' I glare at him but Frank easily ignores me.

What is your plan, Frank?

173

'To live the way of the Almighty and fear no man,' sermons the black addict.

'Sex and money do the trick for me.'

'I see.' He angles his chair disdainfully away from me.

'We are on the same page then,' I challenge.

'How do you figure that out, pray tell me?'

They all glue their eyes to my face.

'We seek mind-bending, worldly experiences and champion us better than the next person.'

'That is one way of putting it.' His smarmy grin is disgusting. 'Do you take on private clients?'

My body language of crossing my arms gives the clear signal he is not welcome by me.

This is his inner circle. Let the game begin. I'm willing to take my best shot.

'Nurse Jean, loves money, and is the business head of our group,' Frank smarms. She has a tidy sum of money that needs to be invested, donations from philanthropists, eager to progress the advancement of medicine. Altruistic pursuits, tax incentives.'

I hear him loud and clear in the outline of the female as the whiz of the group. Very smart, Frank, have no legal ties to the accumulation of funds. Take no accountable responsibility. Let the dame take the hit if an audit is ever sanctioned against a private account. I detest him insanely for his savvy. Does he have accounts off the books?

'I don't bother myself in all that trivia. Thank god.'

'I don't doubt that one bit,' I drip with irony. Then it dawns on me. Drew's cell phone shot, Frank and Nurse Jean were in it, at the lush house party with my mother, sitting with my family. It riles me.

And now I'm an acquaintance seen with them. I have no wish to assimilate into their crew. It's just the law of probability today to frequent the same destination. My equilibrium wobbles as energy zings in the clinic's café. The fine balancing act of living and dying suspended for cappuccino time. The stench of bleach hovers above the tables to remind mingling humans of their destination. As if I could forget. My designer bag has no place to hang in these surrounds. It is not my normal coffee house, I do not have a choice in the matter. A tight feeling clinches my chest.

I offer to get in the coffees, some respite from the group. I can study them from the ordering queue, the cozy troops. They huddle intimately, Mom with Frank. They appear to be tight friends, this support group. The fleeting certainty that I was not intentionally included stung me. Mom notes my place in the line and calculates the separation point of me from them, she keeps me in her line of vision.

I slowly move along to the pay point. How had the day become this strange and unfamiliar? I did not know she had her own relief team. Obviously this is what they are to one another, relief. They share the mental load of ill health, unconditionally. I should have been happy she had this support. But my instincts repel them.

'Ouch!' I almost drop the contents of the tray on the table, a charge of static flicking against my fingers. 'That's the second time this morning - bloody place,' I huff. 'It's full of electricity.' I rub my fingers across my top.

Mom is aware of my annoyance, the displacement from us two as a pair, to numbers making up a group, is bugging me and she has to contend with my grumbling. 'Just as well, dear,' jokes Mom. 'I wouldn't like the doctor looking inside me using a magnifying glass.'

The look of fake tremors, hot on the heels of an image of unorthodox medical practice, mingles comic humor with the group.

Maybe there is hope for us all.

'They offered me a nappy today,' admits Mr Patterson, adding his basic item to the list of the clinic's unsophisticated paraphernalia. I blink. A look of my wide-eyed embarrassment causes another rupture of laughter at the table.

It is good to see Mom relaxing, even if it is with her odd friends. The lightness of the mood is almost annulated as Mom cries out in pain. 'Ouch, my body can't even laugh anymore.' Beleaguered honesty lingers respectfully as they sit comfortably together. Old people make me nervous, all the shouting up of tone, to pronounce words and nothing in common to hold the roaring tirade of conversation, makes me uneasy in their company. It was about being polite but meaningless. I don't usually look at them, in the same way I don't meet the eyes of the homeless in doorways. Too bad for me today, the vacant seat is beside the elderly Mr Patterson. Mom and Frank sit side by side opposite me.

The wheelchair frightens me, but I have no choice but to sit beside it, a scary reminder of wasting-away cartilage. A mirage of congealed blood crowds my table space as the old man lays his hands on the table by me. Purple bruises threading his punctured veins are impossible to ignore as they climb up his limbs.

I stir my latte, the creamy foam offering solace. A woman passes by, as if weights are tied to her shuffling feet, threatening to unbalance her. It is unbalancing me, all this frailty. The others on my table are passive, neutral participants in the scene. This visual disintegration all around me is disintegrating me. But I am the exception in the group. The pungent smell of urine emanating from the old man does not offend. The hunched, quivering Mr P. slurps his coffee as if he were at home.

Nobody complains. I squirm in my seat. I don't have my Mom's medical gene in my make-up. I detest decrepit flesh. Mom smiles over at me like she can read my thoughts. I wink back to her in reply, persuading her to not give up on me. 'I'm getting there,' I reply to an unasked question that I see in her eyes.

The others are oblivious to my disdain at our forced connection this morning. I am being evasive. I had just treated them to coffee and cakes, an act of kindness, they are not to know I am quaking with impatience. Unlike me, they sit unhindered by my addition. Under the pretense of passing the milk and sugar, I scrutinize Frank, the cornerstone, in my opinion. Frank is only a few years older than me, forty years of age tops, I estimate. The scent of lavender is overpowering, he must use it as cologne. Frank is enjoying his doughnut, and Mom's doughnut too, I notice, as she has declined any food. Her appetite is leaving her gradually, like all of her taken-for-granted faculties.

'Have you been working in the clinic for long, Frank?' I try to sound bland, to casually investigate him in an indifferent manner. I stir my coffee. Mom shoots me a look of parental instruction to behave. I ignore her.

He engages with me reluctantly. He has to stop stuffing his mouth, acknowledging my piqued interest in him with a nod of his head to me, placing his coffee cup on the saucer with such tender deliberation, almost stalling for time, I think, to consider his reply to me. Then conveniently, Mr Patterson directs the heat off Frank because he needs to use his oxygen mask. Mom, to my surprise, comes to the elderly man's aid as she leaves her chair and leans over to help him and adjust his strap. I do not take my eyes off Frank's face, trying to read him through all the distraction. He sits impassively while Mom's attempt to secure the band around the old man's head eludes her nimble fingers.

'Let me,' I say, my impatience spilling over. Background intrusions almost prevent our continuance

177

with the formalities, but I hold my ground. 'You were saying,' I instruct continuance.

'I do not work here, as such.' Frank lets his coffee cup sit, to give me his full attention, giving me the feeling that he was expecting this little inquisition. The rasping and gritty sounds of the oxygen ventilator attached on Mr P.'s wheelchair almost camouflage my combative approach.

'I don't understand,' I say honestly. Now it was my time to pointedly place my latte down and give him my full observation.

He smiles a serene smile that does not match his slated eyes. 'I volunteer my services.' He speaks in a voice as smooth as honey. 'Thank god.' The group responds to him in unison, 'thank god.'

'Volunteer,' I repeat, trying to keep my critical opinion from being exactingly personal. My voice is intense, I repeat his dialogue, almost rendering the technique of a lawyer in court. I just don't like the man. The simple words, thank god, jar within my brain's cavity.

Volunteering, not a notion I easily understood. It was incomprehensible to me, almost as much this big-boned enigma. Frank could easily become obese, a protruding large belly and fleshy, full cheeks hinted to unhealthy indulgences. Asexual to the eye, this indifference does not warm me to him, there is no aura of masculinity to him at all. I have no level on which to engage him.

A battle of wills ensues. He prefers my mother's company to mine, even though I am the younger female. My youthfulness has no appeal for him, I can tell as he constantly leans in towards Mom, lapping up her every word, basking in her essence. He has the utmost respect for her, I am dismissed.

Very strange territorial diversion to take. I sum up Frank's uptake, the bodies nearing death intrigue him more than a fertile, voluptuous body across from him. Maybe he is a priest? I think. My intrusion goes further into his business.

'Mom said you are a member of the pastoral team?' I sit completely still as I stroke his ego by giving him some form of status in my estimation.

Mom comes to his rescue in a protective manner. 'We all aren't accomplished accountants like you, dear and have an extortionate charge rate per hour, Olive.' Her lead of parental care did not escape me. Mom can sense my determination. I feel jealous. 'Frank would earn more than I did in my heyday if he were to account for all the time he freely spends with patients. He gives of himself like no other professional I have worked with.' My agitation seeks respite as I shift in my chair. I was always trying to match up to my mom's professional success and now she has placed this stranger on a par with her. I dislike him more for it. Why does my mom hold him in such high esteem? My flushed face is my only tell tale sign that I am tackling myself as well as Frank. Mom's friendship with Frank repels me as much as it transfixes me.

'So you're a humanitarian worker?' I push on. I sit upright to feign interest in his work. 'Like Mom, she had volunteered her services pro bono over the years. I remember going downtown to the temporary clinics set up on community health days. I had been made sit at a desk, and take the names of the patients forming long waiting lists. I'm good at noting pointers.' Recalling my astonishment that Mom would work long into the night for free never left my memory. Am I touching a raw nerve, as I have to associate with Frank's persona? Is his apparent ultimate goal, equal to my mom's, to serve fellow human beings? How altruistic of this team. Is this why Mom has such time for Frank, a kindred spirit perhaps? My head angles to judge him further.

179

'Indeed, one could say I am a humanitarian worker,' he concedes easily with a smile towards me. 'Thank god.' I note his desire to agree with me. It unnerves me. A gap opens as I leave him some rope to hang himself. He sips more coffee and he extols as he sips. 'I do help marginalized individuals the system does not provide for,' he answers, linking an arm with my mom as if to visually show me a point of solidarity. She taps his arm in acknowledgement. Acknowledgement of what? I wonder, as I scrutinize the pair. I am not pacified, I shift tack toward the elderly gentleman. This leads me nicely to address such a patient Frank has helped. 'Does Frank hang out with you too, Mr Patterson?' I ask, my steady course of enquiry breaking through the ventilation noise. Nurse Jean is too busy eating to partake in the chinwag.

'Yes,' splutters Mr P., the spit and condensation clouding his mouthpiece, almost obliterating his uptake in the conversation. With all my might, I cringe as my fingers slip on the frothy spit-dripping elastic band. I release the taut hold from the man's mouth to open up his crumbled face to me. I want to hear him clearly. Had he been wearing a ventilator mask when I first seen him in the prayer room earlier? I quizzed myself, trying to recall the facts. 'Frank is a good friend,' he wheezes out panted words. 'A kind man.'

'Frank is a fellow pioneer, like me, dear, with his humane acts of kindness.' Mom tenderly agrees with the picture Mr P. has painted for me about the volunteer.

Interesting that no one is labeling Frank's IMCA status to me. He is more a mental case himself than a mental advocate. Yet Mom holds Frank in her high esteem. Does he have a medical background? Kindness is a hard value to estimate in my way of thinking. I seek hard facts.

'What's your training in?' I directly ask Frank in a smart tone.

He acts in the reverse to me, almost pausing my affront. Sitting back in his chair, unperturbed, a man of peace, his well-known identity shared with the patients. He has to have heard the edge in my voice, they all did. Frank chooses to ignore it. Reaching for his coffee cup, engrossed the moment, eternity visits as he enacts the slowest of motions possible. The slower he moves, the faster my agitation spirals. Was he purposely egging me on to lose my cool? When he has placed the cup back down with a gracefulness a ballet dancer aspired to imitate, he gives me time again.

'I am in training,' he replies. 'Thank god.'

'Training for what?' It is out of me before I can censor the words. The directness is evident to all at the table. Maybe I should adopt a softer tone to belie my sharpness of mind? Too late now.

'I am a man of the cloth, in training.' He speaks the English language but I still needed a translator. 'Thank god.' The after-kick he has to adjoin to his chitchat incenses me. 'I am in between churches at present.' Frank tips at my reserves some more. Mom senses my frustration and speaks on behalf of the elusive Frank to quell my outbreak. 'Frank is trying to join the priesthood, dear. He has experienced a calling.'

'Well well,' I exasperate, the sentiment laced with irony. 'I have never met a person who has a calling.' I'm talking in a breathless manner, to distract from my cumbersome attempt of assignation. This was true. I don't go to church. Did this give him an advantage over me, I tot?

Nobody reacts to the exchange, they all sit in a surreal stillness. I view the party of misfits in my company. Mom has a unique character of openness, it was part and parcel of her medical life but more so, it

181

was part of her natural kindness toward people. She often cares for stray cats that meander past her doorway. Was Frank a stray predator? I am more calculative by nature and talk plainly. 'My mom has no wealth to speak of,' I state, the accountant in me representing her interests, the combination of church and wealth a given historical footing even I am aware of. How do I stop the heaviness I am bringing to the table as I tackle this man?

'Olive,' streamlines Mom. 'Please don't be so rude, dear.'

His eyebrows arch an ironic twist, 'I'm not interested in money. My interests are with the people.' The staunch denial of any interest in monetary activities perplexes me more. Why would a man in his prime want to keep constant company with weak, dying people?

'A calling,' I repeat. 'Hell if I know what that means.'

'Dear, there are elements of life you don't know the full meaning of,' adds Mom lovingly. My parent was on my side again. I purposely include a standing of family at this juncture.

'Will Dad be here soon, Mom?' I ask, while smiling kindly although I am hyperventilating. Fuck off, the lot of you hangers-on, I want to say out loud, but I would isolate them as soon as possible.

I can only cut myself up into so many pieces. Even I could not be in two places at the one time. I make a mental note to connect with Dad later. For now, I feel like a magnet, the forces of opposite decisions pulling me in two different ways. I love Mom. My mom is my mom. I love Dad. Just as much. But differently. Did my father get it? I never wondered about this fact, but I do now, within this forming of a self-help support group, this play of improvising actors, all of us playing a part in the final scene.

182

Am I playing a lead role? Was I doing enough for my parents? Do my parents know I'm here for them? That they can come to me and rely on me? I had never included this dimension of our lives in any reasonable discussion with my mom, but sitting here, making up a group, in this domain, I may be too late to join the soiree. I shudder. I have to know about these people who are so important to my mom. I had to find a way to incorporate the older man, Mr Patterson, into the dialogue.

'Do you have family joining you today?' I innocently enquire.

His head drops a little further, his spittled chin dampening his sweater. 'I am the last one left.' He tries to speak coherently in between his gasps.

My eyes mist over. And then it occurs to me. I direct my next question to my mother. 'Do you know Mr Patterson's final wishes, Mom?'

'Yes, Olive,' she answers in a clear manner. 'We all here at this table have talked about our final wishes with one another.' I gasp in private pain. 'His wife and only son have passed away before him, Olive,' Mom tells me pointedly.

'I'm sorry for you.' I can only speak the truth.

He raises his beady eyes to try and meet my face halfway. 'I don't want to die alone.'

My stomach twists with guilt. I was pursuing him, but I have my reasons.

'I'm tired,' he musters up with great difficulty, three little words.

I seek my mom's help. 'Should we take him to his room?'

'He does not have a room,' Frank answers impatiently.

'Mr Patterson is an outpatient, dear,' offers Mom, playing peacemaker.

I was being given details but they were unquestionable facts. My instinct tinges a color of royal purple. I can tell I am being spoken to but being told very little.

'We sit in here. This café becomes our living room. We know what is in the fridge, we make it homely with our morning meet-up. And give thanks in the prayer room, thank god.' Frank speaks to me again, gaining momentum. 'After we have sat through Mr Patterson's daily three hour drainage procedure, we visit our friends.'

'Is Drew a friend?' I ask. Not one cup is raised.

'Drew is welcome,' propositions Mom and as a reminder, she lifts the gun and places it on the table. No one moves again. I wait to see who would lift the weapon off the table, surely it could not stay there in broad daylight. Nurse Jean takes it and puts it under her skirt and into a leather hold, strapped to her thigh. I note, no one mentions the foundation's pastoral house, Round Wood.

'I have to take this too tight jacket off,' squeezes Frank. 'I'm bursting.' He undoes his buttons.

'I'm keeping mine snug,' wiggles Nurse Jean.

'I'm tired of living,' gargles the thick mucus reply, as though his system was flooding. Frank leans over and straps the ventilator mask over Mr Patterson's face. I want to ask the old man more questions but what is apparent to me is that this is not the intention of the caring minder. The refreshments have gone cold. Full to the brim coffee is left to puddle, soiled patterns in the cups. The routine of having a morning cup of coffee, a last visage of existing; even if one did not want to drink. Patterns of ingrained behavior continue. Mr Patterson hardly touched his coffee. The illusion of choice. Mom did not drink her coffee either, only Frank enjoyed his, but his hand shook I noticed as he drained the cup. I

184

wished with all my might that the day was over, and I would be gone. I wished this time would end.

Mom looks straight at me. 'Life and death are bigger than your mind can comprehend dear.'

I am stunned by her philosophy; here of all places, a tired canteen, my mother wants to engage in mind boggling actualities.

Then Frank frustratingly pushes back his chair. 'I have to take it off. I'm stuffed after eating two buns.'

'Now?' flusters Mom.

'Now, Dr Tully. Forgive me.' And he unbuttons his black shirt.

'Unzip it only,' scolds Mom.

'It's too tight.'

'Do as you are told. Loosening it will help.'

'No,' puffs Frank. 'It won't help.'

Dumbfounded, my jaw drops. That was why he was rotund in appearance. Frank is wearing a bulletproof vest. I have clear visibility now as he wings his outer garments.

'The public can be so fickle,' colours Nurse Jean. 'Drew got bail. Unfortunately, as you know we would be locked up in the State of Florida for defending ourselves. Where dreams come true and everything is possible. Codswallop. If only we were tourists,' she laughs. The confusion is not comical to me.

'The ethics of a society we live in rule the day for the minority,' expounds Mom.

And Frank continues in attendant agreement. 'Never changes. They look for lessons but they repeat terrible mistakes -'

Mom hastily interrupts him lording himself over mere society. 'Jim, my husband,' Mom imparts, rudely cutting him short, 'has texted an X to me.' And she holds up her cell phone, waving the screen for all to see, changing the direction the conversation has been taking.

185

'Jim's recall of lettering is proving too difficult for him at this stage of his dementia so the symbolic kiss is more than a full alphabet's worth.' It is shocking to me that Mom was divulging personal details to others. 'For me, it's a perfect love poem,' she smiles. Her inclusiveness has startled me. 'Another social admission in time,' her eyes cloud as she communicates to me. 'Mr P. is a social admission today on our humanitarian mission,' Mom says eloquently.

We were quite a magnetic field.

Not one syllable could I mutter. It is obvious Mom has a different disclosure setting with these people.

'At least you're getting some action, Lily,' teases the hearty nurse, her freckled face beaming with merriment. 'I'm sperm dating meself,' she earnestly adds. 'Hand over the goods Frank.'

I laugh loudly, the intense setting I was enduring, welcomed the release of stress facilitated by this candid woman.

The comic relief is short lived.

Frank takes a small plastic bag with a small container inside, out of his pocket and Nurse Jean, holds out her hand.

He deposits it in her grasp.

'You can take of the syringing.' My jaw drops. She stashes the container in her pocket.

'You're a sperm-worthy woman,' extols Mr P. 'If only my body had not let me down.'

Nurse Jean chuckles back at the old man, pinching his cheek. 'I'll be having a virgin birth,' she says to me.

'A what?' I ask her, and sit up straight.

'Well I've never been in a relationship,' her cheeks blush, 'but I want a baby.'

'Have this to aid the process,' echoes Mr P. and he pulls a wad of dollars out of his trouser pocket. 'I've no need of it anymore.'

Encouraged by this mercenary surplus, Nurse Jean engrosses her desires, turning her ample chest into Frank's face.

He splutters his gulp of coffee.

'Mr P.,' issues Mom. 'You have already paid your contribution, as have I.'

The intimacy within the cohort is astounding.

I tunnel for more information.

'Why the protective vest, Frank?' The words burst out of me, unable to hold on to my reserve any longer.

'To protect me against,' a slight pause as he fumbles, 'misunderstandings.'

LIARS.

Weaving their web of lies.

'Misunderstandings?' I repeat his misleading description.

'People gift their carers in the clinic,' Mom butts in. 'At times, family members can be peeved because of the proximity and close relationship the support group establishes with the patients. Sometimes it is easier to trust strangers than members of your own family with private details. Feelings run high, misunderstandings occur.'

'High enough to commit a murder?' I yelp.

'There can be a high price to pay, dear.'

'Pro-lifers have no respect for life,' discloses Nurse Jean.

'Very angry mad hatters they can be,' says Frank.

'That will do just dandy,' she proclaims and grabs the money with such zeal, as if on a rescue mission. 'You're a pet Mr P.'

What deal had just gone down?

'It was my suggestion to Frank that he should protect himself,' mom says.

My mother is almost the spokeswoman for this group.

'I have god's family.' He stoically delivers his sermon to eradicate any images of the workings of the flesh.

Nurse Jean is practically throwing herself at him. He wants no action apparently, an odd specimen of a man in my reckoning. How she could even consider him is a conundrum to me. I chew on my lip as I try to figure Frank out.

'Financial matters are all taken care of,' espouses Nurse Jean, playing her last card. 'There is no cost factor for you, Frank, I'm managing meself. Look at all these dollars flowing in. The foundation is a gold mine.'

I wondered how a nurse, around my age bracket had thousands of dollars to spend on fertility treatments.

But then I wipe out the numerical.

I would not be interested in doing her books, she can continue to look after the administration.

'I have no need of money,' monotones Frank, as if he could calculate the workings of my brain. 'Money comes and goes, adoration is immortal.'

'Have as much sex as you can,' expounds Mr Patterson with roguish charm, a flash of zest reappearing across his eyes.

'Too true,' says Mom, twinkling over at him. 'And not just viewing porn.'

Mom looks directly in my direction.

'Mom!' I morph back to teenage angst around this table, when is she going to stop with her disclosures today and in front of strangers? Well, strangers to me.

'What?' She shakes her head at me and insists on continuing. 'Don't waste your hard-earned money,' she goads me. 'And Jean, get yourself out there.' And when I had hoped she was finished, Mom adds, 'Enjoy the fun of sex while you can, both of you. You can't beat the real thing. We met the shuttle driver, Mike, earlier. A fine specimen, Jean.'

Was Mom derailing my line of enquiry by throwing in bum steers?

'I only require a fresh needle-full - and you are always around the place.' Nurse Jean restarts on Frank, encouraged by the lose talk. 'What man would turn down a wank?' she remarks with disbelief towards me.

'Or woman,' I dutifully bat for the side. Nurse Jean roars laughing. Frank is not amused, he sits poker-stiff. Indeed, I think, why would Frank be so disinterested in the available sex on offer?

'You don't do drugs, you don't smoke, you don't drink.'

Frank earnestly interrupts Jean's flow of compliments and requirements by offering to get her a coffee. What do you do, Frank? Spirals in my brain. This unlikely group of misfits could not be lethal if they tried.

'And you are so tall.' She keeps going on and on as Frank purposely leaves the table, calling after him. 'Oh, I like a bit of meat,' the big-framed girl admits for all to hear. So talk of humping and bumping was the decoy to get him to exit and give me some free space without him within earshot. The smell of his vile, overtly sweet lavender remains. This gives me an opportunity, the assistance of qualified personnel in the clinic was a bonus.

'Nurse Jean, I think Mr Patterson needs further medical attention,' I outline to the nurse persuasively. She seems taken aback by my lack of interest in her personal medical needs. Funny how my remark shuts everyone up, the silence is deafening. They all just stare at me. Mr Patterson becomes eerily quiet. 'Can't you tell he is breathing with difficulty?'

'Olive, dear, what do you mean further medical assistance?' asks Mom in an exact manner. I am wearing her patience thin, I can tell by her curtness towards me.

Did I accuse Frank of criminal activity? I was near enough in the prayer room to see the drain line being tampered with by him but how could I phrase the incident. I don't want a defamation liability case taken out against me. I proceed tentatively. Threading my fingers along Mr Patterson's waist, copying the earlier route of the culprit, I source the freely-flapping line and lift it up for all to view. I am determined to implicate Frank. I will show them he is a shady man. An intake of breath from my Mom forces my concentration onto her now. She has turned ghostly pale.

Then I feel a warm hand. Mr P.'s quivering hand steadily places over mine.

'Everyone wants an easy death,' he says.

Leading the mindset of the jury by saying for us all to hear, 'All is as it should be.'

Then he takes the line out of my hand and places it back down along his side, out of sight again. 'Old people can feel like ghosts in their own lives,' he explains. 'I'm invisible as a person. Thank you, dear one, for seeing me today.' And he gives me the warmest pat. 'What a beautiful day today is. My friends are with me.' The head-nodding respectful interaction within the members of the support group at the table demonstrates to me a solidity of opinion, evidently in contrast to mine.

'We are here for you,' I hear them harmonize. 'Thank god.'

Mom stares at me with exasperation.

Nurse Jean cements the gaping hole. 'We'll take great care of our friend, don't you worry yourself, Olive.' She softens the harshness of my forced action by placing a tender kiss on the top of the old man's head. 'Thank god.'

The old man leans toward me and speaks quietly. 'I'm good. I've made my decision.'

'It's a grim task,' offers Nurse Jean. 'You face the day with the spirit you choose.'

'I'm grateful for the help,' he splutters his gratitude.

'No more false hope from the doctors,' adds Nurse Jean vehemently. 'The blunders that occur in this place,' she scowls. 'I could tell you a tale or two meself.'

I sit there, stunned.

Nurse Jean mistakes my speechlessness for uniformity; she continues in vain. But I am paralyzed. The analysis of these people confounds me. My fears increase, I'm catastrophising internally. Is my mom safe with these people? I can barely register what she is saying. The "what if?" syndrome is insurmountable in my head.

I do not want my mother hanging around with this support group. I can see the tall dark fucker, he is coming back, gaining ground, closer to me, closer to my mom.

'His lungs cannot function anymore. CLD, chronic lung disease.' Mom frowns as she continues. 'Unintentional suffering. Our Mr P. fills up to bursting point, then they painfully drain him and it restarts all over again. Everyday.'

Mr P. whimpers in tandem.

'Words come easy when they are true,' my mother softly intervenes.

'Lily,' the nurse directs towards my mother. 'You need to bring your nearest and dearest on board, today of all days.'

I blank momentarily, and then refocus on my mother. Did she take direction from these people?

Mom notices the look on my face. 'For all of your life, Olive, the telling has been developing, the revealing of me to you. A strong, conscientious, independent female is how you were raised, dear. We are of the same flesh and blood.'

191

Joining the dots should be easier than this. That's the problem, the unknowns, they have the upper hand.

Maybe the medical environment gives them an impunity?

There is no hardness to their appearance. The only person acting all hard is me. The back of the chair digging into my back, my head slanted a slight way to act composed. Purposely, no obvious directional eye contact with any of them was my strategy. My fear was diagnosed by me, not them. Scared is putting it mildly. Their normality is beyond my reckoning.

'Frank will walk with me to my room, dear.'

Glowering, I go to disagree, my frustrated telltale sign of rustling my hair giving her the advantage.

'No, Olive. You should take a break for yourself. You will need strength for this place. Have another latte or something. There is wifi in the café.' Mom arches her eyebrows.

They all get up together, the quirkiest group ever, with my mother, walking away from me, walking together.

The symbolism of the act invades my head, their exact intention.

I am alone, stinking of the lavender, reeking from the lot of them.

I'm reeking of lavender.

LILY

The time is never right; there are the birthdays, weddings, funerals, and family occasions, Thanksgiving is next month, then Christmas. I could delay, delay, delay.

There is always a reason to stall.

I'm dragging my heels today, because Olive is here, with me. Her work will save her, mentally challenge and stimulate her. I purposely chose the end of the year accounts, her active, time consuming career engagements, to impinge on her heart. She cannot cut herself off from life, if the emotions pull her under. I waited for Missy, my choice was to go in the summer, on a long evening, in Round Wood. Then she miscarried and I promised myself, I could not wait for her next attempt at pregnancy; I made myself set a date and meet the target, doctor.

Today is the day, now is the time.

Jim is Jim, he knows I love him.

I pierce my skin efficiently with the needle, insert a few inches into the vein, twist the seal of the IV catheter and align the drip. Before I catch it, a droplet of my blood defies my neat expertise and rolls along my wrist, over the swell of my palm and lands on my top.

A perfect, vibrant droplet. My eye is drawn to the artist circular plop of my blood.

I pull a tissue from the floral box Olive has put on the bedside locker. I can clean the skin but the stubborn stain remains on the cotton.

I tap the feed line, adjust the dial and see air bubbles dance in the morphine sac. It is up and running, I feel the drug enter my body. I am on course. Nothing important in life worth doing is easy. I moved to America, left my home, as soon as I was qualified, to find the baby I adopted out, to an affluent American, well-educated couple, or so Sr. Agnes assured me. The nuns could be scarce with the truth, there is very little paperwork on John, I called him John. Everyone takes a secret, a private sin, to the grave. Maybe that's why graveyards top generations of families on top of the last buried body, the ravine is dug deep. My girls have a half-brother they know nothing of.

I lift my handbag, sit on the bed and take out the old, well worn, black and white photograph of my first born. A piece of my heart is waiting, right up to this point, until the very last breath of my life, to wish he will find me. I have been looking for him.

Jim has the same initial as my son. It was a sign, I think, that closed the deal when I fell in love with my American hunk. The ending I hope for, is that they will all meet, after the initial shock, and they will become family and tell tales of me, and laugh.

I'm lucky I never buried a child, the order of life has favoured that blessing on me, thank god. My will outlines the search fee, set aside, to continue to search for and find John. I smile a sad smile, kiss the photo and put it back in my bag. Enough waiting, I scold myself.

Time is up.

I've made a mess of telling Olive and taking her onboard. My stupid selfishness, the wasted moments,

194

describing what I want, long-winded discussions, what about Olive?

I would not have believed, in the end, I was engrossed in me.

Maybe she will remember tidbits of information, intermittently they will fill her mind, and she will understand today, respect my way. And she will find comfort in the memory.

I mean my child no harm. No mother means her child harm.

When I see her, she will be back, I know my Olive, I should just come out and say it: 'I'm ending my life.' No harsh words, like 'killing' or 'suicide.'

Harsh words are not for a child, not in the final hours.

OLIVE

The smell of the clinic is nauseating. I walk in the opposite direction and reach the front doors to exit the stench of the building. I need fresh air.

Where is my place today in this world inside a world?

LIAR.

My inclusion is my mother's wish, not mine.

Acceptance of difference is easier for my mom in her line of work with the multi diversity of cultures amalgamating under this roof. I can't put my finger on it, but there is a desperation emanating from my mother that I've never experienced. My elderly mother is becoming more stubborn by the hour. Another slap in the face for me, another facet of old age, I don't understand. I feel like I need to scream. Looking up to the grey sky, the blanket of cloud covers me up. I do not want to bite the head off my mom, so I welcome my temporary release, on the point of freedom, gulping rejuvenating air, for my sanity. I have a pulling force to search out life: Mike. I crave stimulation, not pjs and slippers. Entrenched in the universe of ailments, I have to exist. Maybe he could give me information on Frank; Mom is a loyal ally, and is secretive about him.

Natural breeze fluffs me, reminding me of the existence of energy that air conditioning cannot replicate. When I'm inside the clinic, the reality of the real world vanishes; two separate universes co-exist, when I'm outside, I can forget the clinic. People just walk on by. I'm ignored, an irrelevant person, their dismissal of me is liberating. We are all strangers, the strangeness a comforting buffer. I wait for the shuttle to pull in and approach him.

'Mike.'

'Olive,' his return intensifies my decision.

I want time out from my maddening morning. 'Can we talk?' I smile my respectful wish.

He smiles, the two of us respond to one another automatically. 'Sure, wait until the last passenger disembarks.'

When there is the two of us, he shuts the double door, enclosing us within. I felt secretive within the private pod. 'What can you tell me about Frank?'

'Frank?' He follows my lead. 'Only what I see of him onboard the shuttle.'

'How does he come across to you?' I interrogate.

'Is everything alright, Olive?' His look of concern is endearing.

But I have no space for distraction.

'Yes,' I reply and then change my mind. 'I think so.' I sit down beside Mike before realizing …

Frank, he sat here, when I first came across him. The aftermath of his fixture, lingering oils, taunt me almost.

I shake the image off. Mike does not understand where I am coming from, how could he? I restart to try and clear the confusion in my head. 'Tell me everything you know about Frank.'

'Well, I don't know much about him.' And noticing my crestfallen face, Mike adds some more tidbits. 'He comes to the clinic everyday, even at weekends.' As

197

soon as he says it, the addictive routine registers with me.

'How does he treat the other passengers?' I interject.

'Frank is always kind to the feeble passengers, Olive.'

This is not what I wanted to hear.

'Assisting them with their bags, walking with them, constantly talking to them. Very few people talk to the sick, I have found in this country. Most patients are embarrassed but Frank knows them by name and case.' Mike sounds proud of Frank.

I sit on my rising temper.

The last piece of information interests me the most.

'Does he ever ask people about their wills or their final wishes?' I paraphrase my mom.

'I have never heard him talk of such with the patients,' Mike affirms. 'He is always reassuring, telling them all will be well in the end. The patients ask to be anointed. Frank volunteers this service.'

'Fuck,' my eyes slit closely with impatience. I feel strongly that Frank has a tincture of darkness to him. Then Mike adds a teaser.

'I know he was turned away from entering the priesthood. Frank told me, blaming a know-all female psychologist for failing him on the result of his personality assessment test.'

'Really?' I echo smugly.

'He regularly gives testament to the fact that the so-called experts don't know what they are talking about.'

'What experts is he referring to? The doctors?'

'I don't know, Olive, but he expounds such advice daily. Everyone has to listen in the small shuttle. Frank spurns daily that the bureaucratic system is losing sight of the humanity of patients.' I furrow my thoughts, my mom is such an expert, yet her and Frank seem to have mutual trust. But then my mom always talked with Dad about how the health system was failing the sick.

'Frank has never offended me, Olive,' and Mike reveals, 'which is not the way with the majority of this country's folk.'

Mike becomes a curious mixture of masculinity and vulnerability, my spirit of femininity races. A yearning spasm leaps inside of me, I see the fine man before me. Drawn to him magnetically, I want to blend myself in his make-up. My life is stressful, overwhelming. I crave distractions, oblivion. Without hesitation, my courageous ancestral instincts hone in to capture my prey, I bravely close the distance between us, kissing his lips, I reel him in. I instigate a deepening of the kiss to explore.

He momentarily stalls, confused by my change of tack, the highly rational woman before him had shed her inhibitions in an instant. The extremes of my emotions tantalize me to distraction, from paralyzing worry, to existential escapism, I excel. A woman before him, the daughter role left behind inside the building. I need to evade one entanglement and swap it for another.

'Go with this?' I ask him and butterfly intimate kisses along his lips.

'Mike?' I proposition, a hunger for life, the clinic has stalled my liberation. The responsibilities of the day hem me in. My championing nature boosted, both sides of life's tales too closely linked. I want to widen the gap, to live wildly, to revert back to the old Olive of just hours before, to undo my psychological restraints.

Mom had only minutes before advised me to have more real sex in my life. I had no qualms with one night stands; this was just that, a pick up, but in daylight. The diurnal clock is reversed, that's all, I tempt my wanton desire. Go with it, urges my inner beauty, you fancy him, embrace life and all its challenges. This moment, this is life, this is living, this is all I have.

That is what we all have to be sure of. Why plan for later, the plan is happening right now, my inner voice directs me, as sure as my outer body takes the lead. Matching the sweet rhythm resounding in me, I sway to him, melting into his contours, appraising his maleness.

'Oh, you're a gorgeous kisser,' I tease as Mike lifts his head slightly from my face to look into my clouded eyes.

'So are you,' he praises.

We lean in.

This is happening. I'm distressed and need a fix. I pay no more homage to limiting boundaries. I am healing myself, administering my own medicine. I need this more than Mike understands.

Bravo to me … When I get out of here I'm having lots more sex …

Adrenaline swirls in my bloodstream as I heat up.

'Mike, I want sex.' I pull him closer. 'Now.'

'Now?' he gasps.

'Yes, now,' and my addiction goes into overdrive. Existentially, I need to blot out the clinical world. 'Put the out of service sign on the front screen and then quickly service me.'

The words are too direct for him. With pure strength of character, Mike halts the hormonal rush overtaking him.

'You want sex here? On the shuttle?' Mike has to state the facts, whereas I was ignoring the blatant fact that I had to have titillation to make it through my day. Like an alcoholic needs a drink or a smoker a cigarette, I need a sexual high to rescue me from my low. I act on compulsion, pouncing on him with intent, the victor claiming her prize. I have to have this reference of bravery in my life today. This is my never to be forgotten risk, to live beyond my known entity. Go with this, I tell myself.

200

For eternity, I will not regret myself in this moment of wonder.

'I want you, too,' he pants as he holds my face in his hands. He places soft kisses on my nose, forehead, eyes and back to my lips. My welcoming invitation translates to him. We are lucky lovers, grasping our time. Take the joy, no matter how short lived. I greedily kiss him back, teasingly trying to catch his lips in a longer duet.

'I need a slam buddy right now,' I demand.

There is no hiding the intensity, rubbing my loins against him. I relish in my ballsy ways as his hardened balls line against me. His sculpting fingers rest on the small of my back as he stares into my eyes. The slamming term a little harsh for him, I sense his loss of footing. 'Make love to me, Mike. I want you to.'

'If you are sure Olive.'

'I am. Let's do it,' I command.

'Yes.' Mike's voice is hoarse.

'Yes.'

I sum up the situation.

'There is more body room on the back seat of your vehicle than in my car. So here will do.'

Mike's eyes glisten.

'Right, I will lock up and flick on the sign.'

I laugh by way of an answer, not at all sure about a shuttle bus.

But I don't want to tame the growing spike of orgasm. My imagination plays erotic images of being bold on the back seat.

My laughter heals me, the joyous melody echoing in the chambers of my soul.

I can just about block out the reality of the shuttle, if I close my eyes. But I want them wide open. Pulling off my top and bra, the lingering scent of lavender sinking in the membrane of my skin. 'Do you have a hat with your uniform?' I tease.

'No,' he answers, now a little scared of the tigress before him and not the caring lady he had built up in his imagination only a few hours earlier.

'Pity,' I tease some more. 'That's all I had intended on allowing you to wear.'

He gulps. I immediately take action. Taking him by the hand, I lead the way down the aisle to the long back row of joined seats.

'We don't have much time,' explains Mike.

He hears my life-affirming willingness. 'Come on,' I jest.

'I'm coming already,' he jokes.

'Me too,' I joke back giddily.

'Shush,' Mike orders as I squeal with delight, his sucking on my nipple pumping me for action. 'We will have to be quiet,' he hisses.

'I can't promise you that,' I purr, pushing him down, unzipping his trousers.

'What are you doing?' He jerks as I flash my cell phone over the length of his excited penis.

'I'm videoing us,' I state matter of factly.

Mike lifts his head in the mix-up.

'Ah, is it your first time on screen?' I cajole.

He smiles a grin of mixed emotions, of inadequacy mostly. 'It's work. I could lose my job. I cannot go home to my village in Kerala in shame,' he answers sheepishly. 'The filming is no problem.'

'Don't worry, it's just for me, for my personal pleasure.'

The enormity of the pornographic request fades against the erotic pleasure he is receiving.

He waves a continuance.

I ease him into me and position myself below the window line, out of sight. This is my heaven, the best outdoor sex I have had in ages. Quick and intense, life-affirming. A safe haven, free of logical justifications as

202

physical pulsations rule my world. This driver has driven me to paradise.

'Powerful,' I exhale in short breaths.

'Powerful,' replies Mike, gladly following my lead.

There is no room for solutions in my head as I instruct, 'Again.'

'Again?' he cries.

'Again. I need this … you,' I correct. There is only the two of us. Everyone else is in the distance, I'm not thinking about Mom or Frank. I hum to my own unique rhythm. I become my full self. Life and its difficulties do not rule supreme, I do. I excel in these fleeting orgasmic minutes before my dilemmas will return. With a flick of my fingers, I zoom out my camera lens for a repeat performance from another angle.

*****

Deviate or accept. These are my options. Mom waits for me. Motionless, I stare at the revolving door. Interaction fires up self-analysis. I exist in the context of others, I work within a system along with the next person. Today is not about me. And yet it's all about me. I can't get away from me. Insane, I know. I'm muttering to myself like a mad woman. Something is up, I just know it. My instincts are raw. How can I put my finger on what is annoying me if I don't know what I'm looking at? Relief of sex is transitional. The orgasm can only last so long.

The afternoon looms ahead. Authenticity reigned supreme, now I find myself in the mire. It's impossible to escape from myself. I smirk, a loner, hovering by the doorway. The doorway to heaven or hell?

A flight or fight mode possesses me. A strong compulsion to leave the grounds, to escape the parameters of this medical field pulling me back into the dark pit, floods my system and overcomes me. I chart the unknown. My mother expounded the impossible during my formative years. Always arty, theatre, music and literary events joined the respectful analogue of human potential in our household. This outlook challenged me, sure calculations comforted me. I thrive on certainties, the clinical set-up perturbs me. New settings taxed me, but I always found my footing. I must take after my dad. Mom pushed us all, I can hear her in my inner ear, an encouraging quote from her favorite poet, William Butler Yeats, there are no strangers, only friends you haven't yet become acquainted with. Maybe I should give these strangers a chance? My mother has. What to do?

I hop from one foot to the other. My just-fucked hair is raked. Directionless, I remain unsure. The wild animal scratching at the surface does not want to be subdued. I'm not my mother, I'm me. I can't escape from myself. Life with its conditioning rules reins me in, overruling my strong impulse to turn and walk away. The survival instinct is so strong. I love my mom. It is not a lack of love that prevents me from spending more time with ailing parent, it is a lack of courage. I could just leave, but then I could not. My love for Mom overpowers my cowardice.

I re-enter the clinic.

I thought I had it all sewn up. My way is the only way, but life is kicking me in the ass by letting me know differently. All does not go according to my plan, even the best made plans. Especially not the best laid plans. I have to tell my Mom I am not canceling my work commitment. My work dissolves private dilemmas, swamps me in the details. As it is, I have less and less time for my mom, I cannot give her this full day. Life is busy for me by personal choice. I'm being challenged on all levels today. I could stagnate or thrive. Scared of myself because of this unfamiliar domain, am I the meal ticket or the beggar in this institution? The old reliables are not of this location. Tickling with zest, a latest craze of gym drills, overtime, shopping to the extreme. Cookery demonstrations had become my religion, reservations for newly opened restaurants and multiple partners, anything and everything to dismantle my leisure time up into neat segments and avoid other areas of my life. I had condoned picking Mike up and burying myself deeply into him on this complicated day. My era can only handle fun-filled activities. I have no idea how to handle sorrowful events. Why would I? I have never had to.

I mentally bang off the walls. My tendency to side-track delicate issues is a testament to my personal inclination of avoidance. This day is not about me, but it will not leave my sense of being intact. Maybe that was why I could not sleep deeply last night. I dreamt of the red ladybird, flying over my eyes, my spirit injecting into the physical, to alert me. The American Dream is to build a person up; how great I am, my personal potential can overcome and surmount any difficulty. Participating in the predicament of life, the ultimate assurance of contentment, what bull; this fractured society, the groupies, are the source of my discontentment. The group will assimilate me. Why am I not running to the pack? I will rejoin, regurgitated, within this dull dreary place, for her, because my mom is here, waiting for me. Minutes earlier, I nearly left this cursed ground.

LIAR.

I nearly left this cursed ground.

Tracing the outlined route to her, I had never understood how I deplete my reserves when I'm not in control. I did not have control of the situation and there lay the problem. Situation was the term I coined to encapsulate the strangeness of the predicament of mixing with strange people and having to share my mother. I want to dismiss them. My mother wants to discuss with me the burden of dying when I cannot even get a grip on the burden of living. The medics have no medicine to administer to me. Drab corridors, swallowing me as I pass through, challenge me to dissolve. All is as I pictured, the cohort hanging with Mom.

This is a groundhog day, the repetition of a visit in a clinic is mind numbing. Mom has never been a patient before, in any clinic. Is this what a person does when they accompany a patient? No wonder I searched out excitement, I had to remind myself I'm alive.

'I am sorry for your troubles, Lily.' Frank's low voice is the first to reach my ears as I walk into Mom's private quarters, the puke green cube confinement continues to curdle my bile. His scent of lavender softens the harsh reality for them but I find the corrosive sentiment unbearable, just like I find him. Him and his aura are intrusive to my senses.

'Thanks, Frank.' Mom smiles at him warmly.

Frank humbly nods. 'Families -' He stops, notes my arrival, then continues. 'Thank god for them. My mother,' he opts for a safer route of discussion. 'My mother wanted me to move out and on.' I could well believe that, the smirk on my face as I sit on the bed is revealing. I hold Mom's hand and bend in to kiss her. My swinging leg accidentally kicks the wheelchair frame.

'Sorry Mr P.' I grin but he is asleep.

There is no malice in the room, the accepting atmosphere seeps into me.

I'm tired.

Frank gently proceeds with the chit chat. 'I did not know what to do after leaving college,' he explains.

'Oh, you have a domineering mother too?' supposes Nurse Jean. 'Like meself.'

'No,' offers Frank. 'Quite the opposite, my mother just lets me get on with my vocation, she is too busy living this life to think of the next one.' Please don't give a sermon, I privately cajole. 'Vera, my mom,' he titles his parent to include me, 'is worried her money is not out-lasting her lifespan.' He takes a badly timed deep breath. 'She swears the church is loaded and that I would be taken care of, if I could only get into one order and train as a minister. It would let her get rid of her pressing burden.' He turns to Mr P. 'That would be me.' The old man is still in a deep, deep sleep. Frank lets him rest. 'I don't know where she gets these notions. I've told her they will not just let any Tom, Dick or Harry into the orders nowadays.'

Mom interrupts. 'Your mother does not know about Round Wood?'

'No,' Frank's voice drops an octave, looking at me he adds, 'I don't know where she is half the time. Vera collects coupons and loyalty points with the cruise liners. She is on a fourteen day cruise somewhere around the Caribbean as we speak. No coverage, or so she tells me when I don't hear from her for weeks on end.'

'Good for her,' issues Mom just as I am thinking the same.

The interesting topic of parental autonomy up for discussion within the cohort is not lost on me. They are not here for me.

I'm not stupid.

I investigate them suspiciously as they rest their gaze on me too. The gauntlet has been placed down. Who would dual proficiently? Who would divulge a private matter next? No takers, the crowd is quiet. Their boldness stirs my resolve to continue with my own course of action. I want to scream: 'GET OUT! LEAVE MY MOTHER ALONE!' Instead I ask politely, my mother has raised me well, 'Can I have some private time with my mother, please?'

'Olive, dear.' Mom speaks in an intermediary role but I will not be distracted from my mission.

'I would like you all to leave her room, now.'

Nobody moves even though I had been direct in my approach. I turn to Mom. It was only her permission I sought. 'I need to talk with you. Alone.' Mom nods an affirmation to me firstly and then to the others. Movement proceeds at the foot of her bed.

'I have Mr P.,' states Frank. 'Thank god.' And he wheels the deathly still patient out the door.

'Lily, I have recorded the last monitoring of your stats. The intravenous drip is running.' I shoot a look at Nurse Jean. She is ready for my enquiry.

'Is everything alright?' I ask. My voice is not strong.

'Everything is in order,' says Frank.

'Lily requires a higher dosage of pain management. A constant flow of morphine into her bloodstream is recommended.' Clear, crisp words resound from Nurse Jean, not dueling for clarity. I am hoodwinked by her professional approach. No further explanation is given.

'Thank you, Nurse Jean. And my team,' mom blows them farewell kisses.

'Anything you wish for, Lily,' confirms Nurse Jean.

'Thank god,' includes Frank. Jean follows Frank out of the room. 'Say nothing,' she orders him but I cannot hear the rest of their conversation when she closes the door.

Mom is pale looking.

Why is it so unbelievable and hard to accept? Someday I will not have a mommy. How can that make sense? A child resonates in life along the lineage of their parents. The rules, as one understands them as a child, have no natural law in adulthood. I have not the same rights of my childhood, it is time to be the grown-up in the partnership with my parent, while the child within me begs for reassurance. I like being the daughter who has a strong mother. I do not like how the order of my life, the way it is meant to be, is changing. Mom is a tower of strength, always has been, but her encasing limbs, collapsing in on her, tell a different story. She looks older, lying in the medical bed. There is no getting away from my emotions in these highly emotive surroundings. My mother can hear the short intake of breaths from me, they synchronize with her own.

'You came back to me,' her voice catches. 'I'm glad you are here with me, dear.' She makes a sign of the cross over herself and prays a silent prayer. 'It is one of my final wishes.'

'Mom? STOP talking like that.'

'Just because I'm old, please do not tell me what I can and cannot say. The elderly lose enough independence, without taking that trait from me.' Mom commands her timescale. 'I'm sorry I keep reminiscing dear, but today is the day for memories. Your entity was more than I could ever claim ownership of. There is more to you and life than I understand. My mind cannot grasp the enormity of you, dear Olive.'

Our intimate bubble lifts and drifts beyond physicality.

She is reminiscing but it is my mother's privilege to relive and retell stories of times gone by. 'Having my children were catalytic events for me, personally and professionally. The unknown became as valuable as the known. Quite a turning point for a doctor, dear. You're the most tangible beauty I've ever experienced, dear.'

'Bootilicious,' I sing, trying to lighten my anxious feelings.

'You're an entity beyond me, dear. As I am an entity beyond you.' The intellectual's profound note embeds in my mind. Mom squeezes my hand tightly, then she lets go to purposely divide us, to let our minds work independently. 'You have to know about my death, Olive.'

My body shudders. Mom places her wrinkled fingers on my moist cheek, pressing me, willing me to understand the meaning of this message. 'Promise me you will let me go, dear. Respect me enough to let it happen.'

I swallow a hard lump. 'I promise, Mom, I'll try.'

'Good girl.'

I cannot explain why her memory was full of passing on history over the last few hours; my mom is so futuristic, a forward-thinking woman. She had made headway in her field of palliative medicine. A patient's wishes were of utmost importance, even I learnt that under her roof.

'I don't want you to be lost with indiscernible grief, dear Olive. I want you to understand.'

'Understand what, Mom?'

'What every parent wants for their own child, dear. To shield their loved ones, from the incurable pain of loss. No parent wants their child to be afraid of death.'

Is she trying to ease my burden. I thought I had kept my anxiety from her this morning. But she knows me, even more than I possibly know myself. Why she has to talk with me about accepting the end escapes me, she is not terminally ill. But Mom feels impelled to have this discussion about final wishes. Funny how we had avoided this conversation until we came to the clinic today. Mom knows I have an unwillingness to think about the inevitable.

'I'm full to the brim with gratitude for having our time together, dear Olive.'

'And I am so grateful for having you too, Mom, for having us.'

We cry in sync.

I speak softly, to comfort my mom. 'Please don't worry about me, Mom.'

'Oh, but I do, dear, more than I worry about myself.' Mom rests back against the pillow. 'There is no book on parenting that covered the chapter of leaving your child by dying.' My body aches in insurmountable jabs of sorrow. I make myself be still, make myself listen to her. 'Sharing how you would like to die, your funeral arrangements, even the simple things like the last dress you will wear.' She wipes the tears from my cheek first, and then she wipes her own tears away. 'Asking the person who you want to be the one to prepare and bathe you, to have possession of the last touch to your being, may be selfish for one to talk about with loved ones but sure, who else would you be discussing these important facts with, an attorney?'

I cry anew. She waits for me. Then the elder continues on the road she had started down on. 'Even when a candle melts, it's still made of wax dear. Our entities are intertwined forever.'

'Ah, Mom,' I weep. She consoles me by patting my back.

'I'm glad my Aunt Peggy asked me to help bathe my mother in preparation for her sending off. But I deeply regret my own mother never discussed this tradition with me, before our time was up.'

I massage my mom's hands.

The rhythmic movement consistent and soothing.

I fear any talk of funerals. But I understand it has to be on my mother's mind coming in here today.

And my parents regularly attend ceremonies now that it was the main part of their social outings. As they had got older, they both talked more about people dying, it was part of their every day. Passing over was normalized. They seemed to be going to funerals all the time. This was the norm for them. I know I have to listen to my mother and respect this rite of passage, but I disintegrate internally.

'I will be close by you, Mom. I promise.' I give her my solemn word. Reverent silence settles with us.

'Love adjoining love,' expresses Mom.

But no one can cover every eventuality, no love is so strong to protect your loved ones from all realities. I know this. Mom could try and attempt to keep the painful moments little ones, especially for me, her little one.

'I will not die an unlived life, dear.'

The words resonate within me.

'Olive, I am ready to die.'

'I'm not ready for you to die, Mom.'

'I know that, dear, and you never will be.'

The truth speaks volumes.

'You're right Mom, I would never be ready for your death.' We recharge in one another's company as the respected agreement nurtures our souls. Our breathing deepens in sync. I could be anywhere with my mom and feel at home. Peace and tranquility transcend in the room. We let ourselves be.

Mom is ready to continue. 'Did I ever tell you I was a mistake?'

'A mistake?'

'Yes, dear.' Mom softly paints the tainted history of her past. 'I went back to Dublin for a long overdue visit. I flew in the kitchen door. Mother was busy kneading the bread dough with dedication, a pseudo-religious daily ritual in her routine. The modern Dublin shops did not cater for the wholesome food that my mother, your Granma Kay, insisted on providing. Endless hours of domesticity were employed to put healthy food on the table. It was her way of providing the only nourishment she was capable of giving her family. Time-consuming labour and the intensive effort she gave to such household details delayed her acknowledgement of the shortcomings to the emotional daily diet she should have been providing. Who needs bread when you are on a hunger strike of love? No food can fill an endless pit of emotional depravity.'

We repeat together a mantra my professional mother brought me up on: 'You can always buy cake but you can't buy love.' We giggle in unison, our private pact against Mom's sad past. My mother's professional working life had rendered takeaways a weekly ritual in our home. But we never went without love. 'Granma Kay was a strong, stubborn woman, with an amazing work ethic. She did not have time for chit chat.' How sad, I think. My mother was a great doctor and a great mother, but not a good baker, we never made cupcakes together, but we went to the best bakeries in town. The butter cream icing swirls, built high and proud, joined our duet as we happily munched, I lick my lips in recall. Simple pleasures that topped my happiness. Now, I got the relevance of her mantra.

Mom continues.

'The minute I entered the kitchen I should have known not to disturb the matriarch with trivial details of a happy, happening life. Mother had more important things to attend to, the oven was preheated and ready, awaiting the arrival of the loaf tin.' And my mom squeezes my hand before continuing. 'Only I was bursting to unload my own little bun, tell my unexpected happy news that I myself was going to be a married mother. The irony of the moment was that it was my own mother I chose to be the first person to share with. Or was about to. With a sharp all-seeing glance from a parent to a child, your Granma Kay noticed me looking flushed and fuller in the tummy and as a mother's right, went straight to the attack. 'Are you pregnant?' scolded my mother in a high-pitched voice.

'Yes, mother.' I remember I gasped in excitement as I told her. 'I am.' Mother abruptly stopped interrogating, but the tone applied was not lost on me. She stood rigid by the solid pine kitchen table. I nod. This is a story I had never heard my mom speak of before.

'Mom, are you sure you want to tell me this?'

'Yes, Olive dear. Let me finish and you will understand me and today a little more. I did not take one more step toward Mother, I could not. The sorrow from her harshly asked question had wounded my very soul. I, the doctor, was incapacitated. Other private torments hounded me at that moment Olive, I will tell you this firstly, then I will tell you about my mistake with baby John.'

Mom's eyes bulge in her head. I can almost see her heart swell in her chest, like a red robin standing proudly rounded on a branch. 'Let me finish this story first. Then the oven bell chimed reminding Granma Kay to turn the temperature down so she distracted herself officiating the knobs and adjusting the dials. After that job, she went to wash her hands not wanting to dirty her crisp apron. Mother turned her back on me and put on the cold water tap. The falling drops mirrored the sting of shame moistening my sea blue eyes. Maybe Mother had forgotten her daughter was all grown up, no longer a child but a married woman. I had done nothing wrong. Opportunities for a mother's and daughter's intimate encounter were always lost to me. Olive, I do not want history to repeat itself.' She grasps my hand, she is so adamant.

But I'm close to Mom, closer than her own maternal ties to her mother, Granma Kay. I only met my maternal grandmother three times in her lifetime. Instead of inclusion, there was isolation for them. We had purposely overcome that link in our history. Mom continues.

214

'I started as usual to justify myself and to do justice to my miraculous predicament. Raw honesty leaves an opening for raw hurt as I found out to my peril. I told mother, 'I didn't mean to get pregnant. It just happened,' and I went crimson, becoming agitated with myself for not acting my twenty-four year old self. I was an adult yet felt like a guilty child. I tried to get a grip and said, 'I mean, it was not planned.' Mother turned around from the sink and clutched the fresh towel, she meticulously dried each finger of each hand. I obediently waited and followed mother's initiative. 'It happens,' replied Mother, and then the lethal injection was administered. 'You were a mistake.''

'Oh, Mom.' I swear, my mother shielded the blow afresh, because her chest dropped. 'What a terrible thing for Granma Kay to say to you.'

'Yes, dear,' Mom agrees. 'And it hurt the more because I have made mistakes in my day. The time is running out on me, that is why I have to speak my mind and tell you I do not want my death to be a mistake too. That would be the ultimate atrocity in my life plan, dear. Olive, do you understand?'

'I think so.' I try to gauge where Mom is going on this. Mom appears to have a premeditated notion of her death. Is this normal? Do all older people have a set picture?

'I do not want the end of my life to replicate the start of my life,' Mom impassions.

'Your death will not be accidental, Mom,' I console.

'No, Olive, it will not be. I know that my death will not be a mistake.'

'I want to tell you something, Mom. Something I have not discussed with you before. I feel the timing is appropriate, based on the baby stories.'

'Go on, dear, but I have more to tell.'

'I don't want to have a baby.'

'Ever?'

'No. Not ever.'

'I see. Right, dear. The timing can be wrong. I have experienced such,' her eyes are sad pools of loss, 'but you may change your mind.'

I can tell Mom is finding symmetry to this fact. She stays perfectly still.

'No … I've opted for the sterilization procedure.' Maybe that was why the clinic gave me the heebeejeebees.

The facts hold center stage. 'I'm not maternal, Mom, you know this.' I just stop myself from including there was no point in Mom passing on her family traditions to me, I am a sole trader and have no intention of having a clan of my own. Everything changes with the passage of time. 'You have addressed such options in your blog, Mom. Personal responsibility; I would not be a good mother.' I encourage the professional dialogue and lift her iPad up from the bedside locker.

'It's your choice, dear. Conscientious decision, I do purport such morality. Have you read my blog lately, Olive? Free choice and free practice have yet to concur in so many areas in the medical field.'

'Sorry, Mom, I've been busy over the last few weeks after my promotion in work, in all honesty the opportunity to flick over your altruistic free medical advice was not my website for chilling.'

'So you said. My site is free,' she jibes.

'I have a surprise on the iPad for you.'

'Mistakes feature in a large percentage of discussions in the blog. Fear, fright around dying, such as afraid a friend will not hear the middle of the night phone call, or going on holidays and not being in the country at the time of death,' lists Dr Lily Tully. 'Needless tragedy. Such frenzy, the heart-wrenching testimonials of guilt when a loved one dies without family around them.'

216

Mom clenches my hand. 'I want you to be with me when I die, dear. We are a mighty pair. Olive-' Mom continues but a knock on the door misdirects her intent.

Today was a day of improbable junctions. Three foreign medical staff follows the tap. I do not care about the specifics of nationalities. Care is universal once they can speak English, all is fine by me.

Our privacy is of no relevance.

'We are going to take swabs off the surfaces in the room,' one explains, stating to us her identity of in-house microbiologist and that they are tracking a superbug to counteract the infection spreading.

'Is this the normal routine?' I enquire.

'Oh, yes. Hygienic protocol is of the utmost importance. 'Once a strain has been detected in a ward, we have strict policies to adhere to. Patient blood samples are needed to quarantine rooms.' Mom tries to rest between the racks of pain rattling her frame, her eyes are heavy looking, too big for her head somehow. The sight of needles is a necessity and a vein is multi-pierced by the second doctor before a strong bloodline is found.

'I've taken one blood sample,' the doctor addresses no one, head down, intent on her job. 'I need three samples.' A second cylinder climbs and fills with swirling bright red blood. It rises and rises, filling my eyes with redness. I feel faint. 'The sample will be sent down to the lab. If antibiotics are required in this case, we will be back to insert a second drip line into the patient. What is this line for?'

'Morphine,' says Mom. 'I require pain relief. We all need a helping hand.'

Consensual agreement enshrouds us.

'Don't be fooled by penicillin,' counteracts Mom to the head down interns, busily writing up the paper work. They don't even look at her.

'Lily.' I speak up on her behalf. 'My Mom's name is Lily. Lily is the patient.'

A nod of confirmation is accorded. While the doctor respects the patient, she has to add, 'It is impossible to recall all the names I would meet during the course of a day and time is of the essence so I could not partake long with tedious formalities.' The look of astonishment on my face insists she explain further. 'We are chasing the tail of the bug, trying to catch and contain the virus.' Modern medicine I understand, if at times I could not respect. 'I admire you, the daughter's tenacity. It was your intent to I.D. this case.'

'Yes, and to give the patient number an identity, to prevent the paperwork being lost within the system. Will you recall the name Lily?'

'I will try. Good move,' and she draws a flower on the file.

Does she think I'm playing a game of chess? I have reservations and condemnation for the well-oiled machine of the clinic. There is more insistence on the large-scale machine than on the care of the individual. They never asked for Mom's name. And the astronomical cost of this clinic. We still have not been topped up with fresh water bottles. Infact our room is undisturbed for the most part. No wonder elderly patients become dehydrated.

Mom is constantly asking for water. I feel dehydrated myself.

The false air and stale environment of the clinic is scratching at my throat. And I'm aware of the stories of medicine being as much about struggling with ineptitude. Human error, the out for all predicaments. Basic errors in medical care can make a mockery of the modern equipment available. 'Put my mom's name on her capsules, not just her numerical digits,' I insist in case of a misdiagnosis.

218

'Lily,' she repeats as she plants the name by memory. 'It is a flower I associate with a funeral.' She has the audacity to look mortified at the slip of tongue.

'The ambience of lavender in this room is soothing.' The other trainee doctor speaks innocently as he registers the old lady looks frail enough and her pulse is falling drastically by the records of the last hour.

The completion of the round is written up and filed and no one bothers with the mannerisms of further conversation. There is not enough time in the day.

'There is so much activity in the clinic that we cannot be ahead of the curve,' the young doctor apologizes for inventions which undid connectivity. 'I have met you but I may never see you or your mother again, it is not unusual to never see a patient twice. That is the sure prognosis of modern medicine,' offers the young, inexperienced but observant and faithful doctor who condones the obvious care by me surrounding this loved lady in the cubicle, among the multiple floors of floating cubicles.

A hasty exit is executed. Not one of them washes their hands. I spot the flashing light on the CCTV. Fine, they are on camera. I turn to her but Mom has fallen asleep. Now what will I do. I text Mike. **Can u come in the clinic** He replies instantly. **Woman do u have a thing for public places?** I reply, **Not usually...I need U**

I'm not dropping my jocks in public locations where we can be seen Mx

I belly laugh. I'm not an exhibitionist. I text **No I need U to DO something else for me. xOx**

I hope he's not getting squeamish on me. Nudity is commonplace to the medical practitioners after all, what was he worried about?

But no, I have another brave plan in mind.

He texts **Ok Meet U at reception in 10 mins**

LILY

Nurse Jean leans tenderly on my shoulder. 'Lily,' she softly speaks, pulling me out of sleepiness. 'Lily.' Focusing my drowsy eyes, I see two people with her, standing at the end of the bed.

'Nurse Jean?' I say, converging my flat brain to inflate.

'Yes, Dr Lily.' She gives me a sip of water. 'You have visitors,' she says and sits me up, adjusting the bed rise. 'The cops are here.'

I wake up as much as is possible, the constant feed of morphine is acting as a numbing relaxant.

'Dr Lily is on strong pain relief.' Nurse Jean looks at them with authority. 'Her words may be mixed up,' she defends for me.

'I will be fine, Jean,' I smile at her but she stands by my side.

The woman, talks up first in a hard tone. 'We have to ask you a few questions, Doctor.'

I condone her professionalism. A little old lady, blood stained and disoriented, in a bed, is not going to prevent her from doing her job. I don't ask her to take a seat.

Let them stand.

The second officer, profiling me and the room, talks next. 'Shelley Dunn was a patient of yours, is that correct?' he asks, straight to the point. He has sized up that this interrogation cannot take long.

'Yes,' I reply. 'Shelley was a heart transplant client.'

'Client,' the female repeats.

'I prefer loyal sentiment for all my patients, case is too cold, client is personal.'

I boldly slap her down.

'So you were her doctor, who attended to her needs?' She steps in a foot, and rubs her finger along the end of the bed rail, in an intimidating manner.

'Yes.' I swallow but a hard stone like lump sits in my throat.

'We have her husband, ranting on, earlier in the station,' and she stops and lets the image grow in the room.

My eyes do not blink and I hold her stare. The male counterpart speaks up. 'Was she treated in this clinic?'

He knows the answer to this question, I'm not a fool. 'Yes,' I reply.

'You became pals,' the female drips with sarcastic imagery.

'Yes, you could say that.'

'You invited her and Drew to a country,' and she pauses, to let sink, 'to a recuperation house, what's it called again?'

Nurse Jean speaks up for me. 'Dr Lily volunteers, in her spare time, to visit patients resting in Round Wood.'

'You own this grand home, Doctor?' she asks.

He watches me intensively.

The female cop puts both her hands in her pockets, giving the impression of waiting.

'Round Wood is the property of a foundation, a charity dwelling.' Factually, my words are delivered precisely, but my head is swaying with concentration.

'A registered charity?' The female prompts me to reveal as much as possible.

'How long is this going to take,' imposes Nurse Jean. 'I have buzzed Dr Doran's on call bleeper, he will be here very shortly.'

He should be here by now, I'm thinking.

They listen to Jean intently.

'Only a few more questions, please,' Jean adds but they seize the gap.

He sits in the chair and crosses his legs, giving the impression he can wait for the medic to arrive.

'And you are in for tests today and resting?' he asks me.

'Yes.'

'Drew claims a misconduct of treatment, a malpractice of sorts,' she drips. 'A lot of patients die in your care.'

'Have you read Shelley Dunn's medical file?' I ask.

Darts of embarrassment colour her cheek.

I continue. 'My field is palliative care. In that area, all my clients die.'

The sharp words cut the air. I am straight to the point and comply. 'I will come in to the station,' I smile. 'After the drug tolerance tests, I'm undergoing, are concluded.'

They look at one another, which one is going to retreat first? 'Thank you,' he says. 'We will be in touch.'

'We will read the files,' the hard woman adds and swaggers out the door, leaving her partner to follow her.

OLIVE

I could have jumped him again as Mike walked toward me. He has an aura of sensuality that is gifted to him. Mike lifts my hand and places a gentleman's kiss on it. We have passed a juncture of no return, too late for me to worry how much I can trust the man, so I procure a partnership of such.

'I have a plan. I need you, to work with me, to execute it.'

'As ever, Olive, you are both direct and brave towards me.'

I take this as a compliment, never registering that such audacity could be a western attribute.

'Due to your ethnic background,' I start, noticing his eyes widen.

Mike's nationality had not been an issue. I proceed tentatively. My next point of conversation could add insult. 'Most doctors at the clinic are foreigners ...' I pause to gauge how Mike is configuring my argument of factual persuasion. He stands still and nods silently. 'I want you to impersonate a doctor and check out Frank's character, by dropping his name among patients and letting them tell us about him.' There, I had said all I needed to in one sentence.

Mike swears under his breath but it is in Hindi so I cannot understand his sharp sentence. He takes my arm by the elbow and leads me away to the side of the corridor, to stand by a sixteen foot bamboo plant. 'Are you mad?' he expresses.

'Fuckin' right, I am,' I reply. 'Mom has told me she has entrusted Frank with her medical records. Why Frank?'

'I don't know.'

'Exactly. No one is spilling the beans about Frank and I know he isn't as pristine as he has all believe.'

'Why are you not asking your mother?'

This time it is Mike's turn to be direct with me.

'I'm just not.' I am aware it is a lame reply and it hits me that the very person I should be asking the questions of is the very last person I can confront. It is easier to be competent when the stakes are not high. Mom is my goddess, on the highest pedestal. How could I dare to doubt her? The rawness of my emotions prevents me from questioning my own mother. 'I'm afraid,' I confess. 'No one in the world could hurt me like my mother because she is the person I love the most.' It was the whole truth. I had to hear the words aloud to acknowledge it.

'I understand.' His face of clarity is reassuring.

'Well, I don't. I'm uncertain of myself,' I try to explain. 'I need to find my ground on the relief team.'
'Before I can talk to her about it.' The straggles of confusion sound illogical to me. I try again to get him on my side. 'This is my way of getting to the heart of the problem.' I look into his eyes, willing him to believe my sincere quest.

'What problem?'

'I don't have answers, I can feel it in my bones, mom is not being honest with me. It's intuition.'

He studies me intently.

'But the logistics of this clinic are not adding up for me today and I mean to figure it out. No one is outlining her treatment plan with me, not the doctor, Paul Doran or the nurse, Jean. Her care team do not include me.'

He says nothing.

'I can do this with or without your help.' My voice sounds stronger than I feel.

'Right then,' he instructs. 'Follow me.'

And we are off, walking down the corridor. 'Where are we going?' I mutter to him.

'To the staff's changing rooms, I will borrow a white coat.' I keep up with his determined stride. 'My coat is back in my apartment.'

'You're studying to be a doctor?' I squeak.

'Don't sound so shocked,' he says, with dismay. 'I have one more year of studies before I graduate legally in this country as a vet to set up a practice. I am a qualified vet in India but I drive a bus in America.'

We stop by a vending machine and Mike asks me to wait there while he ventures alone past two doors and then enters a third one, the staff room, out of my vision. There is so much I have to learn about Mike.

I welcome the joy of that process.

Within minutes he is out again with a medical coat draped over his left arm. Continuing along, we head for the elevators. Luckily only the two of us enter the empty lift. We push the level we want. 'What now?' Mike asks.

'Do you know a female patient? In her sixties maybe, with a huge, curly auburn wig? No old doll could have such thick red hair. I saw her being very cozy with Frank in the prayer room earlier.'

'Yeah, I do actually. Her name is Tia Wayne. Her limousine chauffeur takes a food break with me some days. Why are you looking for her?'

I stall. How much am I going to tell Mike? And then it hits me that I am as bad as the others, giving just small dribbles of information. I will not collude with them. 'I saw Tia tip Frank with dollars in the prayer room, after I witnessed Frank detach Mr P.'s drain line. My gut tells me that old doll knows more than I do and I intend to play catch-up.'

'Wow. I am beginning to think you are a dangerous woman. Are you?' Mike understands very little about me.

'I don't have time for this interlude right now, Mike. Later, babe. Come on.' We both jerk in memory. 'If only,' I smirk and plant a swift kiss on his lips. 'Do you know where her room is?'

But before he can reply, the elevator stops at a floor and the doors open. One doctor enters and places his over-loaded bag, full of files and paperwork on the floor. We all nod silently and then look away from one another. The silent etiquette of sharing an elevator resumes. Before the doors reopen, Mike bends down and with professional, nifty finger-work, he lifts the exposed stethoscope and brings it up under the draping coat, out of sight.

'Thank you,' I offer to the oblivious third person in our company as we make our way to the forefront to exit as the elevator doors chime. I lean into Mike and place a loud smacker of a kiss on his lips and then gave him a hearty slap across his buttocks. The intrigue of this secrecy spurs me on and elevators are so boring. The embarrassed on-looking doctor coughs and looks away from us as we exit with his possession in our possession. The laughter escaping from us criminals is a mixture of fright and bravery.

'Tia Wayne is a heavy smoker,' Mike informs me. 'We will be lucky to find her in the privacy of her quarters.'

226

We approach her room and sure enough, her bed is empty. My courage is starting to fade; it was all going so well, something had to give. The state of the art clinic could not be conned surely.

'I think it would be safer to hide in her room.'

'But what happens if we are seen in there and a nurse asks us why we are there?' worries Mike.

'We can say we are visitors, family even.'

Mike's eyebrows raise a notch. Even he cannot change Mrs Wayne's all-American nationality to Indian heritage. And then, we receive a shift in tandem.

Mrs Wayne steps on by.

We watch her enter her room and close the door, I catch air, I've been holding my breath

'Quickly, put on the doctor's coat and let's go in,' I order Mike and without thinking of how we were going to work as a team, I knock on her door.

'Hello, Mrs Wayne,' I shout the words out. When she turns to me, the bursting boils simmering along the top and bottom outline of her mouth catch me off guard. That's why she is donning an over sized wig, it's to take the emphasis off her lips. How did I miss seeing the swellness in the prayer room, my instincts had been sharp. My shapely mouth curdles in reaction, mirroring her lips distortion. An immediate sense of shame stings my skin, equally burning my nerve endings. Mike tips his weight from one foot to the other, waiting for me to find my mental balance.

Tia Wayne is surprised by another round of medics to her today, she is puffing a cigarette that hangs suspended mid-way from her puss-oozing lips, the thick cloud of smoke stuck in the thatch of dense synthetic curls of her wig. We have her at a disadvantage because she becomes flustered and acts all welcoming now that she has been caught breaking the accommodation rules of smoking in bed. The smell of marijuana nearly over-rides the rot of dead flesh hanging on the tips of her lips' membranes.

'Hey there, doll,' drawls her Texan accent, the steady, cool tone confirming the drug's embrace. 'Medicinal purposes,' she taps the roley.

'Apologies for disturbing you,' intervenes Mike.

The notion of a truce is established because the doctor doesn't scold her.

'I'm Doctor Boyle.'

Is he for real, how did he come up with a name mirroring her diagnosis.

Mike tries to continue, but we are in trouble, 'Wait a minute, don't you drive the shuttle around the grounds?' asks the beady-eyed Texan, the drug-releasing inhibitors vying for the upper hand.

I look at Mike.

She stares at Mike. I cannot help myself, my eyes return to her mouth, my insides sour, I could never be a doctor like mom. I transfix on the abscesses overtaking her lips, smeared in red lipstick, the greenish infectious scales force supremacy and discolor the hue to a disdainful brownish rim. Oh, I could never touch them, there was no way I could treat open volcanic sores like that.

'I do.' His simple answer does not make things any simpler. 'I double job,' he discloses, 'to pay for my medical school fees.'

I breathe easy again.

She knows his kind would not have money normally. Good call, Mike, but it was a short rescue.

'You should ask for tips, others in this place do. They can, and do get you anything in here, if you ask the right crew.' My heart misses a beat, I am getting places. 'I don't want any trainee doctor,' scolds Mrs Wayne.

Mike's cheeks color a little, like I had made them do earlier. I can tell his emotions are heightened. This is a

228

racist attack on his being this time, not a passionate attack.

What this old prune really wanted to say is that she wants a white doctor.

Without hesitating, I speak. 'Hello, Tia. Frank asked me to call in and see you, he asked both of us, Doctor …' a break mid-sentence almost swallows my brain up; I nearly use Mike's real name and search for the makeshift identity he had chosen. 'Frank asked Doctor Boyle and myself to thank you for your kindness,' and I take a further gamble as I gesture, 'To thank you for your fiscal generosity this morning at the prayer gathering.'

The air hangs heavy, screens of smoke hiding us.

'Frank is on his way up to see you as we speak.' And I rattle on as I approach her and offer my hand. I am ready now to be humane to her, my empathic gene keener than my glamorous cosmetic pastime. Before me is a sick lady and this takes precedence over my sick world view of beauty. The very fact of witnessing human weakness all around me today tilts my loyalty from perfection. We are all striving human beings, wrapped in bodies with intricate systems. I did not mean this woman any harm. My intentions are honest, even if my means to the end are astray. 'You are far too generous. My name is Olive and I'm a member of Frank's pastoral team.' The tone of my voice is sincere and clear. 'Thank god.' The old adage of chant does the trick.

'Oh, you work with Frank,' scratches the nicotined voice.

'Yes, I'm a leader on his team, we both are.' I gesture towards Mike who follows my lead.

'Well then, doll, y'all are welcome. Take a seat, honey,' Tia instructs. 'So you won't be examining me, doctor?'

229

'No,' specifies Mike. 'We are here to chat.'

'A chat,' hisses Mrs Wayne.

'Yes,' I intervene, 'To go over, your final wishes.'

'Nobody has time to chat in here. Only Frank. I frighten people away, with this face of mine.' She laughs sorrowfully. 'I was married three times you know, doll, but I was never in love.'

'Not to worry,' I support her. Jeepers, she could not be in love with Frank, could she? I am a little unsettled. I have to stay put and try to decipher what Frank is about in this clinic. I continue on track. 'We are to keep you company while we wait for Frank,' a reflex answer springs, one lie leads to another lie too easily. 'He will be here shortly.'

'That's good,' sounds a relieved Mrs Wayne.

Now that I have established that we want to talk, how the hell am I going to get the answers. I curse my inquisitive nature. 'Frank is a fine boss,' I lie. 'My role is to answer any questions that you may have.' I let a pause fill the space. Did I sound real? My head bursts off my shoulders with the strain.

'Do you volunteer for free too, doll?'

'Sure do.'

'Hah,' Tia squirms. I think the game is up. 'No such thing as a free lunch. In all my wheelings and dealings, everyone is looking for something.'

I change tack and play familiarity to the fore. 'Mr P. is doing as well as can be expected.' I see a glimpse of recognition in her eyes. 'Frank and I had coffee with him, after the morning blessing.'

My adaptation of the truth becomes believable even to me, it dispels doubt. The catchment of emotion in the room alters. Strangely, I settle. The chair with four solid legs grounds me. I let the world, outside these walls fade from me. All that matters is the four by four square foot piece of ground we humble souls settle on. Never would I have visited such a patient. But life had brought me to this point of humanity. Empathy becomes me. I did not give much tenure to the contemplative dimension of the human experience, but this moment is unique. I could not, as the competent numerical specialist, give an accurate estimate of this fact. I just have to acknowledge it. It could be me in that bed, the vulnerable one. I'm due in my own private clinic soon. I made the appointment.

'Good on Mr P.,' Mrs Wayne says tenderly.

This is not the sentiment I am expecting. 'Ye Good on,' I lie, the venture to understand this day spurring me on.

'Not to be on his own,' she opens up. 'That was his final wish.'

'Yes, that was his wish,' interjects Mike, the medical uniform adding authenticity to his inclusion.

I poke further. 'And we take on board all the wishes.'

Tia Wayne stares at me now. She was not born yesterday. 'Is that why y'all let me smoke myself to death?' she asks and looks at the two of us.

Tricky is the word that thunders in my head. I nod involuntarily, playing for time.

'Yes,' confirms Mike, in his acting medic role.

'If that is what you wish,' I reply in all honesty, fully believing in a person's freedom to choose their own path in life and an image of Mom screens in my mind. Without realizing it, my eyes go to the CCTV camera. I stall as surely as the technology; no red light emanates from the camera. Motivating me to pursue, a flash of temper flares. I have to bring that odd character Frank into the frame. Tia Wayne is very impressionable, there is an alluring eccentricity to her. I bet her real name is not Tia, as sure as the hair on her head is not her own. The Texan ticks to a finer keeper, catching my investigative eyes.

231

'I unplugged the machine,' she says.

'Oh. Yes?'

'Can't be caught on camera, doll.'

'Frank is very understanding,' I comment and lean back in the chair and wait, letting his name float around in the trio. But the old doll goes down a different road.

'The botched surgery cannot be undone,' she resounds in regret. 'Frank understands this.'

I conclude she must have had a lip procedure that went horribly wrong. My heart searches within me to move towards her.

'Hollywood lips, I ordered. I had liquid silicone injections, threaded into my lips but the silicon migrated,' and in a swift movement Tia removed her bouncy wig.

I gasp.

Bumps and boils percolate on her skull, larger than the protrusions on her lips, like a volcanic overflow. Irreverently, I stare at her hideous growths, which she takes for concentration and continues to include us in her trust.

'Bloody doctors,' she spits. 'The chemo for the cancer has aggravated the inflammatory process. Hell, such was my luck, doll.' Her voice is raised and angry, spitting with self-criticism and hatred for her fate. 'And the medical team treating me have gone and made me worse,' she spits as she continues. 'Try vomiting with your lips stitched shut.' She makes a zipping shut action across her mouth.

I could have vomited there and then myself, my insides churning involuntarily. I do not feel well in the clinical environs. It is hard to be myself in this prison-like existence. Continual self-questioning of how I fit in this domain is leaking my reserves to a thin dripping continuance, I almost have no pulse. My usual vibrancy dissipates away in here. I do not trust myself to speak.

232

There is another mitigating factor in the room; I am the owner of my own silicone empire, and my breasts are impressive double Ds. Implosions are known to occur over time, wear and tear. I cross my arms and cradle my buxom babies.

Mike's kind manner listens to Tia wholeheartedly. 'Did the swelling happen quickly?'

'No,' Tia huffs. 'That would have been far too easy. The blood vessels grew into the substance and then after the consultants started treating me for the cancer, the boils.'

She ebbs off, the evidence there for all to see. 'The boils started growing, so the doctors decided to operate and the incisions incited the inflammatory process some more. Hell, if the cancer doesn't get me, then the greasy silicone can take a shot cos the docs have had their pop and left me popping open all over my head.'

I try, to offer my condolences, my rationale can not disregard her appearance. I feel the lesser being as I choose to keep a safe distance. Who is the most fragmented? I tango with my morality. Mrs Wayne coughs and her eyes glaze with pain as the burst of output tares a new rupture. I have to look away from the leakage. The odor sticks in the archives of the room. There is no lavender lingering in this room.

'As a doctor I have to advise you the nicotine will aggravate the infections,' offers Mike in a gentle manner befitting a caring profession, his own physiological studies coming to the fore.

I believe him as I listen. He pulls a sterile wipe from the tray on her bedside locker and hands it to Tia, 'you're a sweetheart,' she chats him up, he pulls a second wipe and gingerly treats the area.

'Sure will, doc,' she agrees and winks as she sucks up on another ciggie, and the coughing, puffing and pussing lips mangle.

233

'We do not expect you to pay us,' I try again in a non-confrontational manner but I feel like bouncing off the walls. I am wasting my time. I need to be with Mom, not sitting by the bedside of a stranger. And Dad would be in by now.

'Hell, doll, I paid a few hundred thousand dollars over the years to swindlers and pirates,' she spits. 'That's what I call those plastic thieving surgeons.' She puffs wholeheartedly, the inhalations deepening with her dark anger. 'They promised my lips would be show stoppers.'

'Put in all the medical bills for tax exemptions,' I say before I can stop myself. Re-entering the pastoral mode, I try to filter more details. 'Well, Frank appreciates it. We all do,' I include.

'I was never lucky with men.' She veers off again. I sit on my hands so I would not visibly express my agitation. 'Never gave me any peace,' she continues.

'Peace,' I repeat, nodding affirmation to her, taking her direction as the cue to proceed on the line of final wishes.

'Sure, doll, peace of mind. No one could promise me that.'

'But Frank can?'

'Sure, doll. Frank has promised me peace of mind.' She puffs out the words, they almost get lost in the smoke but I cling onto them. 'And free of charge, I'll be damned with that rate,' includes Mrs Wayne. 'Y'all a bit cookoo in this place?'

'Maybe. Frank can be ...' I search for the words. How was he promising peace of mind? He would be some guru to produce a state of being yet to be captured by humankind.

'Frank is the only person I have ever met who is not interested in my money.

'Yep,' I agree.

'But Nurse Jean has told me I can leave her a token of appreciation. She's a double-dealer that one, more Irish than like us.'

'Fine big girl,' I say.

'Hussy,' she puffs. 'It's not the first time I've heard her requesting monetary favors either.'

'Really?'

'Sure, doll. Mr P. has left her a shit load, something about not wanting to cock block her. What's that all about, doll?'

'Oh, I couldn't say.'

'Can't put a price on life. Do you know she accepted Mr P.'s proposal of marriage.'

'No,' I splutter. 'Is he mad.'

'She had him tested. His sperm was swimming erratically so she declined his offer and his goods. Still taking his money, goddammit. Well, I suppose we can't take it with us. Mr P. has no more need of the dollar. I might tip her, I'll think on it.'

'Yes, you think on it,' I affirm with her.

This lady must have the funds to squander on improvements if she has spent vast money on surgery. The cosmetic wig could have come from a dollar thrift store, resembling pronounced clown attire, but it was probably a hand-made bespoke piece with real hair, costing a fortune. Gold chains hang from her neckline, almost distracted the eye away form her mouth. Those funds her downfall.

Tia is man made surgically grotesque.

'Frank listens to me. He truly listened, without judging me.' Tia's voice is intense, almost deranged with sincerity.

There, suddenly, in one word, like a solid thump of a heavy hammer, I feel flattened. Judging ... I was judging, without realizing it or the implications of my attitude.

Frank had superseded me in the humility stakes. Self-criticism is exactingly personal as it is indelible. At my age, I should not be jaded. My continual striving for perfection, professional and physical, has made me lose sight of human inadequacies.

'The smartest medical heads are running out of ideas. Frank knows if the fags don't get me then he has my permission.' And Tia lights up another cigarette. 'On the inside, my lungs are as engorged with cancerous cannibalistic growths. So, doll, I've signed the dotted line.' And she laughs a sad laugh. 'A deformed geriatric may have to have her last procedure after all.' Puffing earnestly, she fumigates the room some more.

Mike and I glance quickly at one another and then resume our impassive stance of not registering the information with one another so as not to give ourselves away.

But I am internally erupting. What procedure? What would I want? If I was in a no-win situation. Does anyone know what I'd want? How come these people in this clinic are on a different page to me? And what dotted line has to be signed? What permission is given? Mom! 'I have to go,' I blurt.

'Sure doll.'

The door opens. Mike reacts before me. He actually leans in over the bed, bringing his face closer to her face and oozing lips. My stomach churns. 'All looks fine here,' he instigates in the role of a medic.

My heart throbs painfully. I swing my face around to the door, my investigating brain overriding my natural impulse to hide. Lavender balm swirls. Frank. I scream in fright.

Mike doesn't understand why I am so terrified. But I am being affronted beyond belief. Frank is linking arms with another weak soul. He is accompanying another elderly, frail man.

236

'Dad,' I holler.

'I don't want to die in a hospital,' I hear my father, Jim, declare to Frank.

'But this is a private clinic. We will talk about this again, Jim,' answers Frank as they come through the door. 'Everything going smoothly, Tia?' He registers the crowding of her private room. 'Olive – Mike, all getting acquainted, are we?'

Ignoring Frank, instinctively I rush to my father, in giant leaps, I embrace him. 'Dad, are you alright?'

Dad smiles at me and pats my back gingerly. 'My little star.' This fleeting intimate moment passes when he notices other people are in the room and now Dad looks confused, adding, 'Where is Lily?' quickly followed by a blank, unblinking nothingness. I know not to tax him and allow him time to steady himself before I can try and impress on him for coherent answers. I decide to question Frank.

'Why are you with my dad?' I hurl at him.

'Your mother asked me to mind Jim and to look for you,' states Frank. 'Lily did not know where you had gone.'

The truth hurts, as the facts of the situation roll me into a thinner cloth.

His smile is fixed softly. 'I knew you would be in the clinic, Olive, somewhere. We would find one another.'

The syrup of his voice sticks to the walls.

I hold my hands on my hips, to let him know I am a strong contender.

'We decided to call in as we were passing Tia's door, thank god,' and he sets the precedence by addressing me squarely, 'while on our little expedition.'

I am fit to implode from these incessant mind games.

I know I am being mentally restrained. Being enclosed in the clinic has me at a disadvantage. I am on

237

his turf. I refuse to be minimized or made irrelevant. Using my dad as a decoy was clever but I will not be put off. And the dawning knowledge of my father's constant constraints was the closest I could come to understanding the debilitating mind robbing of dementia's memory loss. I have un-joined pieces of information. It is so frustrating. Like losing a piece of a jigsaw, preventing a complete picture.

'Tia, you've met Olive,' confirms Frank.

'Sure have, Frank,' teases Tia. 'And she ain't offering the olive branch.'

I spin in her direction. This smart woman knew who I was all along.

'Olive, your mother wants to have a word with you,' outlines Frank.

It bugs me that he is a step ahead of me today. The clock is ticking. Dad sways, with no warning, he weakens. His feet give out from under him and he slumps to the floor. Frank lifts Jim to the chair but I want Frank to back away. I physically push him away from us. Mike holds me aside and asks me to tread lightly, he does not want to be sued. Tia pours Dad a glass of water from her glass, my skin crawls as I watch Dad bring it to his lips.

Mike apologizes, 'I have to go back to work, I can't afford to lose my job Olive.'

I take three long breaths. The existence of life running along outside this place has become a lost reality to me. 'I'm fine. Thanks for your help… Here,' and I butterfly a soft kiss on his cheek.

'See you later,' he promises.

'Goodbye, Mike.' I cannot commit, there is too much going on in my mind. 'Sit for a moment, Dad,' I insist as Dad makes an attempt to stand up. I do not want Frank keeping my dad company. Then I think. 'Will you take my dad on the shuttle with you?' I ask Mike, he looks bewildered. 'Please,' I request. Mike exasperatedly shakes his head but agrees to take my dad for me. 'I don't know where his minder is gone. Mom hired a helper for today. I will ring my sister, Missy, and insist she comes to the clinic, so we are talking about an hour or so, tops,' I negotiate. Mike nods an affirmation. Frank says nothing, listening intently to the outline.

'Okay, Dad. Time to go.'

Involving two directives confuses my dad some more.

I know my dad misses having an input on decision making points and misses being taken seriously. It was as infuriating as not remembering things he had been told. The worst part of the exposing wrinkles was the assumption of stupidity.

'What was that young man's name again?' Jim racks his memory but it is no use.

'Mike, Dad, and you are going with Mike now.' Mike approaches.

'No, not him. What was this nice young man's name?' Dad points over to Frank.

It is the brink of bad manners as I ignore my dad, exactly what he finds the most disturbing of all. 'Don't worry about him, Dad.' I contend with practicalities, diffusing his enquiry.

Dad recalls it starts with an F, or is it like his name, with a J in it? But that is all he is capable of figuring out. 'Nice young man.'

Frank does not intrude and lets me manage my dad as we exit out the door.

'Take care, doll,' calls Tia after me.

I stop leaving, turn around and walk back to her. 'You too, Tia,' I whisper and place a tender kiss on her cosmetic cheek. 'Stay sharp.' There is no catastrophe, I surmise. This woman does not need my shit today. She entrusts an emotional thank you to me.

We leave.

I measure my father's wise way of coping. Own up to nothing and take no blame, this was my dad's survival plan. And blame no one in return. Quite a fixture to operate by but it works for Dad in his present state. He could easily join and fit in with Mom's support group, because Frank had remained steely silent back there. Registering an opening slot floors me. I stop in my tracks; my hand flies to my mouth to try and suppress the mewling noise escaping me through the gape of my shocked lips. Mr P. Where is Mr Patterson? He must be with Mom.

'Please mind my dad for me,' I plead. 'Don't let Frank have my dad, promise me, Mike.'

'I swear to you, Olive. Your Dad will be safe in my hands.'

'Please, I have to go,' I plead. The men look at me, worried for me, aghast with fear, the reflections on their faces mirroring my angst. 'I will hurry back, Dad, I promise. I'm sorry. I have to go.' I reiterate. Dad nods his head even though he doesn't understand me. My brain is functioning on numerous levels. 'Mike, do you have a pen and paper?' Mike hands me some. I write a point of reference for my dad: In black ink, I commission: DO NOT SIT WITH FRANK. I add this directive to the page and place the warmed piece of paper into Dad's sticky hands.

'Dad, keep reading this and follow my instruction, okay. Do not lose this piece of paper.'

'Okay, Olive, my love,' Dad holds the piece of paper in both his hands. 'I will try.'

'It will be okay, Dad.'

I hug him so tightly I hurt my ribs.

'I love you, Dad.' I see his fingers tremble as they retrieve a similar sized note from his pocket. 'Let me see that, Dad?'

'No. Lily told me this paper was for me,' he stubbornly answers me. Reaching over, I pull the sheet from him, he tightens his grip, and spindly, weedy fingers rip a tear. 'No!' Dad agonizes. 'I promised Lily.'

The mix up is flustering Dad, a child-like innocence, the only redeemable aspect of his mental predicament.

He releases his hold. 'Thanks, Dad,' I reassure him in his distress. In my mother's hand writing, in heavy, gilded print lettering, I read: Follow Frank. Cringing as if my body has broken in the middle, my stature reacts. Winded but not defeated, I rip the page in two and throw in on the floor. Dad starts complaining to me, raising his voice. Mike holds my arm just by my elbow.

'Olive,' he whispers. I turn. The man I had lost myself in gloriously only hours before, still supports me. 'Go do what you have to do. I can take care of your dad.'

'Thanks Mike.' His lean body strengthens me. I place a soft farewell kiss on his lips. 'We are good?' I say to him; he nods. 'But we're in the wrong place and the wrong time,' I say and kiss him, a short, strong command of pureness. 'Just for the hour Mike. I'll be back Dad.' I hug my dad, then Mike, tenderly leads my dad away.

'Quite a girl you have Jim,' befriends Mike.

'Yes, quite a girl. My little star.' The absence of names is of no matter to my dad. Even if he has forgotten my name, he still remembers me, for now. This time is ours. That is all anyone has a guarantee of. I am torn. My dad needs me and my mother needs me. The neat personal compilation where the two of them normally resided together is no more. The pair were splitting apart and pulling me apart in the separation. Now I have to go in opposite directions. The corridors are quiet yet I sense I'm being watched. I look over my shoulder and remember Drew's paranoia, I now feel it.

241

FRANK

'Mr P., you are making too much noise,' I jump up and down in frustration. Mr P. coughs in clumps of three or four croaky clearances, all to no avail, the gunk will not expel that easily.

The fool of a man is going to give me away.

'Take my handkerchief, put it in your mouth.'

He looks shocked.

'For a few minutes,' I say to him. It's the best I can think of under duress, he will have to breathe through his congested nasal passages.

Mr P. is offended.

We do not want to give our hiding place away, so I push his hand up to his face, sternly eyeing him to do as he is told. There are not many spare double rooms in the busy clinic, we cannot risk getting tossed out.

I peer out the door, no cops are on this floor.

'Get up from the wheelchair,' I order him, acting on an impulse.

He tries to lift his weight up off the chair.

I lean in and manhandle him, dragging him to the bed. 'Sorry pal, but we have to hurry.'

Mr P. shakes his head to nod okay.

Pulling the bedclothes down, I easily toss his body into the bed and draw the blankets up around his chin. My handkerchief is soggy and slipping out of his mouth, the chesty wheezes are audible.

I think it - maybe I will pull the sheets over him, but I can't do it, I leave the sheets tucked. If a cop passes this door, he may see a covered head.

Next I push the chair into the adjoining rest room. They will be looking for a wheel-chaired patient, I'm sure Drew has given the cops details, like Mr P.'s medical history and his final wishes, which the old fool illustrated around the bonfire. We should never have duplicated Shelley's and Mr P.'s farewell send-offs on the same evening in Round Wood.

What was Dr Lily thinking? She must have loaded extra work on her plate before the end of her care. Drew knows too much, he's a loose cannon.

Mr P. is waving his hands at me to gain my awareness.

I hold up one finger and mime I will be over, just after I get out of these clothes. 'In a minute, Mr P.' I whisper.

I go into the rest room and start to undress. The cops will be looking for a tall, black-suited man. I strip to my white vest and blue boxers. I tip toe out to the storage wardrobe in the room, lift a clothes
hanger and hang my clothes up. I could not allow them to crinkle, this is an important, official day, for Dr Lily, and for me. 'Thank god.'

I climb into the second bed beside him. He lies stiff and still.

My heart is racing. I feel like I'm shaking but I know I'm perfectly still. My mind maps a plan; if I get caught, I will blame Dr Lily. With what little time she has left, the cops won't have time to tease the in-and-outs of her role. The dead can't talk.

I will deny, deny, deny.

Good plan, I congratulate myself, thank god.

My shallow breathing evens out. My ears are bursting with my erratic pulse. I stare at the ceiling. This is boring. Nothing to do, but wait, for a knock on the door. No wonder the patients befriend me. Most times we talk dribble, the weather, the news headlines, eventually they talk of their illnesses. I listen. I like to listen, it makes me feel important. Soon enough, I can tell if a patient wants to become a client. They make up their own mind, I'm just a facilitator, thank god.

Mr P. must have fallen asleep, he has gone very quiet.

My phone vibrates. Jean has sent me a message:

All clear – Cops gone.

OLIVE

The circumstances of the day are derailing me. My blood is pounding. Marching to her room I decide I've had enough of this bullshit. My mother has morphed into a stranger in this arena. Mothers are not supposed to change over night. I find my mom in a weaker condition than that of only an hour before.

Nurse Jean is attentively caring for her. 'There you are,' she says with a sarcastic Irish humor, stating the obvious yet the truth implied contains not one ounce of truth. 'We were wondering about you,' and she includes my mom in her ridicule, 'weren't we, Lily?'

Now the nurse is speaking up for my mother.

Who gave this staff member guardianship? I refuse to vocally answer the nurse, just realign the hospitable smile that befits a hospital. My relaxed public face cannot mask the dart of pain in my eyes or the tightening of my heart when the daughter in me makes eye contact with Mom.

Mom looks tired as she nestles against a high pillow. Irregular crackling of heavy rain nosily fills the room and the grayness of afternoon showers dulls it. Raising and lowering, the volume on the window panes, is mimicking the heightening and rescinding of my emotions. I have to go to the most frightening, secretive center of my core. I do not like being vulnerable.

How does a child tackle a parent?

'Olive, dear.' Two little words lovingly fill the space. Mom naturally raises her arms to me. I naturally fill her embrace, I cannot help myself.

'Mom.' I nestle my nose and chin along her slender collarbone.

'Where were you, dear? I'm starting to feel weaker from the trials of this day.'

'I needed some fresh air, Mom.' Our honest connection does not have to be censored. 'And to line up the dots.'

Kissing the top of her head, I smell my mother's essence and become my true self, a woman of bravery and individualistic intrigue.

I breathe. If life could stay at one sure definite point then living would be simple. I would gladly sit in this spot forever if it would make the prognosis for my mother better and the dread of our situation go away. Pure intimacy is everlasting peace. I will never forget this moment. My soul sings and rejoices in this precise moment.

My mommy and I.

Pure love.

Disjointed levels of my inquisitive mind fragment me to pieces. I try to quiet my brain and let my heart continue to beat a harmonious melody. But the tempo is quickening, reacting to my stress level. I am ready to take my mother on. The confusing people and this confusing health centre have pushed me to my limits.

'Why are you checked into this clinic today, Mom?'

'Lily is doing just fine,' answers Nurse Jean for my mother. I presumed Jean had left us with some privacy. 'We have administered pain relief to make Lily as comfortable as is possible.'

I had not noticed the intravenous pole and drip, part and parcel of my mother's attire now.

'We have upped the dose to maximum levels, haven't we, Lily?'

'The morphine will do the trick, dear,' cajoles Mom to me.

'Trick or treat,' I cajole in return; Autumn beholds the witching season. We both smile. I'm scared as shit, the season befits my mood.

'We could lend you another white coat or a nurse's uniform,' offers Nurse Jean and I shoot her a glance as she wore a know-all smile. 'If you want to play doctors and nurses again.' Jean's smile hardens. So news travels fast in the clinic. Frank keeps close tabs.

'I saw Dad with Frank.' It was not the term I had intended to use but the outing of my decoy referenced my word.

'Good, dear. I asked Frank to take care of Dad.'

'Well that is not the plan Olive put in action, Lily. Jim's having a great time driving up and down the avenue with Mike,' laughs Jean. 'Jim's a gentleman.'

I shoot a startled look at Nurse Jean. Is she friend or foe? 'Dad wanted to take a spin in the clinic's shuttle, Mom.' I tell a white lie. But I want to have no distractions to put off the dirty deed. I had not counted on the clinical team in my face at every juncture. In the face of adversity I persevere.

I am aware I'm out numbered.

But I'm the daughter of Dr Lily.

'Mom?' I sit upright, still close but separate.

'Yes, dear?' I creak my head and mouth: 'Nurse.'

The professional of old instructs the surrounds of the room. 'Nurse Jean, we will monitor my stats on the hour. I think that is all for now.'

With a respectful silence, the nurse vacates the chair and room.

I stay sitting by Mom's side, so close to one another yet teetering on a terrain that is a million miles apart. It's now or never. I start.

'What form did you sign in the clinic today, Mom?' I start gently but in a direct tone.

The directness is matched in equal calm measure. 'I signed a non disclosure consent form,' Mom replies.

'Was a witness necessary at the signing?'

'Yes.'

I wait for Mom to bring me up to speed and fully disclose the full details of the morning. 'Frank witnessed the paperwork and Nurse Jean co-signed.'

The tone of the conversation is intellectual but if that is the necessary protocol to insist on the facts then so be it. I continue in an exact manner. 'Can I read it?'

'No, Olive, I handed over the form. I can explain the finer details to you. I do not wish you to read this paperwork.' Her words hurt. 'I would prefer to talk you through the contents of the form.'

'Why, Mom? What did you consent to?'

'I signed my name to leave no room for error.'

The air cracks along with the whip of the rain. I am a statue, poised and stiff. I do not interrupt the doctor as she continues. 'The form stipulates I have full use of my faculties today to instigate my final wishes. The procedure - It outlines my chosen medical plan, such as organ donor status.' Mom makes the criteria sound like minor tribulations; a trained medic can think ahead to end-of-life issues. 'I do not want to be resuscitated or to remain in a drawn-out coma, for instance.'

I had not ever thought of these finer details. Why should I? 'What about taking newly-tested drugs on the market?' I want my Mom to take everything and anything that might be a cure.

'Olive, dear, there is no cure for motor neuron disease.' She cements my eyes to her studious face like a practicing consultant, to impart the truth of the matter. Remaining the doctor yet fusing it with her utmost cherished role of a mother. Maybe this was why this day was so hard for my mom, I reckon. As the academic, she knew too much and as the mother, she loved too much.

'Not yet, Mom. There are always headways in medicine. We will find a way. I will not give up, don't you give up, Mom.'

I challenge an identity so strong.

Mom can withstand the condemnation.

'I do not have the luxury of time, dear.' She continues into doctor mode after slipping momentarily into her mothering calling. 'Neither do you.'

The cognitive closure Mom is expressing frightens me, a shocking psychological trait of clarity is in her voice. I hear her mind is set. 'I know how this goes, Olive. It is the first time I have ever wished I was not a doctor, not a mother even,' and a teary throat prevents her from issuing another word. But she holds up a hand to signal I was to let her gain her strength and continue with the momentum. It is her physical strength Mom could no longer be a master of. 'My mind is very clear, Olive.'

What a point to make.

'This horror I must confront you with is about values. Values are arranged in order of importance, when one is placed at the top. Other values such as your rights, are subordinate, I have to dispense with your needs. My needs dictate as the highest value. I know I am right, Olive.'

My mind is spiraling.

The wrong values given the wrong importance can take us to dark places.

I'm crystal clear of thought when I am doing numbers. I play my professional card to get me through this tough conversation. 'Has this become a numbers game, Mom?' I speak pointedly. I have to seek certainty in an uncertain world. This is not my world.

'Yes, Olive. I suppose it has.'

'How long, Mom?'

'Twenty-four hours max.'

I'm stunned. The mathematician in me tots up twenty-four hours in a second. That could not be right. My mother had not just said twenty-four hours to me. Wait, had she said weeks, months? Maybe I had misheard the time frame.

'Mom, you said hours but did you mean weeks or months?' The inquisition deepens. 'You are not that sick.' Bombs burst in my head. What is happening?

'No, Olive. I said hours.'

Mom does not blink. The trained professional could deliver the exact prognosis.

I knew my mother had a debilitating illness, but not this timescale. The room swayed by the strong current I was sailing along. 'What will happen today, Mom?' My voice cascades with my body. My brain remains poker sharp. I will not give an inch, mentally or physically. I do not budge.

Mom does not move an inch either.

The strong, stubborn lineage of our gene pool to the fore, we are freeze-framed. I could be the trained medic now as I hold her eyes firmly in my level of vision. I am cognizant of the reality that my mother has the upper hand technically.

'I'm an advocate of death-with-dignity, Olive,' the elegance of her voice, backing her belief, stuns me. 'I am ending my life. Today.'

'No, Mom!'

A guttural sound hits the four walls of the caged quarters. I feel like a wild animal as I try to reign in my instincts. 'Death with dignity,' I repeat in a heightened voice. There is no beauty in my tone. Crudeness spins. 'Do you mean assisted suicide?' The logic comes to my assistance, like a loaded gun.

Mom affirms my line of thought. 'Yes.'

'Euthanasia,' my head shakes a forcible negative. 'No way. I cannot believe you want to die, Mom.' I travel on a completely different path to where my mom has placed herself. 'You can't be making this possible, Mom.' A coldness of tone surprises me.

We are actually discussing voluntary death.

'I knew you would find this position hard to accept, Olive.'

But I am not paying attention to Mom's words, emotional shutdown cuts me off.

'That is why I have you close to me today. I have been trying to help you understand my decision.'

I struggle to listen to her. Mom holds out her arms to me but I will not go to her. Seeing her in a medical bed flares my distress. This conversation should have occurred well before this place, before this image.

'I chose you to be here, Olive,' she implores. 'It is my ultimate gift to you, to have selected you to be with me.'

'Gift?' My voice has risen octaves. 'Should I be grateful?' I spit. 'Time to live,' I shout, as if I haven't heard her expression of honor to me. 'I want you to live, to stay with me.' Heated slay of words escalate, the urgency of two opposing sides without respectful listenership muddies the waters.

'You have a life. Live it with dignity. That is the gift I want from you, not a parting accolade. You're not terminally ill, Mom.' The words sound irreverent. 'You're not dying yet.'

'Debilitating sickness is mentally terminal, Olive. There is no relief for me. I can see no other way out.'

Her words swarm, the buzzing, prevents me from listening to her side humanely. My mother is putting herself beyond the pale of forgivable behavior. How could she be spearheading such extremist activities? How did I not know? Revulsion, selfishness, anger, I'm not sure which emotion clouds me the most. They are all splattered across my heart. The living can be so selfish in their smugness of good health, there is no capacity for adherence to her beliefs in my inertia. 'What about us? You would be leaving us intentionally.' My intellectual intelligence loses the battle to my emotional intelligence. Suddenly, I am roaring. 'What about me?' I cry out harshly.

'This is about you, you stupid girl.' Mom meets my harshness with her own menace. 'I'm doing this for you.'

'For me?' My voice shrieks higher. Best mother in the world crown will be presented to the scenario next. Demented, I implore, 'I'm the child, I'll always want my mother around. You're asking me to be superhuman. Euthanasia, Mom!'

'I am asking you to be humane. Death is inevitable.'

'Yes, it is about me,' I roar back. 'Mom, please don't do this to me.'

'Olive, you have to know when enough is enough. Life is good for you and your sister. Why can you not see this as a moment of gratitude? To say goodbye. Don't make it only a time of commiseration, Olive. You have a choice how you will manage this.'

'I am afraid of myself, Mom,' my voice shrills to a high pitch.

Nurse Jean enters the room and we both turn to her and say the exact same words, 'Not now.'

The door closes and we let all of three seconds run on before we rush ahead, further meshing our entangled lives. I have to get some leverage. The bodyguards are close by. I'm out numbered. I walk around the foot of the bed. Mom studies me. Wrangling with my thoughts, my hands rake my scalp. 'Mom, you cannot end your life,' I issue; my first line of defense is to control the situation.

'Yes, I can, Olive. Let me be my own person,' implores a mother to her child.

My heart clenches with sorrow as if Mom was gone already. I can see her right in front of me but I feel she is gone. The exactness of her words, the room shadows into grays and dark reflections of the storm.

'I can die today, Olive, and I will.'

We battle on an invisible battlefield. Feet away from one another, on a parallel universe of choice. A piercing cry folds me in two. 'Mom, I don't want you to. Put it off. Please, Mom.'

The parent cannot withstand the agonizing grief surging through her child.

'Try to hear me, Olive.'

Mom cries with me.

I am not empathizing with her grief.

'I don't want to die.'

She cries tears of despair.

'But I will go, sooner, rather than later, for you, for you all.'

I can't help myself, rushing to her side I hug and kiss her, my torment, preventing me from instilling life into my arguments against death, as I cling onto her for dear life. 'Mom I don't want you to die,' I plead.

'I don't want to be a burden to you all.'

'You won't be,' I proclaim in vain.

'Oh, Olive, you are so wrong. The onset of immobility was the victor. I did everything to keep my brain sharpened. Very soon, I will not be able to move, the muscle function will be gone, my voice will be gone, but the pain is still present. I will always be in pain. Do you want me to be in terminal pain?'

'How could you even say that?'

253

'Think woman,' Mom's mantra resounds. 'Thinking is what I am doing. I will need around the clock care. Your dad cannot take care of himself, how could he look after me?'

She plays with me. We stall, each aware of the power we yield.

'I will take care of you, Mom, of you both, I promise.' The reality was as clear to me as it was unclear.

'But I will not be able to speak, to tell you what I want. I can today, dear. Please listen to me, please hear me. Today I have a voice.'

'I want to take care of you, please let me.'

'No, dear.' She grabs my arms with all the might her painful hands could muster. 'I do not want you to. It is no way for a young woman to live. Just as it is no way for an old woman to live.' She holds her hands up to the heavens.

'I can do it, Mom, I can … I will be all right. Let me.'

'Because I love you so much, Olive, I cannot let you,' and she tries to keep me on board. 'I can attest, Olive, I will have no semblance of life. Your apartment will be kitted out to be a nursing home with hoists, wheelchair and a deathbed. I do not wish your place to have such vibrations.'

I recoil in horror.

'You are no nurse, Olive. I know you.'

'Oh, Mom,' I cry.

There is no picture of tranquility, of positive, light flooding lives. No euphoric finale.

Mom says it as it is. 'Eventually, after you are devastated, wretched beyond belief, you will have to accede to the medical attitude and hand me over. I will be back here,' and she lets her eyes fuse with the puke green walls. 'I will be right back here Olive.'

I understand Mom. But I start to convince myself the scenario would be okay.

'The social admission, unable to cope, the humiliation,' she paints a sad picture.

The branches, pulled every way in the wind, skew angrily in no synchronization; we are privy to a bad day outdoors and indoors.

The natural storm will pass.

In this instant, I hate her. 'Do not hold back, Mom,' I irk her on. 'You don't want to deteriorate, it is beyond your remit as a physician to condone it.'

The flash of anger crossing her eyes tells me the truth of matter that my own mother, the acclaimed consultant, would not take responsibility or ownership of. 'Yes, dear, I have sat with dying people all my life and witnessed unbearable pain and miserable deaths. I know a horrible death. You are correct, it is not for me.'

We mattered in the whole scheme of things, that I am sure of. But Dr Lily Tully was operating the schematic turn of events.

'Your dad cannot take all that upheaval, Olive, none of us can. Love does not conquer all.'

'Dad!' An upsurge of pain fills my ribcage allowing me a tight airwave to call out.

'I would have moved to a state appropriate for my final wishes to be-'

I interrupt her.

'To be legal.'

She does not repeat the accurate facts but continues along her own line of thought.

'I could not go across states because of your dad. He has settled and he would go downhill quickly with all the readjustment if we moved up to Washington. Don't you understand I cannot do all of this carnage to you and your dad? Or to myself. I'm important in this decision. I have rights, Olive,' she swears.

'How are you planning this death with dignity?' I lace precisely.

Mom surveys me, gaging the authenticity of my inquisition.

She proceeds, there is no going back for either of us. We will never be the same women before this moment, ever. 'I will clinically overdose on morphine,' and she lifts the drip by her bed. 'The dosage is being upped as we speak.'

I reel, the procedure is active, before my very eyes.

'An ordinary, everyday occurrence in the health field. That way the medical practice of the clinic will not be called into question. These are fine people on my team.'

She never mentions his name, the smell is enough, the room stinks.

'I have mentored such timely deaths throughout my career, Olive.'

I am shocked.

Mom continues. 'Or if I am interrupted.' She taps the line with her finger as she looks straight into my eyes. 'I will swallow a prescription barbiturate that will end my life.' Noticing my confusion of the medical term, Mom leans into her locker and produces a slim bottle. 'This is the lethal dose.' Her outline is specific. I try to remain calm, like my mother. But I cannot. We are of the same lineage, yes, yet different entities.

'You are being selfish, Mom.'

'Ditto, Olive.'

A realization hits me, expanding my anger. 'Am I the last to know, Mom?'

Mom tries to unload the question. She pulls the bed-sheet up, her body language speaks volumes.

'Please don't stop with the hard-hitting facts of the case. Tell me,' I order.

In mere minutes we had gone from being true friends to true enemies. Mom glares at me now.

Maybe it is typical of me to pitch the argument back to my stance but this is my life too that we are talking about. 'Mom, does Missy know of your final wishes?' And here was the scenario every parent dreads to be put in, and the scenario a child wants to clear, the sibling dilemma of who is loved the most. I can see the color draining from her face as I answer for her. 'I'm the last to know.'

We have gone way off course. I should be listening to and not interrogating my mother. To accompany my dying mother, I should be truly listening to what she is saying, without judging her intellectually and without upping the emotional tension. To listen and do nothing more, forgetting about myself, is the most difficult thing. I am the daughter, not the medic.

Mom we should have been friends in the dessert.

'You have this all wrong, Olive,' cries my mom. 'What you don't know can't hurt you,' she advises in the medic tone. I know she is not acting as a mother on purpose, avoiding areas, damage limitation. She is a trained doctor after all. 'I asked of you to be with me, the ultimate pinnacle of me, an accolade to bestow on you.'

'Please,' I reiterate, irony calling upon to spare me my excruciating pain. 'Don't add insult to injury. You told Dad even. Mom, are you using us as a guard against your own fears?'

'That is preposterous,' Mom howls. 'You are the most like me, Olive. She holds up her fist, a pump action of solidarity. 'Intelligent, competent. My greatest adversary. I knew you would not want to let me go. I truly love you, Olive, dear. That is why you are here today. I give praise before I take my leave.' Mom lists the evidence. 'But that is also why you are the last to know.'

She places her hands on her head, almost to clear it to persuade and win me over. 'You are my beautiful, courageous girl,' and she brings her hands together in a prayerful motion. 'I knew you would want to save me more than anyone else in this world. I just knew it.'

This is a time for supporting silence, to meditate, pray and love. Maybe it is the betrayal and the displacement I feel, but a force of nature incites me to defend the life we have together, that is still pulsing in my mother. I am not ready to lose my parent so why should I? Existential evolution drives me on.

'You always said a doctor is the worst patient,' I explode. 'I think you are not capable of making this serious decision.' And the warrior, my mother knows me to be, cannot concede. I continue to fight for her life. Our raised voices bring the nurse and Dr Doran to our door. 'I can't let you do this, Mom.'

'Don't do this, Olive. Please, Olive. I do not tell you how you should live. Do not tell me how I should die.'

The words sound strange, even to me.

'We are both intelligent adults. I do not critique your al la carte sexual appetites or your lack of maternal genes. I would never offend you and your choices so why insult me and be offensive just because I'm an old woman. You made a decision to mar your future.'

I fuse my anger to prevent a spark of destruction. I want to slap her, my fists close tightly.

'That is a permanent invasive action, Olive. It is your choice because it is your body. And I am proud of decision making medicine, I always have been and always will be. Support me.'

Mom clings to every tenet of persuasion. 'This is a free world, do not be repressive. I brought you up to be a self thinking independent woman, Olive. You are censoring me.'

The medics freeze, unsure when or how to tip the scales in their favor.

'You play unfair, Mom.' I wrestle with my conscience. 'Do not use indication of age as a prerequisite of authenticity. I will not scratch your back because you scratch mine, Mother.'

'Don't kick me when I'm down, Olive.'

'Emotional blackmail won't work this time, Mom.'

'Such derision,' Mom fumes. 'Have I raised a coward?'

'Oh, please,' I slay. 'You were cruel today to allow me to doubt my own mind, Mom.'

'You will ruin my reputation and the work of these fine people. They will all be implicated.'

All heads lock in on me. If they could, I would be restrained on the spot by this cultural inoculation.

'You will regret this, Olive, until the end of your time.'

'Quite the orator, Mother.' The hair on the back of my neck stands to attention. Forever the optimist, I devise a game plan. I am not to be stopped. Why had I not acknowledged her self obsession before now? I cannot think of my Mom's legacy or her eulogy. 'I'm ringing our legal advisors, Mom, to put a stop to this lunacy,' I declare.

Feeling resentful too cruel an ending.

I turn away from the end of her bed. My body tries to keep up with my racing mind. Embattled, I go to flee from her of my own free will. 'Don't you dare to pre-empt to know how I would feel, Mom.'

Mom tries to get out of the bed, but the line, the medical assistance she is partaking of has her strapped in, the drip line apparatus restricts her freedom. She is tied down; this hostage drama a symbiosis of reality. I hear my mother call out to me.

'I'm doing this because I love you, Olive.'

'And I'm doing this because I love you, Mom.'

My departing words ring true.

Spasms in my blood vessels feel like they are bursting. I fled from her room. Then I see it, the solitary wheelchair with the solitary occupant assaults me. I smell the lavender. Frank is sitting with Mr P.

'We were waiting to go in,' he has the manners to look mortified, 'to see your mother, but I heard you. We stayed put, out here.' Frank squirms guiltily.

'Stay away from my mother, you mad fucker,' I snarl.

Mr P. makes no comment, no reaction at all. 'Mr Patterson,' I warn vehemently, 'look after yourself.' I'm about to turn away. Then I know. His rigor stance. He is dead. Frank sits placidly beside him. There is no professional to be seen, all is like a ghost ward. Frank has free rein. 'Did you get him a doctor?' I hurl at the ever-caring companion.

'Olive,' he answers me respectfully. 'Mr P. only wanted to see your mother, she is his doctor, he wanted only her. So we waited by her door.'

Tears sting my eyes. Mom is so revered in here by these people, her friends.

'I did not disturb you,' Frank adds for my attention. 'And I stayed by Mr P.'s side. That was my promise to him. He wanted us here with him, that was his final wish, his perfect imperfection. We were all close by for him, thank god.'

Now I comprehend the meaning of Frank's sermons, his simmering orchestration.

LIARS.

Even nature's lavender wilts and a pungency remains. All I can see in Frank is disgusting, worming images. This clinic is like an open ventilator for Frank and his aura. He is a super spreader, a virus in the system, that hides in his host body and can jump across barriers - age, sex, race.

The frailty of living Frank's domain.

He has been seduced by his art. 'We all do the same thing,' he continues to badger me. 'Do not bring out the beast in me, Olive.' I am stunned. 'Stay with your mother, Olive. Nothing will be the same if you walk through that exit,' he plots.

My breathing hurts my ribcage.

'There are pockets of existing, out there and in here. Every era is afraid of death.' He tries to instill a line of thought in my mind. I don't move. He continues toying with my emotions. 'Stay here.'

A sixth sense to leave propels me. I move, and walk away. Just as I reach the door, I turn and take a picture on my phone of Frank by a dead man's side. I'm going to nail this guy if it's the last thing I do. I send on the image to all my contacts. The day is almost over and I have not been in the sun. I would forget all I have witnessed today, as if it never happened, unless I have backup. I hear Frank's final reply.

'Olive, you always had the measure of me.'

He frightens me with his ministry. He is feet away from my mom. My heart hurts, more than my lungs, I push my physical boundaries. Mental, emotional hemispheres stray, off kilter in the universe, I travel solo.

LILY

Olive is right. I have years left in me. That is not the argument I'm pursuing. I don't wish to be incapacitated. Why should I be beholden to anyone? This is my life. I've lived it well and I will die it well.

Lifting the dial, I monitor the flow of my drug, morphine. An overdose is acceptable, a lightness of lifting, flying off, will soon overcome me. I will be unconscious, the poisoning will drown my system. A few hours tops.

I've held this medical belief since before I graduated. One cannot explain a belief. How did I expect Olive to agree to my belief?

The twelve hour shifts tire the mind, body and soul. I sat with the dying.

Graciously, I did my best. I'm a good doctor.

A practitioner, who can see the evidence right before their eyes, even if a patient cannot detail the ailment, is a doctor. One old man still travels with me on the road. I sat with him, held his hand and asked him to work with the nurses and me. His body was covered in blistering sores and infected oozing ulcers. We marked him with the needles and points of the tubes we pushed into him, opening his skin at multiple junctions.

The unfortunate man, he took my hand and brought my hand up to his food tube. We were force feeding him. Placing my fingers on his line, he was too weak to fight. He had spent the hours of energy he could muster, continually tugging at the lines, often pulling them out.

I could see it in his eyes. He was asking me to help him. And I did.

The doctor in me graduated that day.

In my opinion, if I did not want it for myself, how could I force my will and the will of the medical arena on a poorly victim, the patient as we labeled them.

I've sparked Olive's reaction, exactly what I did not want to do. I've set the blazing fire with fuel, there is no telling what she will do.

I'm on my own.

Exactly what I did not wish to happen.

Tears flow down my cheek.

I lift my cell phone and ring Jim.

His phone rings out. Where is he? I text him.

Sirens shrill. I hear doctors running, a sound I hear in my sleep. I know chaos.

Dr Doran calls in for the last visit.

I adjust my morphine strength, dialing up the dosage.

My doctor helps me into bed.

O L I V E

Calling my sister, I warp with disgust, I can't curtail my anger. 'Missy, you bitch,' I screech down the phone as I push through the exit doors.

Freedom of sorts.

My tears melt in the pouring rain, drowning me and drowning my voice.

'Olive, listen to me, listen to me-' Missy begs.

'No,' I demand. 'You listen to me,' and I roar louder. 'I will not let this happen. Do you hear me?'

'I hear you, little sister.' The quiet endearment makes me howl, the breeze snips my sounds away.

No one is aware of my turmoil. Strangers pass me in my strange life. 'Did you hear our mother?' Gently Missy cries down the phone too. 'This is what Mom wants.'

The flow of tears floods our connection. 'Olive, this has been terrible for me. I've known for weeks. Imagine a person disclosing a suicide intention to you,' she gulps to continue. 'And you cannot stop it. I've tried to reason with Mom too. I need her in the next few months, I have four times the trouble, occurring for me,' she blabbers on, 'I'm living in hell today.'

A clump of my hair comes away from my scalp, I had no idea the force of my own strength as I twist my hands through my hair. I do not feel the pain, only witness the strands in my hand. 'We have to do something.' My mind searches for options. 'We need to stop her Missy … I need to stop Mom dying.'

'Today we will all die a little.' Missy speaks in a rehearsed manner. I had forgotten she had more time than me to digest this horrific situation. She was prepared, ready for this insanity.

'Are you in agreement with Mom, Missy?'

Hallowing winds swarm, yet I definitely hear her say, 'No.'

And that is it, I have to take action.

'Olive, I could not go there, to that place today. I have to take care of myself in my predicament.' Then Missy reaches out to me again. 'Olive, be very clear about this. I could not be there today to condone this behavior. But I do understand why our mother is taking this next step. Were you reading Mom's medical blog.'

'Why?'

'After the conference in Luxembourg.'

'What?'

'Skipping the details of the historic imperial square and the best frothy cappuccino in Europe, new and old world discoveries converging, her testament is very altruistic. She has been building up to this point for quite a while, Olive.'

How could I not have known the outline of her proposition or the backdrop to it? 'That medium was for questions to be poised and a professional doctor to voluntarily answer queries,' I say. 'Mom said it was to keep her brain ticking over and to be of service to others.' A primal roar screams from my lips. 'I had pushed her to start that blog, to stay in touch with the real world. But not to reset the settings of medicine.'

'Please, Olive, calm down. Where are you now?' Missy's sympathy enrages me. My mind explodes, I ignore Missy's fussing. Mom had a safety net all along, a back-up plan. I've seen the barbiturates. I instruct Missy as to my course of action. We as a family could stop our mother.

'Missy understand I have to get back the time with our mother?'

'Of course, this is why Mom wished for you to be with her, right to the end today. She specifically requested you to be with her Olive,' and Missy sounds forlorn, searching for sympathy, 'and not me.'

Now I am against my sister and my mom. I can hear the unspoken words.

'I know that.' Bellowing with distress, I add, 'But this is not a competition sister. Will you help me?'   The silent pause is my answer.

'No, Olive. I won't.' I lost my sibling there and then. 'I think we should do as Mom asks of us. We should respect her final wishes.'

'Fuck you,' I stomp. 'You never let me be equal to you, always the big sister. Well, I will not do as I am told anymore by you, Missy.' I am screaming; we should have been talking all along. My fists curl, I would have throttled her, shaken her to come to her senses. My mother knew that too. She planned for me to be on my own. It was all masterminded. The wet cell phone slips down my neck, the curvature of my catch angles the phone over my heart. I can hear my sister calling out my name as I hang up, running along the avenue.

LIARS.

My chest aches with distress. I dial Alistair Winthorp. Please pick up, the ring tone razzes onto its third calling. Our trusted family attorney picks up. 'Yesssss,' I wheeze, out of breath. 'I, Alistair, Mom is in the clinic with her team ...'

'Who is this?' asks Alistair.

266

'Olive. Dr Lily Tully's daughter.' Every word stretching my diaphragm to the max. 'Hold the tee off,' I hear him say down the line.

'How can I help you, Ms Tully?'

'The clinic. My mother, she's sick.' I can barely get out a full sentence. 'Her consent form-'

In quick, successive points, he clarifies, assuming I can't speak because of my lack of understanding to the process. 'Yes. The firm has Dr Tully's paperwork. Your mother came into us and updated her will only recently.'

'No,' I interrupt him. 'My mother is killing herself.' My voice falters. 'Today.' I dig deep for air. 'In this clinic. Right now.'

'Olive, what are you telling me? Does she have a firearm on her?'

The waste of time is frustrating me, my hands plead to the sky for reprieve. 'Yes, but she gave the gun to Nurse Jean.' I know I need to get help. Maybe I should have called 911 first. 'Do I call 911?'

'What for?'

'My mom is commissioning her suicidal death as we speak.'

'Good Lord,' he flusters. 'Are you sure?'

'I have heard it from her very self, the doctor.' I flood the mouthpiece with tears. 'I've seen her lying there.'

I'm a wandering soul as I waiver on the avenue.

'Oh my, I'd no idea.'

His tone is professional and inquisitive. 'The paperwork Dr Tully signed off on was to donate her body to medical science & research.' And he exacts, 'I oversaw the documents, they are in order. I have a signed affidavit from your mother stating that she has freed herself from the fetters of religious divides, I never purported to any illegal barriers.' He pauses. 'I assumed this covered the ownership of her dead remains, the end

267

of line, not the means to the end.' He speaks so logically that I lose my grip and implode.

'They are not in order,' I yell down the phone. 'I've seen paperwork in the morgue.'

Alistair is exact in his manner because he has no emotional tie to this afternoon's events. 'Olive, I have accommodated signed legal documents from your mother instigating her knowledge and consent of medical trials but I had no idea of these proceedings.' Alistair progresses, there is no duality of clients. 'The claims have huge ramifications,' he explains to me. 'Who is the instigator?' I am asked and then it dawns on me.

'Frank,' I answer.

'Frank who?' my legal expert asks.

'I don't know his second name,' I reply.

'The culprit could remain under the radar then, Olive,' notifies Alistair. I feel so stupid and angry. Why was Frank only ever called Frank?

LIARS.

How I was played.

Alistair advises. 'We have to cease the clinic's operational status immediately. If individuals are difficult to identify it is the only way to halt the procedure of euthanasia,' the legal counsel continues. 'The libel arm to this action is of serious magnitude,' states Alistair. I give him my assurances that the deeds of a new penthouse would cover the costly implications of bail.   'Euthanasia? You are a hundred percent sure?' The professional assesses his reputation is up for summation.

'One hundred percent,' the expert in me tallies, the daughter in me wails, pre-empting my mourning. I am trying to coherently work with the legal conversation; my body is dancing a tango in front of the oncoming traffic. I have to reel my brain in as Alistair quizzes me.

'You can give witness to these procedures occurring in the clinic?' he enquires. I tell him I have seen the lethal liquid stored in Mom's private room in the attendance of medical personnel. And that she is working under the radar by over-dosing on the painkiller morphine. I wished now I had stolen it, I tell him, but he assures me they would have more in storage. He gives me an address. 'Meet at the nearest judge's rooms in the courthouse. Your personal testimony, Olive, before a judge would be necessary to succeed with your case.' The speed of his mind accelerates my workings to electrifying output. 'Olive, we do not have a lot of time here,' he states. 'That is why I need you to stand in front of the judge. Hurry, Olive.'

'I'll go as fast as I can.'

Alistair advises sending a private investigator on his books, Megan Toner, to check out the clinic in my absence and build up the case. I agree. We are to meet at the courthouse.

A cold shiver runs down my spine. Polar coldness steams through my burning veins, my physical body at odds with my emotional entity. Intuitively understanding I am skating on thin ice, I am only one person, with a multitude of tasks. Mom had always had a desire for her professional advancement as I was growing up; as an impressionable young daughter, I had no idea how far her progression would take our family.

I am in a deranged tizzy. Dad and Missy have a timidity of heart whereas Mom and I are the adventurous ones. Using the law of probability, specialized mathematics for estimating the uncertainties, I reckon I have a fair shot of success, of staving off this fear and dread hounding me, if I can get to the courthouse. My brain searches for answers. If

269

only I had been more intuitive and not rational. I had been separating the trivial from the important.

Deep down I can tell my instincts were shrieking. Mom had told me this support group allowed her to recalibrate. Why had I not listened? Why had I not thought ahead? Mom had even told me she was proud to manage her death. I was with her today as she prepared to pass through death's door. It was grotesque, to insult my innocence as such. No respect was offered to my cognitive ability by any of them. Visceral anguish doubles my body in two, like I've been punched. The events of this day are going in around in circles. I push on, speeding up events. I don't have time for this pause. I have to go. I should not be here still.

I'm doing two things at the same time, leaving her and thinking of her. A primal wail escapes my lips, I hurry, realizing sabotaging the judge's meeting is not an option. I wrestle with the wasting of time, it is causing me untold distress. I'm terrified. My Mom is going to kill herself, the words are so loud in my head.

The rain is coming down fast, matching my acceleration. The insane pull of opposite forces, life or death, mirrored in the duality of intent in this supposedly safe medical world, compounds my fear. Paradoxically, I am running from the building in order to run back to it. I am told to love and let go at the same time. I have to leave here to go there, but I want to be back here. The upheaval of the crossed wires is disheveling my controlling nature.

I am fighting with myself.

More haste, less speed is the perfect cliché as I rummage in my bag for the car keys. I intentionally drop the bag and its contents out on the ground to hurriedly find the keys. I am putting my lipstick, cell phone and wallet back in the bag when I decide to just leave my items with the tossed bag on the sidewalk. I only need my phone and keys. I am wasting precious time. Mom, Mom, Mom, my inner voice cries.

Frantic, I cannot be sure what level I had parked the car on; my brain is mush as it tries to assimilate the traumatic itinerary continually reeling in my mind. I nearly turn back. Frank, with his obsessive death disorder, is too close to Mom and Dad. Hunger claws at my insides. Crying, I try the first floor in vain to reach my car. Neutral passersby go about their own business, seeing me but ignoring me. I scream to the echoing chamber, 'Why are the forces of nature working against me? I need assistance not obstacles. How many bloody levels are in this cement jungle?'

I blaze with fury.

I'm having a nervous breakdown. People scuttle out of my way. Choking on my tears, blinded almost as I wobble, I continue in earnest. In my mind I am consulting with the judge, my brain runs over my demands. A fine balance, I have to keep a fine balance. Volumes of words clog my head as my soul swells reminiscently. Arguing my case in preparation for standing before a judge, plays out in my drama. Multiple picture frames are screening in my mind's eye. I run the cement steps, pounding off their surface, and land on level two, barely able to breathe.

The irony of time wasting my time.

Pushing the alarm button on my key set, my car sirens loudly and signals its position. Without reserve of energy, I race to the car, my side throbs with a painful muscular stitch. I ignore my physicality, my anxious strength coming to the fore. I drive like a Formula 1 entrant, speeding down the tightly twisting car park, turning the circular bends at speed, taking revenge on the building for having held me captive too long, now it is my time for payback. My exit cannot come quick enough. The release barrier does not lift fast, I'm

271

impatient with life, and life is impatient back, I clip the roof of my car off the rising bar.

The tyres viciously hit the angry curb as I make the last turn out of the car park. I look at the time, the clock confronts unabashedly.

Bad decision. Bad choice.

'For fuck's sake,' I screech. I speed up. The car does what it is told and follows my lead. The engine growls as I put my foot to the floor and max on the accelerator pedal. The road sign reads 30km zone. My personal time zone is at least treble that.

My car speeds onto the avenue. My phone shrills. Pushing the buttons, my speakerphone joins in the action. 'Where are you now?' Alistair's sharp exact voice masters the sequence.

'I have left the car park, I'm on the avenue.'

'Get moving then. The judge is not happy to be kept waiting. She was just finishing up for the day and has agreed to wait for you.'

'Yes, Alistair. I'm driving very fast.'

'I have emailed and texted the address of the courthouse to you,' issues the legal tone and gives succinct directions.

I declare, 'I'll be there.'

At the same time I manoeuvre a bend on the avenue.

'I've taken the liberty of hiring a separate medical expert.'

The idea jars in my mind, will I be placing my mother in legal jeopardy?

'Right.'

The automatic response was agreement.

'Megan Toner, the private investigator, is the best in the business, is minutes away from the clinic. I've outlined she is to stalk this Frank fellow and not let him out of her sight. It does not help we don't have his full name.'

Good idea, I register, overtaking a car moving way too slowly for my agenda. 'I have a snap on my mobile of this guy Frank.'

'Good. Send it to me.'

'There is a dead old man, Mr Patterson, in the wheelchair in the shot. Frank is distinguishable by his black head-to-toe attire and he is a heavy set fortyish geezer,' I spit the term, my spittle hits the windscreen, obstructing my vision. 'Hell,' I howl.

'Excuse me?'

'No, that was not for you.'

'Okay, I will send it onto Megan. You have her number, I forwarded it to you, on your cell phone. Olive, I do not mean to alarm you, but Megan asked for permission to gain entry to your mother's private room. We are sure this Frank fellow will be found there.'

I get a fright.

Will I stay and protect my mom? Should I be driving off? 'Right,' I answer through the haze in my thoughts. 'Room thirteen.'

'Hurry,' he says, 'as if your life depended on it.'

'Yes,' I shout, too loudly, panicked.

He hangs up.

I'm shaking. I have to grip the steering wheel to hold the wheels of the car steady. Should I be leaving my mother? The P.I. will stop any harm, I hope. One eye on the road and the other on my phone, I have to send the shot of Frank to Alistair and Megan. Freeing up one hand is to the detriment of the other, I miss a beat. Dizziness, my blood sugars diluted by the lack of a meal today, I sway due to no sustenance in hours. The front tyre I let air out of now retaliates. Crying, I agonise to the universe. Unknown to me, I was driving Mom to her death today. Her engagement ring catches my eye. I continue to push myself to the max. 'Fuck,' I scream. My last sex video is forwarded accidentally to Alistair as I

273

seek the recent images. I send the snap to Alistair's details. I have no time to delete the video. I'm half doing everything correctly. I press the screen on my cell phone, Mom's voice recording plays on the car system, booming words swirl in the car - 'I love you Olive.'

I'm thinking too far ahead, to see what is right in front of me. Drew. His silver, battered vehicle, swerves across my lane to obstruct me leaving. I instinctively react and turn from the lane.

'What the-'

DO NOT ENTER

Dark, bold words register in my brain as they whizz past by my car, slitting the directive from my vision. Realisation dawns. Too late to react physically, mentally I have the scope of it. How strange, yet clear. I can see it all, in slow motion. The earth, with the limitations of time, spun out with possibility.

On the wrong side of the road, my vehicle pursues life itself. My intelligence overtakes this instant motion and can pause, rewind, then play on the catastrophe. It unfolds. The clarity is striking.

Too late to turn the physical restraints of my arms and brain to work as teamwork. The shuttle, at the stop sign, strong and steadfast, grinds my vehicle to a pulp. All their horrified faces, bright, in the warm enclosure of the shuttle are in my inner eye. I smash into those poor innocent people. It registers, I'm driving myself to my death. And the loss I feel is not for me but for them. I pray not to offend another and take their precious time on earth; all of this I do in a nanosecond.

I don't feel chaotic, I feel emotional. The emotions stay with a soul, imagine that. Plato said every soul returns to it's own star. I feel light - A flash of headlights, an explosive bright beam blinding me, then sudden darkness, a blank effect similar to falling asleep, the unconscious reigns.

Physical body markings with unique engravings slice in my flesh. My soul indents, responsible for my actions, but I feel as light as a feather. The surety is pristine in my being, as a collage of fire, smoke, and broken glass cements me eternally to my distraction. 'Olive,' I hear Mike shout before the crunching metal claims dominance.

An internal equilibrium of energy guides me.

Piercing pain sears through me, then, a contrasting numbness. Nothing. I can feel nothing. Did I imagine the pain? Bare slits, my eyelids strain to open. A glint of emerald catches my eye. Mom's ring is on the ground. A dismembered hand lies there, with the ring on it. Is that my hand cut off from my body? Blackness again, my heavy eyelashes webbed.

Mom.

I try to call out.

The silence is louder than my voice.

My tongue is gritty. I can't speak. I can't move. How did I let this happen? I was fighting for life and I've instigated death. Such heartache, it's almost not human this tortuous turmoil. My brain is taking over bodily functions, assimilating.

Mike.

I hear his voice, full of excruciating pain.

Cruel, only my ears will work for me, my body sleeps. Payment for my destructive deed, a pound of flesh - The Merchant of Venice resounds. I hear the screams, sirens, and the chaos in my motionless entity.

This must be hell, my personal inferno.

I burn. I want to lift my head. My ear is gurgling blood, moist liquid inlets trail down my cheekbone, scorching red. Black dots grain my eyeballs and then they go red. My eyes are red.

His demented agony rests on my hair as he roars for help.

275

Mike, you are alive, give praise. I try to move to him. My arms, legs and body will not respond to me. I beseech the heavens to have mercy.

Mom. I want my mom. She is my safe haven, I remember. Was my safe haven. Where is the beam of light I have heard of, and seen in the movies?
My eyes are swivelling in my head. Mike is calling my name over and over.

Don't cry, Mike ... Please don't cry, Mike.

He pleads to the gods. I wish he could hear me. Why can't he hear me if I can hear him.

I'm sorry ... It's my fault ... I was driving like a mad woman.

He must be kissing me, my face can feel his gentle touches. His lips are reverently warm.

Mike, I did not mean to do you or others harm...

Mike answers 'Olive.'

Yes.

'Olive. Stay with me.' He pleads with Hindu goddesses. 'Yami, Jai, Sai Baba. I will do anything. Anything. Oh, please Asura. In your all mighty wisdom. Please.'

Please Mike, help me ... Bring me to my mom ... I want my mom ... I have to say goodbye ...

'Let her live. Oh live, Olive,' Mike pleads.

I pray to the gods - Leave my mommy ... Take me ... If it is someone's turn to die today ... Take me.

Mike's screams ricochet off the concrete buildings. The mangled vehicles reflect his distraught heart, his mental anguish overtaking his physical haemorrhaging organs. 'I could run from here. I could make it, Olive,' he tells me.

I want my mom ... I try to tell him.

The chill, Mike, I'm so very cold.

Everything stops, even my breathing. My world is dying. Mike, in my stillness, rests his forehead against

mine. With all my will I try to squeezes his hand. I can't.
Mike kisses me. 'Easy with her,' I hear him instruct. I
feel myself being lifted again and I can hear the medics
take over. I smell the scent of essential oils.

Help, Mike ... Not this place, not the clinic ...

I can hear Frank's incantation of prayer over me.

Don't let that fucker Frank near me.

Everywhere I turned today, Frank was there. I grin
with the crazy concoction that in the grip of death,
complexity still haunts a person. Intelligence must be
immortal? If I could use my hands, I would gladly
commit a crime myself and finish off this menacing
maniac. His syrupy tone seeps into my skin.

'Mike, we are here for Olive. We have a part to play
in her time of need,' Frank intonates. 'Thank god.'

I can hear the medics direct, 'One, two, three. Lift.'

*****

The pain comes to my senses. The surgeon's scalpel
unleashes brazen clumps of skin, they peel me back
layer for layer. Extremes of nerve endings zing in my
brain. Warmth again. Who would think? Hot, cold. Hot,
cold. Happier now, I'm warm at last. I drift, ecstatic in
my lightness and blissful recollections.

'Tiny variations little one.'

'Dad, show me again.'

'Peek through the lenses, dear.'

Dad lifted me so my eyes were level with the
telescope.

'Can you see the star?'

'Yes, Dad.'

*'That's my girl, my little star. The star has changed since
we looked at it last night at bed time.'*

'How come, Dad?'

*'The light has to travel back so far, the light must travel,
such a very long way, before we can see it, that the star has*

277

already changed.' Dad spoke plainly and simply for me. He so enjoyed my wonder, he always told me, just as the stars were wondrous.

'Wow,' I gasp.

'The variation of the star is so small, little one, like you, and is barely measurable but the variation is there.'

'How do you know that, Dad?'

'Because we are all variations of life, my little star. The sensitivity of the instrument such as the Hubble Space Telescope has discovered this new discovery.'

'Wow. You are so smart, Dad.'

'Yes, I am and don't you ever forget it.'

'I won't, Dad. I promise.'

'But I am not as smart as you.'

He pinched my nose. I can almost feel it now ... Funny my last recollections are of life's variations and of my Dad's voice and a pinch on my nose.

'Everything changes, Olive, my little star.'

'Everything, Dad?'

'Everything.'

Operatic music plays in the background. Bocelli sings for me, 'Time To Say Goodbye.'

Mom?

I hear her. My heavy eyes, have no option but to remain closed. Only my hearing remains intact. I cannot tell you how many hours the doctors worked to save me because I do not know the time. All is dark because my eyes still will not open. I am in no pain and I laugh ... How strange? I'm laughing in this tragedy. I still have to hang around this place, the damn clinic.

'Come see this, Jean,' and I hear soft patting, as if off a bed. 'Olive had set this up on her iPad. It's a video of our family holiday in Barcelona.'

I'm smiling.

'Oh, Olive, you rascal,' scolded the mother as her two little girls posed for a photo in the sand. 'Olive was covered in sand, not like tidy Missy. Our blessings,' prays Lily in gratitude. I hear mom crying.

'Olive was baptised, Lily,' I hear Dad recount.

Dad ... Oh Dad.

'Yes, dear, I know she was,' replies Mom.

'But she was baptised twice, my little star,' laughs Dad.

'Are you doting now, Jim?' Mom asks Dad. 'Are you confusing Missy and Olive both getting baptised?' she asks him.

I'm enjoying this banter. I have never heard this story before.

'No, I'm not making this up, Lily, not this time. I can remember my little girls.' And he sounds so sure of himself.

Well done, Dad.

'When?' she eggs him on to discern the truth.

'We were arguing, this was more than a disagreement. You did not want the girls to have anything to do with the church.'

'Yes, I remember that juncture in our lives.'

'Well, I snuck off down to the parish priest and told Father Peter that you were on your sick bed, very poorly, and could not attend the mass and we wished to baptise the new baby and her elder sister, the two girls together.' Dad speaks with such clarity and authority, of olden memories. 'Two for the price of one,' he recalls exactly.

The accountant in me rears her head even as I lie in my deep induced coma.

'No way,' Mom says, sounding astonished. Why did you have us do the whole thing again, then? A painful infliction having to sit through the male-dominated show.' I can hear her agitatedly fix my blankets. I feel her fingers run through my hair. I can feel my hair. I must stay hopeful.

Mom?

No one responds to me.

'I can't recall just now,' and the peaceful tone of my dad's voice washes over me.

'Baptised twice, well I never,' Mom repeats. 'Didn't make the rascals holy.'

I hear both my parents sob. Then I feel a soothing cloth of warm balm wash along my hairline, ever so gently. Full of tenderness and love, compassionately the material washes over my eyes as they are bathed. 'Dear Olive,' my mom's endearments soothe me.

Mom, Dad, I love you ... I wish you could hear me.

'A blessing is a blessing in any world, thank god,' Frank lets the tome resonate, trusting his own resolve, his emotions, brimming full, added to his calling. 'I am honoured to have shared time with you, Lily, and with Olive, her essence in this room today.'

'Mom, what do I do now?' Missy sniffles.

Missy?

'Are you up to this, Missy?' snarls Nurse Jean. 'In your condition.'

Condition?

'We don't want you going into labour,' hisses Jean. 'Quadruplets do arrive before their due dates.'

Labour? Quadruplets? Missy – Pregnant by whom?

'I think you should see this, Mike.' Missy distinctly ignores Jean.

'A phone?' Mike says chokingly.

'Yes,' a coy reply, 'It's my cell,' says Missy. 'I'm Olive's sister. Together you and Olive live on in this, are fully alive in this. If you see this, then you will understand.'

'I see,' muffles Mike. 'Thank you.'

I'm a porn star. Thanks, sister.

'Also,' I hear hesitancy in her voice. 'That clip has gone viral. A security camera on the shuttle captured the interlude, and some security guard uploaded it on YouTube.'

'You've both become quite a sensation,' chirps in Nurse Jean. 'I may hook up with you meself, Mike. And-'

Missy hiccups, 'have some decency Jean.'

A famous porn star!

On cue, a ringing tone rings crisply from the evidence. 'Alistair Winthorp is calling you, Missy,' states Mike.

'The family does not wish to answer any phones at the present time,' orders Nurse Jean. 'This time is for intimate undisturbed privacy,' I hear Nurse Jean details the course of action. 'Shall I hold it for you?'

'No,' replies Mike. 'Thank you.'

'Another thing.' Nurse Jean invades the space again. 'The speed camera clocked the erratic speed of Olive's car. The mangled trauma is a massive hit online too. Another moron videoed it.'

'My Olive,' echoes Mike.

'The trippers have titled the two of you Romeo & Juliet. There are the two snippets of you holding Olive in your arms.' Nurse Jean is up on all the latest gadgetry. 'The consensus on the comment pages is that Olive was committing suicide, driving head first into the shuttle at high speed and all.'

'The public opinion will help matters, wrap up the autopsy,' states Dr Doran.

The shrills of my unanswered phone continue.

Answer the phone, Mike.

The stink of the room is so deep I can taste it in my throat.

'It is time for you to take your leave of us now, Mike,' says my mom eloquently. His distress, evident by his heavy breathing, is not addressed. 'Have no fear of man, Mike.'

'If I must, Dr Lily.' He sounds unsure of himself.

A brush stroke of hair along my face and solid lips on my lips lets me know he is close. Mike's personal smell awakening my muscle memory.

How can I think of sensuality now ... Wow, when in a coma, the fantastical wiring of the brain function.

Mike whispers, a soft, loving tone.

'Hold on, for me, my Olive, live.'

Mike ... This is hell ... I can't touch you ... Can you not see my tears?

'You must go, time is up,' responds Mom solidly. My mother, forever the doctor of academia, instructs. Mother sounds so sure of herself, as always. 'Inside, I know my daughter is reminiscent of joy.'

Mike ... I will never forget such passion, my tumescent specimen of a man ... Thank you.

I hear the soft click of a closing door, his silent departure befits me.

'Is the CCTV camera in this room taken care of?' asks Dr Doran.

'Yes sir,' Jean replies. I swear I can hear her eyelids blink in adoration. 'A power outage problem. I listed the faulty camera with the repair department. They will not be on duty this late hour. We will not be disturbed until the morning.'

'Good girl. Drew is caught on the grounds' CCTV system, leaving the scene of the accident,' details Dr Doran. 'The investigation will be pursued,' he points out. 'Be vigilant, team.'

'I tided up the paperwork,' issues Jean. 'Mr P. looked so peaceful. Thank god.'

'Thank god,' they all chant.

Stop saying that.

'Lily, please make your thumbprint mark on the control dial now.'

'Yes Dr Doran,' Mom replies.

282

'And on Olive's line after your own line,' outlines Dr Doran.

What?

I hear a rubbing sound above my head.

Mom, your deformed ideas have atrophied your mind ... Stop this ... Please.

'Well done, Lily. You have achieved what you set out to. A bit like meself,' gushes Nurse Jean. 'Thank you for your wisdom, Frank has inseminated me also.'

Ah, the sideways shuffle of the crabs. But I have felt the sting of your claws. The duo will multiply!

'We will be close in the sisterhood, Missy,' extols Nurse Jean. 'We are blessed with fine specimen.'

Missy and Frank?

While my eyes cannot serve me, my ears are preened to precision.

'I will lead us in.' Missy's voice weakens to a trembling tone.

Missy ... The third angle of our triangle, completing Mom ... I understand your love, honour and loyalty to our mother, I do Missy.

Missy - Why are you crying by my side? I will get better. There is no need to mourn me ... I'm not dead, I don't know if the medication is altering our mother ... This clinic is like the twilight zone, Missy ... I have not been myself all day in this place.

There is a hard knock on the door.

Ha! See what I mean ... There are always intrusions in this place.

Help

The last sense to remain is hope.

'Ms Toner,' comes the sinister tone of Nurse Jean, responding to the vociferousness of this lady stretching her reserve. 'As I have repeatedly conveyed to you, the family do not wish to speak with anyone at this time.'

You are a bitch, Jean.

'As I have explained, I am a close friend of Olive's. She would want me to be with her,' the insistent voice intervenes.

'The family do not wish to have any visitors. This is a private time, Ms Toner.' I hear my mother declare. 'Close over the door, Jean.' And I hear the door shut firmly.

No ... Let my private investigator in ... I've hired her.

A closed door is no soundproof arena, the vibrations of Megan Toner reverberate, as she conveys the situation on her phone, outside in the corridor. 'I can't get in, Alistair. I have tried.' Seconds of silence offer a private reply. 'I think you should come in to the clinic.' Silence. 'Yes, I know it's late, I'm aware of the time.' I can hear the urgency in her review. 'Nothing appears to be out of place. There is nothing untoward occurring as far as I can tell. A doctor and nurse, twenty-four hour watch team, is in the room, so medical personnel is present at all times.' Silence. 'Of what I can see, the position is negligible to the warrant, and without a witness.'

Alistair, help me ...

'There is no family squabble here, Alistair.' Silence. 'The private group is sitting with Olive.' Silence abuses my senses yet again. 'I agree, it will be hard to push the claims through from beyond the grave, let's hope that will not be the case. I don't know if there is a man called Frank in there.' Megan's inert mind relays the facts as she sees them, 'I can't enter the room.' Silence. 'An Indian man just exited the room. Maybe he knows something. We never got the image Frank, from Olive, before the car crash. Will I ascertain if he can point me to Frank?' Silence.

The sermon starts. I hear my big sister read to me. A beautiful poem, almost like a recital, Missy is full of emotion, her voice cracks.

'Leaves.
I am;
A leaf
Happy and carefree
Blowing the breeze
Am me.

Green to amber
Cherished
Cycle
Seasons come, seasons go
Nature's title.

Here, there
Everywhere:
Abundant pleasure
I lay to rest
Life's treasure.'

No one speaks. They accompany me in silence.

I try to remember ... The imbalance of life affronts me ... At death's door - It is the sadness that multiplies not the joy. Missy's crying fills the silent void. I feel lips on my face. Dying is unfinished business, things not said, things not done, dear sister ... Missy, missing in duty, you neither acted or collaborated.

'Frank, I wish to continue with my final wishes as planned today,' issues my mom.

Mom.

The Dawning - I had not pictured the enslavement of myself in the family's invisible handcuffs. The grail of my destiny ... I apologise, dear reader, for my introspection today - this day is the thief among us, as is every day. Funnily, I feel strength in my solitude, it is all

I have left. I try again to move. I will not give up. Patients wake from their comas, it is not unheard of. If I keep talking.

'I am honoured to be accompanied,' Mom's soft voice calms me. 'My euthanasia act becomes a euthanasia pact.'

What the fuck? Mom?

Lavender.

I smell you, Frank. Help anyone, do not let that man near me ... Get that leech of a man away from me, Mom ...

I will end up in a mental asylum before I'm six feet under with that fool for company ... Caesar always had a fool with him to remind him he was mortal.

Mom, you are so much more than Frank ... Why do you find him compulsive? I find him repulsive.

I have never felt so desolate in my Mom's company.

My spiritual essence is revolting.

But my imprisonment contains me, again, today. I feel a cold link on my neck. 'Olive, my ring I gifted to you.'

A chain?

I'm confused. The ring? Why is it not on my hand, Mom? I recall, curling blood, seeped in a circular ladybird shape, oozing from my dismembered limb. Oh no, I lost my hand.

The R'n'B tunes start cracking.

'Ah, music,' echoes Dad. 'To take the devil out of you, my little star.'

The drum-role ... Summoning my ancestors.

'We have put in her in an induced coma, Jim, to alleviate her pain so she can drift off effortlessly with me,' explains Mom, forever the consultant. 'The line of morphine enters her blood as we speak.'

For fuck's sake. No wonder you frequented the morgue, Mom dead bodies can't talk.

Euthanasia, Mom is this your life's ambition?

'These cruel, unfortunate twists have coloured my farewell. I thought I would be alone in my passing. We will always be close, dear.'

If I had power in my feet ... I would flee this place again – never to return ... My soulful voice tried to tell me not to come into this clinic.

That's why I was stalled all day.

'You two, always close. Lily and my little star,' repeats Dad.

Dad.

I converse in vain.

Someone.

This is not self pity.

This is immoral.

Let me tell someone what are my final wishes.

'Mom, I liked that ring,' sulks Missy, wishing for a re-gift.

Fuck off, Missy.

'Daughter, I gave you my wedding band,' corrects Mom to Missy.

'It is a lovely ring,' gushes Nurse Jean. 'Emerald stones are my favourite. It looks well as a pendant.'

I hear the two of them whine!

What about my life? My ultimate possession.

Time and tide wait for no one.

'If I wait, I will be less able ... and all present could be implicated.' Mom re-iterates, beset herself, embattled. 'Greater blame lies in the cock-up of the conspiracy. Let me be.'

I can sense her ideological strength, her identity so strong it can withstand the condemnation.

'Missy, I give you my directive now to oversee your loved ones, the doctors are on stand-by. What we lack in the vocabulary of love, our actions will speak louder.'

Mom.

You have the power here.

'Frank is officiating, the medical personnel is as it should be. It is time for completion, my final wishes,' my mother directs.

I love you, Mom ... Don't do this for me ...

Who has been the less tormented today? Such limpid, dark promise.

Mom... I will never forgive you ... Never.

'Thank god,' Frank expounds.

Frank, I curse you, the man who would rather bury me than poke me you fuckin' weakling. And the morbid distress returns to haunt me, as in my dawns calling, awakenings, only yesterday, a day ago, as then, in my apartment, the pitch darkness here, frightens me also. A psychic chill spikes my skin anew. You face the one day with the spirit you choose. I'm holding my breath. I've been betrayed and ambushed ... My chest enclaves, hurting me. The chill of dread has stayed my constant companion these past 24 hours. All day the premonition has tailed me, even in the sun, I could see the shade. A dusk of deadly quietness, immersed in sharp shrills of screaming, only I can hear. I feel raging anger in the stillness.

Repetition of loaded accusations inflict upon me. I am aware the cultural gravitas of the day is free choice. Mom and I, we both would not want the dramatic. I would watch this on TV, I love reality shows, the hot humiliation enthrals me.

Wait, I do not want the lead role.

I never wanted to star in this, Mom ...

I don't know who I am, until I lose who I am.

I want to live ... The worst part of this day, Mom, was not losing you, it was losing me.

'Do you want to pass with us, Jim?' Mom asks.

Mom, I love you, but you are a mixed blessing.

'No Lily. Not yet, I'm not ready. I may not know where I am but I do know who I am.'

Good for you Dad.

'Open your eyes and look within. Are you satisfied with the life you're living, Jim?' My mom and dad's easy chatter as if they have just met, even after fifty years encapsulates me.

Leave him be, Mom ... Good man, Dad, names are locked away in your head and you have only misplaced the key, but you are still Dad ...

I honour your ailment for the first time.

Father, you will forget you live with the loneliness ... Missy ... You bitch.

This is no Hollywood ending.

'I have Jim,' intersperses Frank. 'Thank god. Rest assured, Dr Tully. We will continue the good work.'

What the fuck? I bet he wanks off on his superiority.

'Follow Frank,' Mom verbally instructs Dad.

'Follow Frank,' repeats Dad.

Steps to oblivion.

'Frank, you know what to do,' Mom says.

'Yes Dr Tully, I do.'

'Good man, Frank.'

The distress is immeasurable, how cruel for my hearing to have remained intact.

Are you my devil in disguise, Frank ... The impersonator? And there will be multiples of you ... Your futuristic fantasies ... Frank and his followers.

'If we have a girl, I will call her Lily and she is to be a medical disciple, just like you. Our fellowship flourishes.'

A fellowship for Frank?

'Because of you, Dr Tully, I am going to advance our work of like-minded minds. Thank god.'

The sultan of the spinning lineage

LIARS.

Irony laces through me. I can't believe Frank is a stud ... Piercing through me - images of Frank masturbating for a cult of misfits. Sperm heading a church of Frank's fellowship, how original and how farcical ... Absurdity is dangling all around me ... Life is weird, not death.

'Jean, bank those dollars Mr P. handed over. Leave no paper or money trail. I have less than a hundred dollars in my purse. But leave that there.'

'Yes, Dr Tully.'

'Missy, are you strong enough?'

'Yes, Mom, I am.'

'Remember in your hour of darkness: We were alive but we were not living.'

The traitors.

Mom, it's not fair to inflict more inflictions on me.

I feel my right cheek being placed in the palm of her hand.

'Olive would not want to live like this, paralysed, a vegetative state with only her eyes to blink.'

Paralysed!

My mind is broken with this diagnosis. What will happen to me? Where will I live? Work? I will lose my job. How will I pay for my care? I will never have sex again ... Who will care for me? Who will care for Dad? Who will feed my dog? Dark visions swirl. Frank ... And Frank's fellowship will sit with me and nurture my soul, they will talk to me of happy families, Missy's babies, my nieces and nephews, in the clutches of Frank, living in a mansion, Round Wood. Nurse Jean will gloat, counting and recounting her happy brood and I will be helpless and lost, left behind. Mike will disappear, Drew, beside himself with guilt, will fall to the side, Alistair will wind up ... Eventually forgotten by all who ever knew me ... All except Frank, his ultimate vision of personal deity, he bestowed onto his being, will necessitate him visiting me everyday ... Informing me of the ever increasing fellowship and the swelling demands, so many clients ... Until he sits with me ... One last time ... Would I follow my Mom's deliverance eventually?

Tears fall down my cheek.

Mom, I understand ... Decision making isn't just about knowledge - It requires judgement and understanding. Her wet cheek rests on mine. 'Out of necessity comes bravery. I know my daughter.' Damp kisses moisten my dry mouth. 'We're together till the very end, Olive dear, as I wished. Love adjoining love.' I call out, the decibel of my voice unrecognisable to them.

A sense of unease invades me, like a bad smell, which should not be here, of something rotten. Damn my puss colluding with the embalmment. Gashed and scarred, the sweetness of the lavender is more sweet. All around me swamped with pungent poison. I can hear my mother in her professional capacity.

'Good teamwork, guys.'

Another medical misadventure I will be ... Midnight claims ... my favourite digits 00.00

I hear Mom decree. 'Death is a guarantee in its unpredictability. Love you all.'

'Love you,' responds a choir. Vices are national, virtues are personal. 'Thank god.'

'Proceed, Frank.'

Mom ... It was you all along ... I curse the lot of you with your obsessive disorder.

'In death we live the divine, thank god.' Mom is blurring the lines of humanity and divinity.

'Thank god,' they chime.

I spit, redundantly. God is a symbol that constantly requires reinterpretation ...

In silence, I scream.

You're wrong ... I don't believe in an afterlife so do not rush me there ...

291

I hack and choke as the fluids flood my blood, disgorging my lifeline.

If you take away my devil ... You will take away my angel.

The group surrounding me are like passengers on a plane that is going to crash. They go through the motions. I wish I wasn't a sentient animal, feeling such joy and pain in one day. My mother's tears bathe my face, mingling with mine; our blending tears, our last bath.

Glistening droplets, just as nature's dignified beauty of this dawn come to greet me at this hour, recycled in the process of my decline. Lavender's oil is dotted on my forehead. Serenity invades. I sense her and feel comforted by my mother's true touch. True love greets me and rests with me.

Mom ... NO!

The emotional satiety and sensory pleasure of embalming.

NO!

I'm baring my soul but I am the waking dead. In the unspoken, trauma lies.

LIAR.

You have done me a disservice, Mom.

Wafts of essential oil assail my nostrils.

'This will be quick, my dear,' Mom lovingly whispers in my ear. 'Essential simplicity. I love you, always, forever.'

Mom, I do not give my permission.

Nobody responds to the octave of my soundless sound. Lost to their own despair.

They ignore me.

All is as it is.

This debacle.

An adherence to beliefs that leave no room for doubt, advances. Cognitive closure is darkening. I must not black out again.

292

For a split second, I think I'm rescued, then the images of a release. Release me to what? I'm not my former self.

I wish I could fly away, like the ladybird.

Frank's voice is triumphant, he holds center stage.

'I read from Proverbs 287. Our passions are the winds that propel our vessel. Our reason is the pilot that steers her. Without winds the vessel would not move. And without a pilot, she would be lost.'

Get Frank away from me.

Reverent silence.

'Our work here is done. Thank god,' says Mom.

'Thank god,' the unison chants.

I hear Frank humming, the group surrounding me, hum with him.

Mom ...

My last touch is not to be Frank ...

'I'm not sure,' speaks up Dad, breaking through the chorus.

'Yes Jim, I know you are not sure, dear.'

The humming resumes.

'No Lily,' I hear Dad shuffle.

'I'm not for turning Jim, this is my choice.'

I hear her lips plant a strong kiss on his lips.

'I'm not sure,' Dad repeats, 'I'm not sure for Olive.'

Dad.

'I want to hear Olive,' his stubbornness affirms.

No one says a thing.

I could hear a pin drop.

'Dr Tully?' asks Dr Doran.

'Jim, her neck is broken, Olive is paralysed. It will take weeks, even months before she will communicate. And that may be by blinking. She may never speak again Jim.'

'Olive is my Olive,' Dad simply says, clear words, his voice strong.

Oh Dad, I love you, your mind is a muddle but you have a lifetime of memories in you.

'Okay Jim,' Mom speaks softly to him.

'Okay,' Dad repeats.

'Team, I will continue. This is my choice. I'm clear in my own mind, not in the mind of others. Wait for Olive to tell you what she wants,' my mother, the doctor, precisely instructs.

'This is for me.'

Mom.

Edel Cushnahan studied English at University under the renowned playwright, poet and author Frank McGuinness.

She continued with further studies in Journalism. Edel is a freelance journalist and lives in North County Dublin, Ireland.

The Ladybird Flies is her first novel. It is being published & sold worldwide and is available on Amazon.

Her second novel, working title – THAW – is out Autumn 2016.

ACKNOWLEDGEMENTS

Thank you, precious family; Kieran, Cian, Ronan & Eryn.

Thank you, sister, Dr. Alison Afra, for reading early chapters & cheering me on.

Many people have helped in the completion of this book. Catherine Moonan, for all your support and encouragement.

Including, Mary Halpenny, Mary O'Hanlon, Susan Foley, Jackie Mc Donagh, Geraldine Freaney.

Stepping in, when I attended the Dublin Book Festival, thanks Edel. The CARI Lunch Ladies, Fiona, Lisa, Marie, Annemarie, Tracy, Suzanne, Sharon, Niamh, Rosari, Louise.

My Book Club - A group of inspirational readers, Sara, Janice, Kevina, Christine, Bronwyn, Jean, Sue, Yvonne. The coffee ladies, That's Amore, Malahide, Maura, Nora, Mary, Lillian. Meghan Wynne's creative writing group. Noelle and local Writers Group, Malahide Library. Denise & Edel, Paperweight, Malahide. The business acumen of Robert, Manor Books, Malahide. The Irish Writer's Centre, Dublin. Editor Emma Jane Golding. Award winning, cover designer Siobhan Foody.

Special thanks to fellow author, Cecelia Ahern.

Dear Readers, who have welcomed me into their lives, smiled and enthusiastically praised my writing. I'm eternally grateful for the honour of sharing my book.

48426091R00181

Made in the USA
Charleston, SC
03 November 2015